DEADLY FORCE

A SCVC Taskforce novel

MISTY EVANS

ROMANTIC SUSPENSE AND MYSTERIES BY MISTY EVANS

The Super Agent Series
Operation Sheba
Operation Paris
Operation Proof of Life
The Blood Code
The Perfect Hostage, A Super Agent Novella

The Deadly Series
Deadly Pursuit
Deadly Deception
Deadly Force

The Justice Team Series (with Adrienne Giordano)
Stealing Justice
Cheating Justice
Holiday Justice
Exposing Justice

The Secret Ingredient Culinary Mystery Series
The Secret Ingredient, A Culinary Romantic Mystery with Bonus Recipes
The Secret Life of Cranberry Sauce, A Secret Ingredient Holiday Novella

DEDICATION

This book is dedicated to all the men and women in the arena
striving to do the deeds that need doing to keep our country
safe and free.

And to those who never stop loving their soul mate,
no matter what.
Thank you, Mark, for loving me.

"It is not the critic who counts, not the man who points out how the strong man stumbled, or where the doer of deeds could have done them better. The credit belongs to the man who is actually in the arena, whose face is marred by dust and sweat and blood; who strives valiantly; who errs, who comes short again and again, because there is no effort without error and shortcoming; but who does actually strive to do the deeds; who knows great enthusiasms, the great devotions; who spends himself on a worthy cause; who at the best in the end knows the triumph of high achievement, and who at the worst, if he fails, at least fails while daring greatly, so that his place shall never be with those cold and timid souls who know neither victory nor defeat."

~ Theodore Roosevelt from The Man in the Arena

~

"You pierce my soul. I am half agony, half hope. Tell me not that I am too late, that such precious feelings are gone for ever. I offer myself to you again with a heart even more your own than when you almost broke it, eight years and a half ago. Dare not say that man forgets sooner than woman, that his love has an earlier death. I have loved none but you."

~ Jane Austin, Persuasion

CHAPTER ONE

Culver's Marina, Chula Vista
0900 hours

Cal Reese's boat rocked hard, waking him. Heart hammering, he reached for his gun.

Assess.

Waves crashed topside. Maggie, the black Lab lying beside his bunk, whined.

Remnants of a nasty nightmare filled his head, lingering snapshots of his last mission. He rubbed his eyes and blinked them away. He was back in the States. No firefights, no shouting, no exploding RPGs. Drawing a deep breath, he let it out slowly as he forced himself upright. Dull pain throbbed at his temples.

Maggie's cold nose nudged his arm. He reached over and patted her head. She was the only one who had his back these days. If not for her, well...he'd probably be six feet under like the rest of the men in his unit.

The feel of her warm breath on his face, and the happy lap of her tongue, made the blood and screams of the nightmare recede. Setting his gun next to the whiskey bottle on the shelf above his bunk, he scratched her ears. Soft thunder echoed in the distance. "Storm moving in, girl. Nothing to worry about."

Except for the fact that he wouldn't be working today. Another day of twiddling his damn thumbs. Maybe that was good considering he'd already overslept, lost in the nightmare of the past.

Night terrors, the doctor called them. Usually followed by sleepwalking.

He glanced around. Nothing seemed out of place. He didn't have much in the run-down boat, but everything he did have was right where he'd left it.

All clear.

Oversleeping was unacceptable, but mostly surprising. Since Afghanistan, his internal clock was as much of a fucked-up disaster as his head, although he'd never had a chance to set a normal work/sleep routine until now anyway. In high school, he'd always stayed up too late, got up too early, working his ass off to get the grades, the girl, and some hope for a future. The day he graduated—twenty-four hours *after* his high school sweetheart tore his world apart—he walked into the Navy recruitment center and signed on. Three years later, he was in BUDs, and up until thirteen days ago, he'd headed a special SEAL commando team hot on the trail of terrorism sponsor Otto Grimes.

The only "normal" in his world had been coffee—black—and his deep-seated love for water.

Now all he had was time to kill and memories to drown. And for the first time in his life, he had a dog.

Rising, Cal ignored the bottle of Jack and the pain in his temples thanks to the brown liquid. He went through the uncomplicated act of filling the coffee pot, scooping grounds, and searching for his single coffee cup.

Normal was…okay. Even good some days. He'd learned to appreciate simple things again. If only the flashbacks would leave him the fuck alone. The goddamn nightmares, yeah, they could go AWOL and he wouldn't miss them a bit.

Stay in the present.

He breathed in the aroma of grounds and hot water and listened to the waves hitting the hull. A glance out the starboard window told him there was no rain yet, but the dark clouds over the ocean were ushering in a doozy.

The incoming storm had just freed up his calendar. No scraping barnacles off yachts or fixing motors for Chewy at the boatyard. Maybe the storm would blow itself out by noon and the Southern Cali tourists would keep him busy at the marina's rental shop wanting their jet skis.

Maggie whined and Cal set down his cup. Time to take care of the love of his life, then hit the shower.

Pathetic. His life had dwindled down to the barest of needs, the loneliest of lives. Thirteen days ago, he'd been in nonstop action. His team had been seconds away from taking down that bastard Otto...

Now Butcher, Avery, and Tank were dead, and he'd been put out to pasture by his country. Worse, he couldn't remember the details of what had happened in those moments after gunfire broke out.

Welcome to PT-fucking-SD.

Snagging a ratty T-shirt and a pair of shorts, he dressed, tossed on a windbreaker, and hooked Maggie to her leash. *Bring on the wind and the rain.* He and Maggie loved water. A run would do them both good. Clear the lingering images of the nightmare and that horrific last mission from his brain.

Maggie's tail wagged furiously as they climbed the four short stairs to the top deck. The dog froze, and Cal looked up.

His heart lurched and so did his cock. *No fucking way.*

Standing on the dock, hands on her curvy hips, was the one woman he thought he'd never see again. Never *wanted* to see again.

Talk about a storm blowing in. "What are you doing here, Bianca?"

She pointed to the name written in flowing script on the boat's side. "*The Love Boat?* Really?"

Maggie danced on her feet, straining at the leash and wagging her tail like Bianca was the best thing she'd seen in days.

Traitor.

B still looked as young, fresh, and innocent as the day she'd broken his heart in high school. But she wasn't innocent. Not by a long shot. She'd ripped his heart to shreds again six months ago.

The NSA agent working on the Southern California Violent Crimes Taskforce never rested in her quest for information. "You're still wearing your ring."

The damn gold band around his finger was an exact match to hers. "You didn't need to bring the divorce papers in person. The post office delivers bad news every day."

The wind toyed with strands of her hair, making his fingers itch to do the same. Her mouth quirked. "Do you even get mail here? On a boat?"

The headache in his temples pounded as hard as his heart. "What do you want?"

The smirk left her mouth and she looked around as if she were worried about the approaching storm. Or maybe she was worried someone would see her talking to him. She stepped forward, lowered her voice, and her pretty blue eyes met his head-on from behind her sexy librarian glasses. "I'm in trouble, Cal. Big trouble."

"Trouble's always been your middle name, B. What's new?"

"If I'm going to live through the next twenty-four hours…" She hesitated a moment, then said the words he'd never thought he'd hear. Ever. "I want—I *need*—you. After what I've stumbled across, you're the only man who can protect me."

What angle was she working to save their marriage now? He climbed the steps and brushed past her. "Drama queen doesn't quite suit you."

Her hand landed on his forearm, stopping him. "I'm serious. I know what happened with Operation Warfighter. At least, I think I do." She looked over her shoulder, back to him. "Something you should know. You're not going to like it."

He couldn't do this today. Not right now. His head hurt and

4

hearing the words *Operation Warfighter* made his heart kick like a jackrabbit inside his chest.

Her paranoia—faked for dramatic effect or otherwise—immediately set his nerves on edge.

Assess. He scanned the boat dock. Was she telling the truth? Did she have details on the operation? Why did that put her in danger?

Fuck. His fingers itched for his gun, even though he saw nothing out of the ordinary in the marina.

Regardless, he'd never been able to deny Bianca anything. His love, his protection, his goddamn loyalty...

She shifted her weight from her right to left foot, watching him—no, *pleading* with him with those big baby blues. Her reach was long and deep inside the NSA, although his instincts told him he didn't know everything about what she did. No telling what dirt she might have dug up.

But dirt that had sent her to him in his current state on the country's blacklist? She must be desperate. The last time she'd made contact was to tell him to pack his things and get out. She wanted a divorce.

Cal glanced past her petite shoulders. A few of the local hardcore boaters were out fastening down their boats in preparation for the storm. Otherwise, the marina was quiet.

Regardless, Cal's instincts were on high alert. He wanted nothing more than to protect the woman in front of him.

Damned instincts. "Go inside and stay there. I'll be back in a few minutes."

He didn't wait to see if Bianca followed orders, giving Maggie her freedom and running with her for the boardwalk.

Bianca watched Cal take off, his muscular legs flexing as he ran with the dog. The wind blew the windbreaker tight against his back, outlining his broad shoulders and V-shaped waist.

Every time she saw him, it was a blow to her senses. He topped six-one, weighed a lean two-ten, and looked like a fighter straight out of an MMA ring.

But it wasn't his gorgeous body or his chiseled jaw and bristling attitude that knocked the air from her lungs every time she saw him. It was his eyes. The chocolate-brown peepers were nearly black thanks to his Spanish lineage.

Gypsy eyes, her mother had called them. Haunted was more like it.

Cal and the dog hit the marina's parking lot, and a few seconds later, disappeared from view.

What's new? During their long and rocky relationship, she'd always been the one staying put while Cal took off for parts unknown. She loved him fiercely, but he was never around.

That's what I get for marrying a military man.

She'd never dreamed when she'd finally caught up with him after high school and said "I do," that Cal would end up career military. He'd run to the Navy to get away from her. Once he had her, she figured he'd serve out his term and come home.

Wrong.

Once he'd served, the Navy had gotten into his blood. He'd become driven and relentless in his quest to serve his country, especially after he realized he couldn't give her the future they'd both dreamed about as innocent kids.

She'd matched him career-step for career-step, graduating top of her class with a double major and an offer from the National Security Agency. When she'd told Cal she had accepted the position, he'd brought her champagne and chocolate truffles and then made her swear on his tattered copy of *The Art of War*—a book he kept close at all times—that she'd keep her nose out of his work.

Hard to do when you worried constantly about your husband's safety and you had access to everything he and his commando team did.

From down below, she caught the whiff of wet dog and screwed up her nose. *The dog's new.*

Cal had always been a dog guy, but with their insane work schedules, having any kind of pet was out of the question. "Someday," he would always say, "I'll retire and we'll have a dozen dogs and a couple of kids."

Devoted as he was to the SEAL team, someday had never come. Not until now.

Bianca scanned the marina, saw no one watching her. *It's the one you can't see that you have to worry about.*

Which was what had brought her here. There was a man looking for her. A man who had a bullet with her name on it.

She'd lost her family, had no friends because of her insane work hours and need for secrecy, and she was in the process of giving up Cal—her only touchstone. Now her job and her life were on the line.

Loser. Her mother had always called her that, and maybe it was true. She'd never done anything right, no matter how hard she'd tried. With her high intelligence and photographic memory, she'd never been normal. Hated the very word. So here she was, on the run and about to screw up Cal's life all over again.

What choice did she have? She'd told the truth...he was the only man in the world who could protect her.

That's what being *ab*normal got you.

Swallowing the sudden lump in her throat, she sought cover inside *The Love Boat.*

CHAPTER TWO

Stark was the only word to describe Cal's new home.

No one would call this place home, Bianca thought, her heels clomping on the deck to the descending wooden stairs. She'd never been sentimental and could appreciate a functional, sparse place, but this was downright sad.

The upper deck held the bridge and navigation station. Below deck, the walls were unadorned except for a set of weather instruments to measure wind speed and barometric pressure. From the looks of their ragged frames and scratched glass, they were originals. Ditto on the sailcloth curtain hanging over the window above the bunk bed, and the cheap, dark paneling lining the galley and head.

Living quarters. That's what Cal would call it. It was definitely no love boat.

The place smelled like freshly brewed coffee, wet dog, and sea air. Bianca's gaze skimmed over the bed with its tussled sheet, a bottle of Jack Daniels on a shelf, a gun next to it, and across from the bed, a small table with a bench seat.

Her eyes came back to the bottle. Cal never touched hard liquor. Was the bottle a left-over remnant, like the weather instruments, of the previous owner?

She picked up a squat glass from the sink and examined it in the low light. A few drops of brown liquid clung to the bottom. She sniffed and the acrid scent of whiskey met her nose.

If the previous owner had left the bottle behind, Cal had

made use of it. As much as it surprised her—he never drank anything stronger than beer—she didn't blame him for seeking comfort with a shot of Jack. Being a SEAL meant everything to him, and now his career was over. He'd lost three men, was suffering from post-traumatic stress disorder, and was facing a military investigation. If she knew him at all, she knew he cared little about the outcome of the investigation compared to the deaths of his friends and teammates. Those men had been closer to him than brothers. He'd carry the responsibility of their deaths, and the families they left behind, forever. Even if, in the end, she proved he wasn't responsible for what had happened in that terrorist compound.

Her eyes fell on the gun. Cal always had guns, but she didn't like what her brain synopses were floating past her frontal lobe. Setting the glass in the sink, she checked the gun's chamber.

One bullet.

Her stomach did a dive.

Cal, suicidal? He wasn't the type. After what had happened, however, who knew what was going on in his head.

Why didn't he come to me?

Because your marriage is over, the voice in her head admonished.

Pain in her chest made her place her hand there. It wasn't logical...her IQ was 146, genius level, but she couldn't figure out how to fix her marriage.

The real irony was that her EQ, emotional intelligence quotient, was so low it caused her all manner of interpersonal problems. Cal had been the only person she'd ever had a real relationship with. He'd brought passion and excitement to her life, to their marriage. He'd protected her from the first day he met her—no small thing to a young girl with no father and an abusive mother.

The floor under Bianca's feet rolled, making her shift to keep her balance. Her stomach was empty, but it threatened to bring up dry heaves. Backing away from the gun and whiskey bottle, she hugged her briefcase and leaned her butt against the cabinet to steady herself. There was nothing inside the briefcase that would prove Cal was a pawn in a government cover-up, but like him, she needed something to hang on to. Cal had given her this briefcase the day she graduated from MIT. It had become her lucky charm.

Right now, she needed all the luck she could get.

The only proof she had that Operation Warfighter had been compromised before Cal's team even hit the ground was in her head—something she'd accidently come across while investigating a cult leader several days ago—and it was circumstantial at best.

But she knew when she was being followed. Knew when her phones had been tapped and her emails were being read. Hell, she was one of the NSA's most elite eavesdroppers. She better damn well know when *she* became a target of the very government she served.

Her encrypted cell phone buzzed inside the briefcase and Bianca startled. She did that a lot these days…jumping at every noise, every shadow. Getting distracted by all the cranial activity inside her head.

Pulling out the phone, she glanced at the display. *Punto.* Bianca shifted her thought process, clearing her head of blown missions, Big Brother, and bullets with her name on them. She had to pretend she was at work and not let on she was about to disappear. She raised her voice to be heard above the waves and growing wind outside. "Hey, Ronni. What's up?"

FBI agent Ronni Punto was part of the Southern California Violent Crimes Taskforce and working undercover on Project Bliss trying to take out a narco-terrorist. "That name I gave you yesterday? Did you have a chance to track it down, land an address?"

Bianca had an eidetic memory. She could recall details of every case she'd ever worked on without the aid of notes or memorization…one of the reasons the NSA had wanted her before the ink was dry on her degree. "The name Fire Chetfler was bogus as you suspected. It's a codename. I played with the letters and came up with Rife Letcher. Ran that through the system and got a hit. His rap sheet includes everything from petty theft to B&E."

"Hot damn," Ronni said. "Where can I find him?"

"Unfortunately, his current physical address won't help you."

"Why not?"

Bianca sank down in the padded bench seat and rested her briefcase on the table. Her roiling stomach seemed to appreciate it and settled down. "It's the state pen. He was convicted of prescription drug tampering and Medicare fraud six months ago."

"You're kidding." Ronni mumbled something Bianca couldn't hear. "Any possibility he's running this ring from inside?"

Bianca shrugged even though Ronni couldn't see her. "Anything's possible." The motto she was currently running on and hoping would save her life. "I'm checking into all the visitors he's had since he's been in there as well as his lawyer's background. If there are any leads, I'll give you a heads-up."

"Thanks, Marx. You okay?"

Ronni Punto hadn't been a fan of Bianca's when she'd joined the taskforce. Bianca was too direct and didn't know how to play well with her coworkers, often saying things that annoyed them. After surviving the cult operation, however, she and Ronni had grown on each other. Neither of them was the touchy-feely type and there was a sort of respect in that. They each recognized that the other was there to get the job done, and they shared the mutual goal of survival in a world of alpha males and giant egos.

What Ronni didn't know was that Bianca's gig on the taskforce was a cover for another mission. One the NSA was keeping off the books and another reason Bianca had to go about business as usual. Whoever was keeping tabs on her knew about Command and Control, but they'd never expected her to come across the damning information she had. "I'm good. Working. You know…"—she cringed—"normal."

"You sound like you're in a tunnel with a vacuum running."

The wind continued to rock *The Love Boat* and it sounded as if the waves were getting serious about toppling it over. "There's a storm here. Must be a bad connection. I better go."

"Before you do, I wanted to say thank you for the books. It's not easy figuring out how to talk to Adam and understand his bipolar disorder, but we're making progress. I appreciate your help."

If anyone knew about mental disorders, it was Bianca. Ronni's brother was an easy case compared to her mother. "As long as he stays on his meds, you two should be fine."

"Do you want to grab some lunch today? I'll be back at the office by noonish."

"Um." Bianca wished she could meet Ronni for lunch, and on some levels, it surprised her. She didn't do the friend thing, but lately it had been nice turning to Ronni for advice. Sharing a laugh with her over a case and learning the art of socializing. "I can't today. I have a…an appointment."

"Okay. No worries." From Ronni's tone, she knew Bianca was lying, but wasn't going to hold it against her. She seemed to understand Bianca's uncomfortableness with relationships. "Talk soon."

Bianca disconnected, a hollowness filling her chest. She liked Ronni and didn't like disappointing her, but it couldn't be helped. She couldn't involve her taskforce coworkers in this.

Fingering the phone, she considered turning it off, maybe even dumping it over the side of the boat. She'd already diverted the GPS signal with a little software code that was all hers, so anyone tracking her phone would think she was miles away at a Starbucks in downtown San Diego. Her usual haunt during the week. But going AWOL from Command and Control would require more than disabling her phone's GPS and would tip her hand to those tracking her. Not the smartest idea. Not yet anyway. Not until she talked to Cal and got his feedback.

She only hoped he would help her.

She sat back and toyed with the zipper on her briefcase. Her fingers shook ever so slightly, and she clenched her hand tight. She was in serious trouble but this wasn't her first rodeo. The information she'd intercepted and decoded may have put her life in danger, but now she was here. If anyone could keep her safe until she figured out how to expose the truth, it was Cal.

She thought she'd made it clear to him that her life was in danger, yet he'd taken off with the dog.

Good to know he puts his dog's wellbeing over my safety.

Cal took Maggie along a familiar route, then doubled back through a less populated area. A week ago, he'd been a mess, anxious every time he went out in public. An expert at threat assessment, he'd never felt unsure of his surroundings. He'd relied on his unit, his team, to always have his back. Once they were gone, his mind continued to be stuck in Afghanistan. Every noise made him jump. Every person who stuck their hands in their pockets was suspect. He felt claustrophobic in every store. The places to hide an IED were too numerous.

Even outside, tall buildings were hide sights for snipers. Every corner was the perfect place for an ambush.

He felt like a walking target.

The only place semi-comfortable for him was on the water. The minute he saw the boat for sale, he knew it was the only place he'd find peace. What he found when he showed up to take ownership, was Maggie.

Since then, she'd become his "unit." She had his back, kept him centered. Calmed him down when the anxiety hit. He still struggled with crowds and entering buildings, but he was doing better thanks to her.

The marina had two escape routes, a parking lot, and the shack with the office and rental equipment. From his location, Cal could see all of it. Vehicles in the lot were few, none with tinted windows or out-of-state licenses. No faces stared out from Chewy's shack or any of the boats. Because of the storm, few souls were out, making his reconnaissance easier.

...After what I've stumbled across, you're the only man who can protect me...

...I know what happened with Operation Warfighter...

Bianca's words looped like a flimsy rubber band through his mind as the wind drove rain into his face. His naturally suspicious nature was conflicted. Maybe she was telling the truth, and in that case, he needed to know what she'd discovered and why she needed protection.

If she was pulling a drama queen act and going for an Oscar, he needed to know the why of that as well. Why not hand him the divorce papers and be done? Why imply she needed him when all she wanted was to kick his ass to the curb like the US government had done thirteen days ago?

Either way, seeing her stirred up feelings he'd tried long and hard to shut down. She was kryptonite. His Achilles heel. Her simple presence—that librarian look and genius IQ behind the glasses—undid him every fucking time. He wanted to strip her naked and kiss every inch of her body, make her groan and beg for more.

And then he wanted to irritate her with some flippant comment about her "desk job" just to listen to her spout words like "autolatrist" and "kosmokrator."

How the hell did I end up with her?

He wiped rain from his eyes, slowed Maggie to a walk. *Because she saw something in you long before the Navy did. She believed in you.*

He wondered if she still did.

...you're the only man who can protect me...

At a lookout site that offered him a view of the entire marina and boatyard, he tucked himself and the dog behind a set of trees and in between some large rocks. Maggie whined, wanting to head home for breakfast. His own stomach gurgled in reply. "Give me ten, Mags," he told the dog. "Better safe than sorry."

He scanned the area, saw nothing and no one out of place. Normally, a few of the old guys would be sitting out on their boats having coffee and reading their papers. This morning, there wasn't a soul out. He searched the hills behind the marina and saw nothing suspicious. If someone was tailing Bianca, they were good.

But he was patient.

He gave it the full thirty minutes, his headache lifting in the humid ocean air. When he couldn't put it off any longer, he took Maggie and doubled around the area again, rechecking the obvious sites a man could hide. Sites Cal himself had scoped out and logged in case he ever needed them.

"Paranoid son-of-a-bitch" Butcher had always called him. Cal had never denied it.

Confident no one was following Bianca, and ready for his shower and breakfast, Cal urged Maggie back to a run and headed for the boat.

CHAPTER THREE

Bianca found a pair of binoculars on the bridge. As she stood hidden behind the navigation controls, wishing she'd worn more sea-worthy clothes, she watched Cal running back to the boat.

As per normal, he was in his element—water. He'd been a gifted swimmer even as a kid and had competed nationally in high school.

She'd never learned to swim. The best she could do was dog-paddle and even that was a struggle. Open water made her feel claustrophobic—the opposite of most people. Being in water over her head sent her into a full-fledged panic.

We really couldn't be more opposite. But opposites *did* attract. In their case, that was both good and bad. From the day they'd met, she and Cal had come together, broken up, and come together again. First as friends, then as more.

Even now, she couldn't deny the sexual chemistry between them. Her pulse jumped at the sight of him, every part of her body tingled when he looked at her. If only there weren't so much bad stuff between them. She wished they could lay all the ugliness down, get out from under it for a few hours, and enjoy coming together once more.

Not just for the physical stuff. For the friendship. Cal had been her best friend since elementary school. She missed him.

While rain pelted the bridge's windows, Bianca stood transfixed, unable to take her eyes off him. He ran with such ease, his tan face turned up to the rain as his long, sure strides ate up the distance between them. Her parts tingled and her heart beat erratically in her chest.

God, I love you.

She understood the science behind what she was feeling— the chemical releases going on in her brain. Cal was familiar. Cal was safe. Her most precious memories were tied to him. Her happiest times were rooted in him.

He may have been her polar opposite, but since the day he'd picked a shy girl up off the playground asphalt, brushed pieces of the sharp cinders from her knees, and raised his fists to the school bully who'd made her life hell, Cal had been her hero.

Even when he'd broken her heart.

Now it was time for her to repay the favor. This time the bully was the government she and Cal had sworn to serve. Standing up to that bully would cost her everything...her job, the quiet existence she enjoyed, and quite possibly her life. But the government had already taken the one thing she held most dear—Cal. She wouldn't let them destroy him as well.

The dog ran by his side, completely soaked and tongue lolling from the side of its mouth. They hit the boardwalk and slowed to a jog. She was sure the dog was smiling.

Through the binoculars, Bianca could see the animal was missing vital male parts, so it must be female. That might explain the adoration in the dog's eyes. Bianca had never met a female yet who could resist the absolute alpha male prowess Cal exuded.

Hell, she'd been at restaurants with him where the *male* waiters hit on him.

The thing none of them realized was that he was a very dangerous man. A weapon the US had trained and given specialized skills. When she told him about Senator Halston, Cal would want to use those skills on the man.

What to do? Could she keep her husband away from the senator until the worst of Cal's anger subsided and she could convince him to go along with her rational, logical plan? Cal would be out for blood, and if he went after the senator his way—with violence—she'd be forced to rein him in.

She couldn't physically stop Cal from doing anything. And she didn't want to notify authorities that he was hunting down a United States senator.

Cooper, the leader of the Southern California Violent Crimes Taskforce, could possibly step in if she needed him. He was a secretive guy himself, and she knew a few of those secrets.

If necessary, she wasn't above blackmailing Cooper to gain his cooperation, but she didn't think she'd need to stoop that low. He valued her—at least her brain—and once you were part of Cooper Harris's team, the man would move mountains for you.

She preferred to do things her way, and if she involved Cooper, he'd take charge. He'd also end up in the crosshairs with her. Best not to involve him unless she was left with no other alternative.

She lowered the binoculars as Cal and the dog came aboard and headed down the stairs, oblivious to her in her hidden vantage point.

"B?" he called over the noisy rain, and his deep voice made her pulse jump. There was the usual irritated edge to his voice, but something else as well. "Where are you?"

Worry? Was that what she heard in his voice? Sure had been a hell of a long time since he'd worried about her.

She had to do this. She had to tell him. What happened after that would be up to him.

Leaving the binoculars behind, she flipped on the tiny camera she'd installed by the boat's windshield so she could keep an eye on the marina's entrance. Grabbing the handrail, she steadied herself. The storm might buy her an hour or two—keep Cal from going anywhere and slow down anyone searching for her—but she needed to figure out a way to keep him sequestered, and her ass out of the line of fire until she could find physical evidence against the senator she could take to the Justice Department. They wouldn't bring him up on charges over hearsay.

And hearsay was all she had.

Bianca sighed. After what she'd put Cal through already, he was more likely to toss her overboard than become her bodyguard.

———————

Cal dried his hair with a towel, watching Bianca descend the stairs. She was as wet as he was, strands of her hair sticking to her graceful neck. She'd removed her glasses, and if not for the clothes and the fear on her face, she'd look like she'd just stepped out of the shower.

Oh, the fun they'd had in the shower. "What were you doing up there?"

She took the other end of the towel and wiped her face off with it. "Watching you."

Warmth spread in his veins. "Afraid I wouldn't come back?"

Her eyes met his. "Yes."

One simple word but it packed a hell of an accusation. "I always came back, B."

"You almost didn't this last time." Her voice was soft but forceful. "I told you that would happen. The odds—"

"The odds?" He took the towel, then wiped off his neck. "Fuck the odds. Three of my men died. I should have died with them."

"You nearly did. You knew that joining the SEALs could leave me a widow."

How many times had they had this discussion? "Being a SEAL is my life."

Was my life.

He didn't miss the flare of hurt in her eyes, but before he

19

could backtrack and try explaining that she'd always been even more important to him, Maggie decided to shake off the rain.

Water flew all over Bianca's legs. She let out a yelp and jumped backward. "There are over a million feral cats in San Diego County and you adopt a dog?"

Cal grabbed a dry towel from a bin above the bed and tossed it at her. She'd always been a cat person, feeding the strays in the neighborhood even after her mother had slapped her for "wasting food." He shook his head. "A million feral cats in one county?" She was a walking book of facts and an expert at exaggeration. "Come on."

"You want to see the stats from Animal Control?" She dried her legs and feet while Maggie panted, looking at Cal and waiting patiently for her kibble. "L.A.'s even worse. The number runs around three mil."

So maybe she wasn't exaggerating. Being married to Bianca was like being married to his own form of Google—except in an annoying, infuriating way. "The towel is for Maggie."

"Maggie?"

He pointed at the Lab. "Dry her off, will you?"

Bianca looked like he'd asked her to sleep with a terrorist, but after Maggie whined and wagged her tail half-heartedly, Bianca conceded and started running the towel over the dog's fur.

Cal filled Maggie's bowl. As she inhaled it with loud, chomping noises, he sidestepped Bianca and headed for the shower. "Make yourself at home."

"Cal." She touched his arm as he passed. "Can we get out of here? We don't have to go far, just...away from San Diego."

The feel of her hand on his arm stopped him. The familiar scent of vanilla and almond came off her skin—the lotion she'd used since high school. His cock gave a twitch, his eyes automatically closing so he could breathe deeper.

Home. She smelled like home.

In that moment, his male instincts told him to follow her anywhere. His heart, however, knew better. He shifted his arm out from under her hand and opened his eyes. "And go where?"

"How about we sail up the coast for a couple of hours?"

"In this storm?"

"*The Love Boat*'s not seaworthy?"

She knew how many cats ran wild in San Diego but not the simple fact that taking a sailboat the size of his out in a storm was a bad idea?

His senior chief had given him orders...stay low and near HQ until the investigation was over. Cal's meeting with the military review board was in two days. They were going to crucify him but he deserved it. "I can't leave San Diego."

She bit her bottom lip, looked away.

This time, he reached for her, snagging her elbow. She jumped, wrenching it away, and he felt like an ass. She'd always had a knee-jerk reaction to people grabbing her, thanks to her bitch of a mother.

Gently, he reached out and took her hand. It was cold, her fingers trembling. "Is someone really after you?"

She looked down and closed her fingers around his. Her eyes were sad when she glanced back up. "I've missed you."

God*damn*. She couldn't do this to him. Not here, not after everything she'd said to him the last time they were together. *I want a divorce.*

For one half-insane moment, he almost wrapped his arms around her. Her body had always fit so perfectly inside the ring of his arms...

"I came to see you in the hospital," she said. Her voice was quiet, so quiet he almost didn't hear the words over the wind and rain beating against the boat. "Your senior chief told me you didn't want to see me."

The hospital? He'd been injured during the raid, a couple of bullets doing some damage as he pulled Tank to cover. "Ramstein?" He'd been transported there for medical care and a debriefing in the aftermath of Warfighter. "You came to Germany?"

She looked down and her lashes fluttered against her skin. In the dim light, she looked pale—too pale. "I heard about what happened. Saw the report. Only, per orders, no names were mentioned. I didn't know who'd been killed and who'd been injured. No one would tell me, and I was going crazy. All I could find out was that only two of you were taken to the base hospital, so I hopped on a plane."

"I didn't know."

Her chest hitched. "Lugmeyer said…" She exhaled hard, her gaze flying up to Cal's again. "He told me to fuck off. That I was the last person in the world you needed by your bedside."

Justin Lugmeyer was Cal's senior chief first, his friend second. He'd been coming to the rescue during the raid and had taken shrapnel in his thigh. "I was in a dark place, Bianca. I was laid up and had amnesia. Seeing you…well, Justin was doing us a both a favor by keeping us apart."

Dropping his hand, she turned away, anger making her movements jerky. She wiped at her face. Tears? He'd only ever seen her cry twice—and never over him.

He reached for her, brought her back, her chest bumping into his. "Forget Lugmeyer. You're here now, and whatever's going on, I will protect you, got it? You don't have to be scared. I won't let anything happen to you."

She went up on her tiptoes to kiss his cheek. A strong wave hit the boat, knocking them both off balance. Cal used the opportunity to draw her closer and brush her lips instead.

Her eyes went round and locked with his for a brief second, and yes indeed, he spotted a damp streak across her left cheekbone. As he went to brush it off, thunder boomed, another wave hit, and her briefcase skidded off the table.

She startled, pushing him away, and made a production out of retrieving it. "You better take that shower." She tossed the briefcase on the bench seat and set her rain-speckled glasses on the table. "We have a lot to talk about."

A part of him wanted to drag her into the shower and wash

the sadness off her face. Forget their damaged past for an hour or so and erase the pain they'd caused each other.

Instead, he grabbed a fresh towel. At the entry to the head, he said over his shoulder, "Help yourself to coffee."

"You know I hate your coffee." The attitude was back in her voice but she still wouldn't meet his eyes. "I'll make a fresh pot."

Smiling, he closed the door behind him.

Her stomach had grown used to the rocking of the boat but the movement still played havoc with her nerves. Or maybe being so close to Cal was making her jittery. The simple touch of his hand nearly made her cry with longing.

Coffee wasn't going to help, but she needed to keep her hands busy and her mind off Cal and his gorgeous, rock-hard body now naked in the shower.

She cleaned her glasses and put them back on. Then she got the coffee pot going with fresh grounds and water, and as it perked, she searched the two cabinets nearby. Cal's food inventory included six boxes of high-protein granola bars, some type of protein drink mix, and—she moved the muscle-building stuff aside and saw a blue box that brightened her day—good, old-fashioned, sugar-filled PopTarts. *Yes.*

The soft hiss of the shower as it came on in the bathroom competed with the sound of the brewing coffee pot and the rain outside. Surrounded by water, Bianca focused on opening the box of breakfast goodness and snagging a foil wrapper to take back to the table. Blueberry. *That's a fruit, right?*

She tore open the wrapper and wished Cal had a toaster. From the heat in his eyes a minute ago, she probably didn't need one. All she needed was to look like the damsel in distress and he went into alpha male, all protective and *me-Tarzan, you-Jane.*

Those eyes. When he went Mr. Intense, the energy radiating off him nearly fried the ends of her hair.

She wasn't a crier—which was probably why Cal had gotten protective when he saw her tear up. Telling him her life might be in danger invoked ridicule—*drama queen*—but a couple of tears, and *bam*, he turned into a knight in shining armor...or in this case, a Navy SEAL.

That used to turn her on. It still did if she were honest. Unfortunately these days, it also annoyed her. She wasn't a kid anymore. Not some teenage girl with her head in the clouds. He might call her a drama queen, but his protective act was a joke after all the times he'd walked away when she needed him.

Marriage. Did anyone ever survive it?

She broke the breakfast pastry in half and took a bite. She would have preferred chocolate, but sugar was sugar. Maybe if she put food in her stomach, she could handle coffee. The smell was certainly appetizing.

Maggie sat at Bianca's feet. Her eyes were dark like Cal's but her energy was bright and playful. Bianca tossed her a corner, and the dog caught it in mid-air and swallowed it whole. She panted, looking like she was smiling again. Bianca ignored her and tapped a few icons on her phone.

Instantly, a black-and-white picture of the marina's land entrance appeared on the screen. Everything looked the same. No new vehicles, no pedestrians out in the storm.

She continued to watch, thinking about what Cal had said. Being a SEAL had been his life. That's why she'd had to let him go. Cal put himself through the training and the danger involved with being a SEAL in order to drown out emotional pain. Every time she'd tried to talk to him about their marriage, her miscarriages, or leaving the navy, he'd shut her down.

During six years of marriage, he'd never been an overly warm person, but he'd never been cold either. Until she'd lost the first baby and he'd lost his father in rapid succession. The SEAL missions had kept coming and Cal had wrapped himself in ice.

The coffee wasn't done percolating when he stepped out of the bathroom. A wave of humid air and the smell of sandalwood came with him. A towel hung low on his waist, beads of moisture covered his chest.

He was inked on his upper shoulders, a rising Phoenix on his right and a trident on the other. Various scars were visible— one under his right pec, another on his left calf, a trio on his lower back. As he dried himself in full view, her eye caught site of an ugly red scar near his left collarbone. He'd been shot during the mission. A little lower and he wouldn't be standing there in all his glory.

Snagging a second towel, he dried his hair as the dog did her best to get his attention, acting like she hadn't seen him in hours rather than minutes.

Bianca's eyes tracked a bead of water as it flowed down over his left pec. It continued down his ribs, one by one, until it hit the first rock-hard ab. As if it were enjoying the terrain, the droplet languidly slid over the muscle. Like a tiny rollercoaster, it dived into the crevice, then topped the next ab before it finally hit the towel wrapped around his hips.

Bianca licked her lips.

Cal's hair was short so it didn't take much buffing to dry. He flipped the towel over his shoulder, the ends of his hair in disarray and sauntered to the sink. There he poured coffee into a mug and offered it to her. "I only have one coffee cup so we'll have to share."

Sharing coffee. Why did that sound so sexy? Bianca glued her eyes to the small screen in front of her. "That's okay. I don't want any."

"After you made a fresh pot, you don't want a cup?" He squeezed into the bench, sliding her sideways. The towel around his waist split over his leg, baring the muscled expanse of skin and daring to reveal more.

He did a chin cock at her phone. "What's that?"

Tongue-tied, Bianca fought to keep her attention above his

waist, above his naked chest for that matter. "It's a... I put a..." She couldn't form a coherent sentence with him this near and this...naked.

Cal slid the cup to her. "Drink. You need caffeine."

What she needed was a good old-fashioned screw on the table. Seeing him, being close to him...it was driving her hormones crazy. Maybe if she got it out of her system, she could concentrate again.

No. *So not going there.* Like an electrical circuit, she and Cal were the positive and negative poles the current ran between. At one time, she'd thought they were a direct circuit—her always the negative pole and him the positive one—but after marriage, she now thought of their relationship as an alternating current, neither of them always positive or always negative. These days, they alternated their polarity on a regular basis.

And yet, always there was that delicious, dangerous electricity between them.

Accepting the cup, she took a sip. Caffeine really was the last thing she needed, but she let her lips linger over the rim, pretending to drink while she fought her natural urge to rip his towel off and put her mouth on something much more satisfying. "Could you put some clothes on?"

He smirked, rose from the seat, and grabbed a dry pair of shorts from a drawer under the bunk bed. Without returning to the bathroom, he dropped the towel and pulled on the shorts. "What's the camera for? You that paranoid?"

Damn him. Like she needed the full Monty after the bench peepshow. Her parts weren't just tingling now, they were exploding like fireworks. She crossed her legs under the table and pretended she hadn't been watching as he turned once more to face her.

"Better?" he said.

He'd never been self-conscious of his body. Not that he flaunted it. Not Cal. But he never worried about how he looked, and for good reason. He was beautiful.

She met his gaze and a little thrill went through her at the heat burning in those dark orbs. He knew he was distracting her, probably had done it on purpose to see how she'd react. She'd known this would be a trial and she had to stay firm. She had to keep the good memories, the ones where Cal loved her and made her feel important, at bay. She had to remember all the reasons she'd filed for divorce.

Hard to do when he was looking at her like that. All that intense, gorgeous male letting her know he still wanted her. Even after she'd ripped off the bandage on their marriage and exposed the fact they weren't good for each other anymore.

Well, she wasn't playing games. It was time to be one-hundred-percent truthful. "I've always loved your body, Cal," she murmured, maintaining eye contact. "There's nothing I'd rather do right now than jump your bones, but I'm not here to seduce you and I'm not repeating the same mistakes with you and our marriage again. The camera is for our protection."

This time he sat on the bed. His shoulders slumped, his eyes went flat. "Fine. Talk. Why are you in danger and from whom? What did you find out about Warfighter?"

She'd irritated him. *Not the first time.* How much should she tell him? "Someone leaked the details of the mission before you were sent in."

Nothing changed on his face, yet she sensed his entire body stiffening, going on alert. "Who?"

Bianca fiddled with her phone, stalling. She was about to go out on a limb here, and she'd always liked Senator Halston. He reminded her of Cal's dad. "I don't have concrete proof, but I—"

"Who the fuck leaked it?" His face was in shadow, his eyes pure black with anger.

She swallowed hard. "Senator Halston."

"Patrick Halston?" He snickered in disbelief. "The man *was* a SEAL back in the day. He's our biggest supporter on the Intelligence Committee."

She knew it would be a hard sell to Cal. Even harder to the

27

Justice Department. Sometimes the truth sucked. "A week ago, I was eavesdropping on a cult outside of the city. Running satellite images, intercepting calls, that kind of thing."

"I know what you do for the NSA."

Oh, but he didn't. Not all of it. "Senator Halston was here for a dog and pony show at Camp Pendleton. He received a call from a top official in D.C. at five o'clock in the morning last Saturday. I intercepted the call...accidentally."

Bianca paused and glanced down at her phone's screen. Was that a seagull she'd seen from the corner of her eye swooping past the camera upstairs or something else? A red sedan backed out of a parking space and headed for the entrance. Probably someone who'd decided not to ride out the storm on their boat.

Cal opened his hands, urging her on. "And?"

The rest of the marina appeared rain-drenched and quiet. "Halston wasn't on base where he should have been. That's one of the reasons my program picked up the call. He was at a hotel in downtown San Diego with a woman. The caller"—she couldn't tell him who it was without revealing too much detail and raising suspicions about her real job inside the NSA—"told him 'loose lips sink ships.'"

"It's just an old saying, B"

He didn't get it yet but he would. "There are people inside the NSA that use everyday common sayings to communicate more...sinister...messages. 'Loose lips sink ships' is a threat, telling Halston to shut his mouth or suffer the consequences. The caller said, 'you've already cost me my best blue elephant, and you've cost the president a second term in office. Haven't you learned your lesson?'"

"Blue elephant?" Cal's brows dipped together. "What's that?"

"That would be me." Bianca tapped her temple. "Because my memory is like an elephant's, and certain people inside the NSA refer to me, and others like me, as that animal."

"Why blue?"

Here's where it could get dicey. "Colors designate which section the elephant works for."

His eyes narrowed slightly. "You work for S2E."

The NSA was made up of a dozen directorates with sub-units and sub-sub-units, all labeled with letters and numbers, many of which were hidden from the general public. Bianca had started with one directorate, ended up with another. Command and Control. Six people in the world knew it existed: the president, vice president, her Command and Control boss, Jonathan Brockmann, Senator Halston, and a couple of people at Homeland.

Even though she'd been yanked out of C&C and sent to California, she was under oath not to expose the truth about her unique job.

If I end up dead, it won't matter. "A blue elephant is one of the highest analyst code names inside the NSA."

One brow arched. "I didn't realize you'd made it that far."

"That's what happens when you're stationed on the west coast and your wife is stationed on the east and you're never home for normal, married-couple conversations over dinner. You know, 'Hi, honey, I'm home. How was your day?'"

His eyes darkened and Bianca dropped her gaze to the screen. This was no time to dig into their marital problems, and she couldn't have told him about the blue elephant status before now anyway.

She eyed a black SUV turning into the marina. It did a slow cruise by the boats on the far end of the docks. All of the boats were larger and nicer than Cal's. In the driving rain, the SUV's wipers slapped furiously back and forth, struggling to clear the windshield.

"I was recently sent here to work with the Southern California Violent Crimes Taskforce and told to make it look like I'm helping them take out a couple of criminal organizations," she told Cal. "My actual assignment is to covertly investigate the high-ranking Bureau agent in charge of the taskforce, Victor Dupé. With my clearance levels and the type of operations I've handled for the past nine months, investigating an FBI agent is below my clearance level and pay grade. Way below. I believe the reason I've been demoted is because I made a call on an operation that went bad. It was a top secret operation that very, very few people knew about, and when it failed, I took the blame. They shipped me across the country on a bogus assignment to get me out of D.C., and now someone is following me and tracking everything I do."

She paused. Accusing a member of Congress—someone she'd trusted emphatically—wasn't easy to do. "After hearing that phone conversation, I've figured out that *I* didn't blow the operation. My intel was accurate and solid. I made the correct call, but someone else, namely Senator Halston, leaked information about the operation before it went live and that's why the mission failed."

Cal shook his head. "You got all of that from a simple sentence about a blue elephant and a reelection bid?"

Bianca had kept her cards close to her chest for so long, the thought of divulging more facts—*the* fact—that would trigger Cal's understanding felt like betraying her country. She'd rather jump off the boat into the cold Pacific than expose the NSA's secrets. "I'm the only blue elephant the NSA currently employs. The other one, Alisha Jamison, was killed in a freak car accident six months ago."

Except for the storm, silence reigned. Bianca glanced at the screen, saw the SUV had made its slow crawl through the docks and parking lot and was now leaving.

Cal rubbed his knuckles over the slight growth of beard on his square jaw. "What does this have to do with Warfighter?"

"I've been with a sub-unit of SE2 for approximately nine months. During that time, I had one assignment. Track down Otto Grimes."

Cal stiffened at the mention of the terrorist's name. "You were on his tail?"

"I was tasked with finding—or creating—a scenario to take him out."

"You?" Skepticism showed on his face. "Why isn't the CIA handling it?"

They'd been "handling" Otto Grimes for years and not getting anywhere. President Norman had had enough. "Grimes was supposed to attend a birthday party for Prince Hamid's son on board his yacht on August 23rd. The CIA had an asset—a crew member—on board the yacht. After careful analysis of all the players and the situation, I recommended the crew member see to it that the ship entered international waters after the party was over and the guests fell asleep. That would allow a SEAL team to board, take out Otto, and disappear. It was a solid plan, so when the birthday party happened, I made the call to send in the SEALs, and my boss agreed. So did the Secretaries of Defense and Homeland."

"*You* made the call? Since when do you decide when and where a SEAL team goes?"

Since she'd been appointed to Command and Control as part of the President's Threat Matrix team. Many people knew about the Threat Matrix team, but C&C didn't exist on paper.

"President Norman pulled the plug on the operation at the last second. The timing was wrong, he said, even though every one of my analyses confirmed we had better than an eighty-three percent chance of success. The next day, Grimes called up three terrorist cells who set off bombs at multiple U.S. universities based overseas, killing fourteen Americans and injuring twenty-six people."

Cal no doubt knew about the bombings. Everyone knew. They'd been all over the news with plenty of mudslinging at the president and his cabinet for letting it happen. Grimes had produced a new YouTube video calling POTUS a little boy hiding behind his mother's skirts.

Cal's forehead creased as he did the mental math. "That's when my unit was called up."

She nodded. "First, I was told to come up with a new approach to take out Otto."

"To save the presidency and win Linc Norman a second term."

Now he was catching on. "Blue elephant, second term for the prez. Still think the caller was talking about someone else?"

Cal got up, drank half the cup of coffee, and refilled the cup. "I'm still struggling with the fact you made the call to send in my team."

The dog watched Cal's every move. So did Bianca. He didn't drink any more coffee. Instead, his jaw set and a muscle jumped under his left cheekbone as he eyed her.

Danger. It radiated off him like heat off a missile.

Cal would never hurt her. His intense stare, however, might make her melt. "I made the call to send in *a* team. I never know which unit will be picked—I'm kept in the dark, and that's how it should be. Most of the time, I don't even know if it will be SEALs or Marines or Berets. All I know is that a Special Forces unit will go in and get the job done. In this case, however, I forecasted it would be a commando unit such as yours who knew the terrain and the terrorist in question better than any other team."

He stewed, still seeming to struggle to wrap his brain around her "desk jockey" job. "But *you* gave the order?"

"I'm an integral player behind the scenes when it comes to tracking and analyzing terrorists, international terrorism hotspots, and hunting down terrorists on Homeland's most wanted list. It's a critical piece in my job to keep POTUS safe."

He zeroed in on her for a long minute, probably hoping she'd break under that intimidating stare.

She didn't.

His gaze was unremitting and challenging. Was he blaming her for sending him and his men into a death trap?

He didn't need to. She'd already castigated herself a million times. "Grimes has always been an unpredictable leader, as you

32

know," she said, "but he always rewards his lieutenants for a job well done. That's the consistent thread I uncovered during my time tracking him. I knew after the bombings successfully went off at those universities, he would find a way to meet with his top lieutenants, Warwick and Meidi, to reward them. Based on my outcome analysis, your team had an eighty-nine-point-six percent chance of success of killing or arresting Grimes and at least one of them. An even higher percentage than the first SEAL unit had."

He sipped the coffee, his dark eyes never leaving her. She could almost see the dozens of questions he had behind those eyes.

She tried to hold his gaze, but on the screen, she saw a dark shadow. The black SUV drove into the marina again.

"I have a lot more to tell you," she said, rising from the bench. "But right now, the most important thing you need to know is that a call was made at three-sixteen this morning. A call to an assassin the CIA has used for off-the-book wet jobs for the past twenty years. His assignment is to kill me."

She grabbed her briefcase and her damp jacket from the hook on the wall. Turning the screen so Cal could see it, she tried to stay composed. "He just pulled into the parking lot."

CHAPTER FOUR

Cal was still so attuned to Bianca's body, the moment she'd stiffened in response to something she saw on her phone, he had too.

Assess.

He'd turned up the heat on her and she'd responded by shutting him down. His ego smarted, but he'd seen the lust in her eyes, felt the energy pouring off of her in the tight quarters. She wasn't immune to him any more than he was to her. Every time he was close to her, his chest tightened with love, and everything below his waist hardened with yearning. Hers, in typical fashion, always responded.

Figures I'd fall for a crazy woman. Beautiful but crazy.

"The CIA sent an assassin after you." Saying it out loud made it sound even more ludicrous. On the phone's screen that she was now shoving at him, he saw a dark vehicle driving slowly through the parking lot. "And he drives a Cadillac Escalade."

Her body tensed even more, not from danger but irritation. She lowered the phone and got in his face. "I know you have a ton of questions, and I'll try to answer them, but I'm not kidding, Cal. There is a man after me."

He moved the curtain aside on the small, round window to his left. A tiny stream of water was leaking in through the worthless seal. *Capillary effect.* Water could find the smallest of cracks and the effect more or less acted as a water pump to keep bringing water in. Kind of like his and Bianca's tumultuous relationship...they'd found each other's cracks long ago, widening them over time with all their petty shit.

Water was also leaking in from a spot near the door. Another thing to fix on the boat. The capillary effect was why water could enter at one point, such as the window, and come out three feet away at the doorframe. Bianca's love did the same thing to him. The brush of her hand or the feel of her thigh next to his circulated heat and love and lust through his entire being.

Who's the crazy one?

The storm had mostly blown itself out, the wind dying off to a light breeze. The rain continued in a steady drizzle.

Cal scanned the parking lot. The SUV was gone. "The CIA can't harm an American citizen on US soil. You know that."

"The CIA is not behind this."

Maggie rose from her spot and walked over to the stairs. Her nose twitched as she sniffed the air. "You just said they were."

Bianca was the queen of exaggerated sighs, yet this time, her sigh was contained. "The assassin is experienced in doing wet work for the CIA—*that's* what I said."

Through the window, Cal saw two men in trench coats carry a net onboard their small fishing vessel. Todd and Hurley. He wasn't the only one in the marina whose work day had been put on hold. "Why would anyone want to kill you, B?"

"Can we talk about this later? We really need to get out of here."

She started to turn away. Maggie whined. Cal reached for Bianca's arm and stopped her. "Who is this assassin, and who hired him?"

"It's—"

Everything happened at once. Maggie barked, Bianca whirled to look at her, and the window beside Cal's shoulder exploded.

Protect.

Without thinking, he barreled into Bianca, taking her down in a hail of glass and rainwater. His arms went around her, one hand cradling her head before it struck the floor.

She let go of an "oomph" when his weight fell on her. Her glasses flew off her face and her briefcase skidded across the floor, smacking into the leg of the table. A fine line of blood blossomed on her right cheek. Cal shifted to the side, keeping her tucked close to his much bigger body.

She'd been hit. By flying glass or something worse? The cut across the top of her cheek appeared thin, as if from a piece of glass, but the blood...

It pooled and ran over her cheekbone, flowing backward into her hair. Into his fingers at the back of her head.

Cal's stomach fell. His chest constricted. "Shit. Are you alright?"

Bianca's eyes were round saucers as she stared up at him, bewilderment and fear clear in their blue depths. She gave a single nod and her throat worked as she swallowed hard.

He glanced up and saw a hole, a depression in the wall across from where they'd been standing. From his position on the floor, all he could see was the indention in the wood paneling, and the faintest gleam of metal, but Cal knew the sound of a bullet punching through glass. Knew the reaction his body had to being shot at.

Shield. In his head, he heard the sounds of battle. Smelled the odor of metal and blood and sand. For a split second, Bianca's body morphed into Tank's...

And then she squirmed, sucking in a breath and bringing him back to the present.

Temples pounding once more, he refocused on her face. Even though it had been months since he'd felt his wife beneath him, he couldn't deny his instant and automatic response to her delicious warmth and feminine softness.

It's only adrenaline. A natural response to the situation.

In the back of his mind, he knew it was more. His body

recognized the familiar feel of the only woman he'd ever loved and was responding accordingly.

Now was not the time for his body to take a fucking stroll down memory lane. Someone had shot at him and Bianca. *Maybe she isn't crazy after all.* Like always, the male inside him rose to the challenge of keeping her safe.

"I thought…," Bianca stuttered, "…that boat windows were made of polycarbonate."

Miss Google was back. Polycarbonate was strong, flexible, and bulletproof. "Windows made from polycarbonate are notorious for leaks and easily scratched by saltwater spray," he told her. "These are good old-fashioned glass."

Maggie whined from somewhere off to his right. Bianca lay ramrod stiff underneath him. His mind flashed back to their shared youth in the Midwest. The way she'd always been fearless about adapting to her environment, no matter how shitty it got, and to trying new things. The only thing she'd ever been scared of was people. "People can hurt you," she'd told him, "in ways Mother Nature never dreamed of."

He wiped blood from her cheek with the pad of his thumb. "I've got you, and I won't let anyone hurt you."

Her teeth chattered. "Do you…believe me…now?"

"Bullets typically get my attention."

She started to say something, but he silenced her with a finger to her lips. Her tongue reached out to lick them at the same moment, and brushed against his finger. A shot of sexual energy shot right to his groin.

Like he needed a second shot.

He lifted an eyebrow and she cringed, realizing how suggestive the habit came across. "Sorry. I'm just…it's just…if I hadn't turned my head to look at your dog… Shouldn't the glass at least be tempered or something?"

"In this old boat?" No telling how many times that window had been replaced. "The previous owner didn't put money into repairs since the boat never left the dock."

There were no more shots. Ignoring his raging hard-on, Cal lifted his head and caught sight of the dog huddled in the corner, panting. Her ears were back, eyes darting from the entrance to him and back. Except for the rain gently hitting the hull, he heard nothing.

Didn't mean the fucker wasn't close by. From the trajectory of the bullet, and the fact the window faced north, the shooter had to be...

Right next door.

Except there was no boat in the slip next to Cal's. His boat sat at the southern-most end of the docks, alone and on its own. His closest neighbor was Gus Madington, five slips away.

Gus was in his fifties and had a long-standing friendship with alcohol. His hands shook so badly, he could barely hold a beer bottle, much less a gun. Cal was pretty sure the guy had never owned or fired a gun in his life.

If it wasn't Gus, then who?

No way. Cal shook his head. Bianca had to be mistaken about her mysterious assassin. Why would anyone, especially the United States government, hire someone to kill her?

Defend. A bullet was a bullet, and until he figured out who'd fired it, he wasn't taking chances.

Cal made a stay motion, first at Maggie, then at Bianca. Keeping one eye on the door and the other on the broken window, he slid completely off Bianca and slithered to the bunk bed. Reaching up, he found the cool steel of his handgun. He checked the chamber and clip. One bullet. *Sloppy.* He needed to reload.

Slipping his hand under his mattress, he found a fresh clip. *Good to go.*

A glance at Bianca gave him pause. Like the dog, she had stayed put, but also like Maggie, her eyes were wide and her body shook with tremors. While Maggie was nervous and unsure, Bianca was frozen with fear.

Not good. He needed her clearheaded and able to move when

he told her to. "Bianca." He said her name out loud—not too loud, but with enough force to break her trance.

Her eyes snapped out of their fear-induced haze. She shifted to look at him.

"Are you armed?" he said.

She shook her head.

Great. "You think some asshole's trying to kill you but you left your weapon at home?"

"I don't...own...a-a-a..." She bit her bottom lip, either out of frustration or to make her teeth stop chattering. "I don't own a gun."

"Why the hell not?"

"I'm an analyst...not a...field agent. I don't n-n-n...need one."

Oh, for the love of...

He had weapons stored in hiding places all over the boat. Not easy to get to at the moment without giving away his position. A sneak-and-peek outside was in order, but he wasn't leaving Bianca unarmed.

"Take this." He handed her the Glock. He'd taught her to handle one years ago, and while she might have been given "analyst" as a job description at the NSA, he knew she'd had weapons training. "Stay down. Belly on the floor."

Her fingers shook as she accepted the weapon but her face firmed with determination. "Where are you going?"

He pointed up. "Need to get eyes on the shooter and grab another gun."

As he stayed low and crab-walked across her body, her free hand locked on his arm. "It's too risky."

Blood continued to pour from her cheek wound. He wanted to grab the nearby towel and press it to the cut but time was of the essence and while there was a lot of blood, she wouldn't die from a graze. "I'm a trained SEAL, B. I know what I'm doing."

She closed her eyes for a split-second as if gathering courage. "It's Tephra."

The name stopped him. *Tephra?* As in Rory Tephra? Cal reared back. He hadn't heard that name in ages.

Rory Tephra didn't exist except as a ghost whispered about in BUDs training. Tephra, the ultimate SEAL who had disappeared on a secret mission in Sarajevo ten years ago. No body had ever been found, but the rumors about him being alive were as abundant as Elvis reports. He'd become an urban legend, a myth that had grown bigger than life. Every SEAL wanted to become Tephra.

Cal almost had.

"Bianca, that's crazy. You're in shock."

"The hell I am." She squeezed his arm. Hard. He got the message. He could count on one hand the number of times he'd heard her swear. "Rory Tephra is a soldier of fortune...a killer. And he's after me."

Cal's brain rejected the idea, but his body and his instincts clearly shouted that Bianca was telling the truth. The unadulterated, although no less dramatic, truth. "Then he's about to meet his maker because anyone who shoots at my wife is going to get his ass handed to him."

CHAPTER FIVE

He found me. Tephra found me. How?

Her heart felt like she'd swallowed it and it now lodged in her throat. Bianca forced herself to breathe in through her nose and out through her lips. No hyperventilating. No going into shock. She'd handled plenty of tough situations before—albeit none involving a hitman—and she would *not* freak out like some wimpy girl regardless of the fact she'd almost taken a bullet in the head a few seconds ago.

Cal, on hands and knees, started to move off her. God, she'd brought Tephra right to his doorstep. She knew it had been a strong possibility, but now...

"I'm sorry," she said to Cal. "I shouldn't have come here."

He paused. "Do what I say and sit tight. Give me fifteen minutes. If I don't return, call 911 and everyone else you can think of, got it?"

Like the police could help her. If Cal died, she was dead—either from Tephra's bullets or from guilt. "You damn well better return or I'll haunt you in the afterlife."

Cal smirked. "I'll be back."

God, she loved that smirk. Loved his cockiness, even though it drove her crazy. "Swear it."

He cocked an eyebrow. When they were young, she'd made him pinky swear to things, like not telling her mother where she'd hid the rent money so her mom couldn't blow it on meth or Shopping Network deals. "We're not kids, anymore, Bianca."

"Swear. It."

His gaze dropped to her lips. Ever so slowly, his face lowered so he was barely a breath away. The tip of his nose brushed hers and his warm breath fell gently on her lips. "I swear on *The Art of War*, I'll be back for you."

A warm rush of love spread through her body. Her nerves tingled. Without thinking, she tilted up her chin and skimmed his lips with hers. A kiss, but not a kiss. "Fifteen minutes, not a second more."

He nodded and crawled off, keeping low as he headed for the steps and the door to the upper deck.

As Bianca rolled onto her stomach, she cursed the fact she'd lost her glasses, but she could still make out his blurry frame as he appeared to open a panel under the stairs and disappear into the bowels of the boat.

The dog, also watching, whined and walked over to the place where he'd vanished, sniffing at the paneling. Bianca rose to her hands and knees, careful of the loaded gun—a Glock with no active safety—and the broken glass littering the floor.

Where are my glasses?

She hated being blind. Grabbing one of the towels, she brushed glass out of the way, then folded the towel and put it under her knees. Her cheek dripped blood on her hands, the gun, and the floor. She shimmied toward the table, stopping every few inches to feel around for her glasses. Her fingers touched leather.

Briefcase.

She stretched, reaching under the table. Everything was a blur. Her fingers threaded over more glass bits and what felt like old dog kibble. "Eww."

She smelled Maggie before she saw her. A heavy head knocked into Bianca's hip and something clattered to the floor next to her. Bianca reached back and felt the cool plastic of her Dior frames.

Thank God.

Or Maggie, in this case.

Bianca rubbed her bleeding cheek against her shoulder and finagled the glasses onto her nose. The world, small as it was under the table in *The Love Boat*, came into focus.

"Good dog," she whispered, giving Maggie a pat on the head. A pink tongue emerged from Maggie's mouth and the dog panted in Bianca's face.

Behind her, the bathroom beckoned. No windows and only one entrance. Good cover where she could point and shoot. "Come on, girl," she said. "Time to hide."

Bianca used the towel to clear a path and crawled to the bathroom, hoping Maggie would follow and not cut her paws. Once inside the door, Bianca turned to see Maggie still standing next to the table, head cocked.

"Maggie, come!"

The Lab obeyed, then stood at the threshold and looked back toward the steps. Bianca snapped her fingers and the dog shifted her sad eyes to Bianca's face. "He's coming back." *I hope.* "Get in here."

The room was so small, Bianca could barely turn around without bumping into something. The dog stepped into the tiny bathroom and laid down on the floor next to the shower, half on top of Bianca. She sniffed the air in the direction of Bianca's face.

Blood. The metallic smell mixed with the scent of salt air blowing in through the broken window. The side of Bianca's face was wet with it. Her hair sticky.

What idiot used non-tempered glass on a boat window?

And how did the shooter know it wasn't?

Keeping an eye on the cabin, and Cal's gun at the ready, Bianca grabbed a washcloth with her free hand and soaked it in the sink. For a brief second, she glanced at her reflection in the mirror and nearly gagged.

This was why she wasn't a nurse, doctor, or EMT. The sight of blood made her queasy. Add that to the fact the rocking boat had already done a number on her stomach and an assassin had taken a shot at her, she was in no position to do anything but...

Yep, there it was. Her stomach clenched, a shot of heat filling her jaws. In the next instant, everything in her system revolted and she hung her head over the toilet.

Great. If Tephra comes after me now, I'm easy pickings.

Tephra wouldn't get to her. Not with Cal standing between them.

She'd been betting on his protective instinct and it had paid off. He stilled cared enough about her to want to keep her safe. Playing on that instinct was low and manipulative. Exactly what Cal hated. But she'd learned at an early age that manipulating others was the way to get her needs met. Being direct got her a slap or a beating. Although she'd worked for years to overcome that awful failsafe of manipulating people, old habits died hard when you were staring death in the face.

Besides, the direct route *had* failed. Cal hadn't believed her until someone took a shot at her. Now he was all Mr. Protective. Exactly what she needed in order to survive.

Guilt nonetheless ate at her. Clawed through her stomach and up into her heart. It was one thing that she'd nearly gotten him killed in action when she'd sent him after Grimes. This was worse. She'd purposely put him in harm's way in order to shield herself.

He deserves better than me. One of the reasons she had to follow through on the divorce.

Even after all these years, all the therapy and telling herself she was no longer a victim, here she was, struggling to survive. And just like when she was a kid, she couldn't do it on her own. She prided herself on being independent, smart, and a bulldog when it came to thriving in the face of abuse and neglect, but underneath it all, she was still that scared, helpless little girl inside. A girl nobody but Cal had ever wanted.

At the thought, her stomach finished emptying its contents. Weak and suddenly exhausted, Bianca removed her glasses and washed her face as best she could with one hand, keeping the other with the gun at the ready.

A steady pressure on the back of her legs told her Maggie was leaning against them. Bianca couldn't hear any sounds except for the normal ones coming from outside the boat, but that didn't mean anything. Cal was quieter and quicker than any ninja, and Tephra no doubt was as well.

She flipped on the skeleton light bulb over the sink, then immediately turned it back off. *Stupid.* Even if Tephra couldn't see the bathroom from outside, there was no sense spotlighting herself.

No sense in scaring herself either. While the mirror was flecked with water spots, and she'd only had a half second to see herself, the light had given her skin a sickly pall. The dark circles under her eyes and the cut across her cheek only added to the zombie effect. She pressed the cool washcloth to her cut. The blood was finally easing up.

She might not be a nurse, but she could guess the thin slash had been caused by glass and not a bullet. She sunk to the floor and put her back against the shower. Maggie eased up next to her and laid down with her head in Bianca's lap.

Keeping her attention trained on the door, Bianca set down the washcloth and stroked the dog's head. The gun was heavy in her right hand, heavier than she remembered the weapons being in her firearm training. But Cal was a big guy. His gun matched.

Firearm training…a memory of the day Cal had taught her to fire a small Walther PPK. Then a Beretta, a Glock, and lastly a Smith and Wesson. He'd figured she needed a variety of experiences with handguns, knowing she'd remember every gun, how to fire it, and how to clean it afterward.

Maggie lifted her head and nudged Bianca's hand, jarring her from her reverie, her body going on alert. "What is it girl?"

She scanned the door and beyond, but the dog was staring up at her. The top of her dark head looked wet. Bianca ran a finger over the spot and realized it was blood. Her blood. The bleeding had kicked up again.

"Sorry." Bianca used the washcloth to wipe off the top of the dog's head. *Too much blood.* The washcloth was a mess. Bianca gained her feet and then had to grab the edge of the sink when the room spun.

Lightheaded.

Not from loss of blood. From the loss of *everything.*

Her footing. Her career.

Cal.

Quickly, she rinsed the washcloth, washed her cheek again, and looked in the flat medicine cabinet. *Too dark. Need light.*

Only stupid heroines in horror movies turned on the lights.

A whitish box caught her eye. Bandages. *Hallelujah.*

She opened the box and fished one out. There was no way she was setting down the gun, so she used her teeth to rip open the stupid paper covering.

She was just about to stick the bandage on her cheek when the boat rocked hard and Maggie bolted from the room.

Bianca shifted to look around the doorway and lifted the gun. Where was that stupid dog going? "Get back here!"

All she could see was the dog's butt and wagging tail. The rest of her was under the table. A second later, Maggie backed out and when she turned around, Bianca nearly laughed at what was in the dog's mouth.

Purple plastic. Sparkles. A screen flashing with a silent incoming call.

My phone.

A modicum of relief swept through her. Maybe she *should* call the police. Or Cooper Harris. Or…

*Wait…*the phone was still connected to the video camera she'd installed above deck.

"Bring it here, girl."

Maggie did, and Bianca retrieved the phone from her mouth, wiping the dog slobber off with the washcloth.

She'd turned off the ringer but it still vibrated in her hand. Speak of the devil...caller ID told her it was Cooper. Her automatic response was to answer, like she had when Ronni called, and pretend everything was normal. While the idea had appealed a minute ago, she didn't want to have to explain the situation. Cooper was miles away. He couldn't help her right here, right now.

She tapped the ignore button.

The call went to voicemail, and she swiped through her screens until she found the camera app. If she could get eyes on the marina again, she'd be able to see what was going on.

If Cal was in stealth mode, she'd never see him. Probably wouldn't see Rory Tephra either. But if she could at least get the license plate of the SUV...

The app opened and the screen blurred. She ticked off a couple of seconds, waiting for it to clear and the marina entrance to come into focus.

It didn't.

The kaleidoscope of white and gray shadows suggested the camera was facedown. She closed the app, reopened it, hoping it was a glitch.

The same picture appeared.

Damn. The wind had done a number on the camera even though she'd secured it as firmly as she could. Either that or the wind had blown something on top of the camera covering the lens.

Or maybe Tephra had covered it.

She needed to go check. Fix the camera and try to zoom in on that SUV if it was still there.

Trust Cal. If the SUV was still out there, hopefully he got a look at it and memorized the plates.

Her heart thumped in her throat again. A part of her hoped the vehicle was gone. That Tephra was gone. That Cal was safe.

Above her head, she heard a soft thud, so soft she nearly missed it. The dog looked up at the same time she did, confirming it wasn't her imagination. Her breath froze in her chest. Just the wind or a footstep?

Lowering the phone, she focused on the area beyond the bathroom. She could see the table and bench seat. Faint light from outside the cabin reflected on the glass littering the floor.

Another thud sounded, then a scrape across the deck off to her left.

The only bad thing about her hiding spot was the fact she couldn't see the stairs. Couldn't see who might be coming down them.

She raised the gun with both hands, keeping her arms straight and pointing toward the bathroom door opening. A Glock was good. Reliable, lightweight, seventeen rounds in the magazine. Trusted by law enforcement officers around the world.

Point and shoot.

She thought she heard a slight rustle...or was that another footstep? The boat seemed to list slightly to the left.

In her peripheral vision, she noticed Maggie had her ears perked. The dog's body, next to Bianca's, vibrated with tension. Excitement or fear?

Either she was losing it, or there was definitely another human presence on board. A bead of sweat rolled down Bianca's neck and under her collar. The strong smell of the ocean after a storm hung in the air, the humidity high.

Something inside of her wanted to call out to Cal. She bit her lip. Giving away her location by not keeping her trap shut would be yet another stupid heroine move.

So she sat tight, debating whether to rise to her feet or stay low. If the presence on board was Tephra, and he came around the corner, he'd expect her to be standing, right? Her advantage lay in staying down and taking him by surprise.

A shadow fell across the floor outside the bathroom door. Her heart spiked with fear. *This is it.*

Bianca took a soundless breath, dragging oxygen deep into her lungs, then let it out halfway, like Cal had taught her, and put her finger on the trigger.

Point and shoot.

Bianca felt something hit her hip, a swipe, swipe, swipe, right before she heard someone whisper "B?"

The only person who ever called her "B" was Cal.

Maggie's tail wagged harder, beating against Bianca's hip. "Cal?"

"Don't shoot."

She automatically lowered the gun, pulling her finger from the trigger and letting the rest of her breath go. Her muscles twitched, flexing and releasing from the surge of adrenaline still pouring through her system.

The shadow grew and Cal's big body came into view. The relief that swamped her nearly laid her out right there on the bathroom floor. A sob caught in her throat and she jammed the back of her hand against her mouth.

Cal frowned, squeezing into the room. He patted the dog and squatted in front of Bianca. Maggie licked his face in greeting and he chuckled before running his hand over Bianca's hair and giving her ponytail a little tug. "Whoever it was is gone. You're safe."

She couldn't help it—she grabbed his shoulders and dropped her forehead to his chest. "Thank you."

One hand rubbed her back. The other stayed at the base of her neck. "We need to move. He may come back."

The smell of him, part soap from his shower and part ocean spray, filled her nostrils. Her cheek burned from the cut. "Where should we go?" she asked.

He released her and confiscated the gun from the floor. "Sit tight. I have a plan."

She didn't want to turn loose of his shoulders, his solidness, but she did anyway. *Distance.* She had to keep some, no matter how vulnerable she felt right now. She couldn't let him and his protectiveness worm their way back under her skin.

But, oh, did she ever want to. Heart sad, she watched him disappear once more, heading for the upper deck. A few seconds later, the boat's engine roared to life.

CHAPTER SIX

Bianca stayed put for several minutes, wondering where they were going. Maggie happily left her, toenails clacking on the steps as she went topside following her master.

I'd like to do that too.

Cal was a conundrum. Always had been. She wouldn't call him nice or even particularly polite. In fact, at times, he was downright unfriendly and inconsiderate, and being married to him was more challenging than decrypting China's North Korea strategy.

But he was brave and loyal to a fault. Duty and honor were the driving motives for everything he did. Those qualities practically oozed from his pores, making her fall for him time and time again, even if he did forget little things like, say, her birthday.

He better make it up to me next year...if I live that long.

Of course, even if she did live to see another birthday, she and Cal would be divorced by then. If he couldn't remember her birthday when they were together, he certainly wouldn't remember it when they were apart.

Granted, this year had been the first time he'd forgotten, and he'd been out of the country for weeks on a mission along the Syrian border, but still...

A therapist had once told her that if there was more than a fifteen point difference in IQ between her and her partner, the chances of them having a successful relationship were extremely low. They would lack the right amount of communication for a healthy relationship.

What Bianca had determined, however, was that it wasn't the difference in their IQ that caused a lack of communication with Cal. It was that they both suffered from a low EQ.

The boat picked up speed, probably clearing the marina and heading for open water. Bianca heard a dull thud in the cabin and a rolling sound. The coffee cup. It must have fallen off the table and rolled along the floor. She grabbed the sink for balance and hauled herself to her feet. A quick splash of water on her face, a new bandage, and she peeked into the cabin.

Sure enough, the coffee in Cal's mug had joined the glass on the floor and the cup was rolling back and forth, whacking the handle against the bench seat. Wind howled through the broken window, mixing with salt spray. The sailcloth curtain hung in tatters.

So much for the boat not being seaworthy. The way the thing was bouncing and gyrating through the water, it seemed to be holding up just fine.

Shuffle-walking to the bed, she held on to the shelf nearby and stole a look outside.

They were heading north, out of the bay. She craned her neck and chanced looking behind them. The marina grew smaller, no black SUV anywhere to be seen.

Drawing in a deep breath, she edged back from the window and let it out slowly. *Safe.*

At least for now.

Where did they go from here? Could Tephra follow them on the water? It wasn't like they could stay out on the ocean forever.

Focus on the here and now.

Her cheek stung and her legs shook, but she forced herself not to sit down on the bed and have a good cry. Instead, she hunted for something to clean up the glass. The last thing she needed was for the dog to cut her paws and Cal to blame her for that on top of everything else.

The two cabinets under the sink held a garbage can and a few cleaning products. A worn-out broom and dustpan sat in a tall cabinet next to the stairs. Bianca moved them aside and started rapping lightly on the cheap plywood wall behind the broom. *This is where Cal disappeared.*

Her knuckles hit a section that had more give and made a lighter sound. A hidden door.

Her fingertips ran over the wood and found a tiny notch. One that looked almost natural in the cheap paneling. When she curled her fingers into it and gave it a tug it didn't budge. But when she pushed, a section gave way.

The hidden door swung open to reveal a compact space. On all three sides, various handguns and knives were meticulously placed, ready for someone to grab. *Cal's own personal gun safe.*

One spot was empty.

He'd grabbed a weapon but where had he gone from there? He hadn't come back into the cabin so there had to be another door.

Crouching, she again ran her fingers around the walls, avoiding touching the weapons. She couldn't find any other hidden door and no funny sounding areas when she knocked on the walls.

Backing out, she closed the secret door and grabbed the broom. Cal...always so secretive.

Just like you.

Sweeping up glass in the dimly lit cabin was challenging, especially when the boat continued to rise and dip as it sped through the water, but it gave her something besides the recent encounter with an assassin to concentrate on. She set the coffee cup in the sink and went to work.

She was under the table, sweeping up the last pieces she could find when Cal startled her. "What are you doing?"

Jerking up, she hit the back of her head on the tabletop. "Ow."

Inching her way out, she sat back on her heels and looked

up. She hadn't even noticed the boat had slowed or that he'd come down the stairs.

Her dustpan held an assortment of grossness. She held it out to show him. "Don't you ever clean under there?"

"It was the next thing on my to-do list, right after saving your ass from a bullet."

"Your dog saved me."

The dog in question was standing by Cal's legs. She wagged her tail and panted.

Cal took the dustpan from Bianca's hand and dumped the contents in the garbage can under the sink. Then he helped her stand. "How's your cheek?"

The boat rose and fell, sending Bianca's face into his chest. His very solid, very muscular chest that she'd always loved. He grabbed her by the arms to steady her, but she didn't immediately pull back. Instead, she tilted her head up and looked into his eyes. "I'm sorry for this. All of it."

He clenched his jaw and pushed her down onto the bench seat. "Sit."

Her balance leaving her, she didn't have much choice, her butt hitting the cushion. Cal went to the bathroom, came back with a blue plastic box with a white top on it. On the lid, red letters spelled out *First Aid Kit* above a red cross.

Without another word, he flipped open the lid and laid out a package of antiseptic ointment, gauze, and bandages. He knelt in front of her and unceremoniously ripped off the bandage on her cheek. "Hey!" she yelled, flinching.

He ignored her protest and opened a flat, square antiseptic wipe package. "This will sting."

She glared at him. "Like ripping off the bandage *didn't?*"

Again, he ignored her. That was Cal. Nothing was ever done slow and easy. Everything with him was a bandage that had to be ripped off fast and hard.

He was right. The antiseptic wipe stung like a bee, but Bianca refused to flinch this time. She wouldn't let him get to her. Wouldn't let him see she was in pain. She'd never be as tough and callous as he was, but she sure as hell wasn't a wimp.

Tossing the used wipe on the table, he fanned her face to dry the alcohol. Ripping open the ointment package, he squirted a small glob on a cotton swab. Gently, he brushed her cut with it, smearing the ointment around. His eyes stayed focused on her wound as he spoke. "You may end up with a scar."

His fingers were light but he continued to clench his jaw. *Tense. Pissed.* "A scar is better than being dead."

The swab went the way of the wipe, landing on the table. Next he grabbed a larger bandage than the one she'd used and removed it from its packaging.

"Where are we headed?"

"North."

She knew that. "Where?"

"A safe place. I need to figure some things out."

"Did you get the plate number on the Escalade?"

He placed the bandage on her cheek, smoothing it gently with one fingertip. "It was gone before I made the dock."

A shiver ran through her, her skin felt tingly and her head light. She opened her mouth to ask him something else but the words disappeared. Thoughts raced through her brain faster than she could catch them. Manic. *No, not now. Focus on something. Breathe.*

As Cal packed up his first aid kit, she kept her eyes pinned on the red cross. She liked the shape—balanced. A symbol of hope and caring. Maggie came over and laid her head on Bianca's lap. Her fur was dry now, thick and soft under Bianca's fingers.

Cal brought her a bottled water, then took out a knife and climbed up on the far side of the bench seat. He dug at something in the wall.

Her tongue felt thick as she took a swig of water, but touching Maggie's head was comforting. Cal's presence was as well. The activity in her brain slowed to its usual level. "What are you doing?"

The muscles in his arm moved as he worked at his task. "Your assassin left behind a token."

The bullet.

Bianca took another drink of water, hand shaking as she lifted the bottle. She stroked Maggie's head and silently thanked the dog once more for saving her life.

A second later, Cal pocketed the knife and pulled the compressed bullet from the wood. He held it up in the light, rolling it around. The pointed end had flattened but it was still an imposing sight. "Fucker used a BTSP. He knew he'd be shooting through a barrier."

She knew a lot of useless facts, some pretty important ones too. "What's a BTSP?"

"Snipers normally use a specific ammo, BTHP. When a sniper knows he'll be shooting through a barrier, like tempered glass, he uses BTSP. Different design."

Bianca's brain seemed to be floating in cotton candy. "Meaning what?"

Cal's eyes met hers. "He was prepared."

Exactly what she feared. Tephra knew she'd be on a boat. Cal's boat. She sat forward and put her forehead in her hands. Her brain cleared for a second as a fresh shot of adrenaline entered her system. "Tephra knew that if I figured out he was after me, I'd run to you. You live on a boat, which under normal circumstances has polycarbonate or tempered glass for windows."

Cal's nimble fingers turned the bullet over and over. Moving closer to the window, he eyed the once-pointed tip in better light. "Huh, that's weird."

The remnants of the bullet looked like a mushroom cap that had been flattened. "What?"

After a moment, he shook his head. "I've seen about every type of ammunition out there. There's something off about this bullet. I just can't put my finger on it."

His palm closed over it and he came back to the bench,

56

sliding down in the seat. He set the bullet on the table, his face was drawn, his eyes hard. "He killed Gus."

"Who?"

"My neighbor a few slips over. The sniper used Gus's boat. I found the body. Gus never stood a chance."

A man was dead because of her. The memory of her mother's face flashed in Bianca's mind. How many more people would die because Bianca hadn't been smart enough to stop their deaths? "I'm so sorry, Cal."

He slid out of the seat and she watched as he pulled out a T-shirt and tacked it up over the open window. "Drink your water," he said when he was done. "And stay down here."

Bianca's ears were ringing. "What now, Cal?"

At the first step, he paused. "We see how far *The Love Boat* can take us."

CHAPTER SEVEN

Cal turned off the autopilot and resumed control of the boat. No one was following them on the water. Didn't mean they wouldn't catch up, but at least he had a minute to think.

His head swam with ideas, questions. There had to be more to Bianca's story. Politicians did stupid things, and sometimes endangered good men and women, but this all seemed too farfetched.

Cal wasn't stupid. He knew the government covered up a lot of shit. But who would hire an assassin to take out an NSA agent because she'd discovered a senator had leaked intel?

Then again, Otto Grimes was no ordinary target. He'd made quite a name for himself, challenging President Norman to a showdown on more than one occasion. The fact he'd issued these challenges and threatened to kill the US leader in cold blood in a series of videos—all widely viewed on a popular video-sharing website by millions of people all over the world—had turned the death threats into a Hollywood spectacle. Congress had demanded the videos be removed, the owners of the video website had refused and lawyers were now involved. The CIA had tried tracing the origins of the video uploads but were still chasing their tails.

President Norman, along with his V.P. and cabinet, was suddenly in a brand new spotlight. The younger generation knew who he was. His campaign advisors saw a way to reach those voters come November. The president made his own video, calling out Grimes and issuing threats at the terrorist sponsor. "Put up or shut up" was the president's new calling card.

Flame wars ensued on the video sharing website, crashing it for several hours. Norman's approval rating went through the roof.

The terrorist sponsor had responded with a *Wanted: Dead or Alive* video, telling Norman he was coming after him personally. A Homeland tech guru had finally gotten a solid lead on where the videos were being made and uploaded. SEAL teams were put on alert, but intel from the area revealed Grimes wasn't there.

Norman decided to up the ante. He'd challenged Grimes to put his money where his mouth was—Norman would give the order to let Grimes enter the country if Grimes would meet him at the end of his campaign trail in Chicago at a dinner fundraiser.

The V.P., the First Lady, and a host of other people had gone ballistic. There was no way anyone wanted Grimes to get near the US or POTUS. Cal's SEAL team had been put on alert.

But Norman was crafty and so was the CIA, FBI, and NSA...all working the Hollywood terrorist and his ego to their advantage. Grimes would never endanger himself by entering America, and in order for him to save face, he'd have to attack Norman in other ways. If they got Grimes moving and planning a terror "spectacular" on American soil, the SEALs' odds of capturing the man increased three-fold.

It had seemed like the plan was going to work. Grimes, as suspected, had made several moves, one of them being the attack on the universities.

There was an outcry from many inside the US, but instead of blaming Norman for provoking Grimes, the majority of people— especially the younger generation who'd grown up on movies like *The Hunger Games, Divergent,* and *Ender's Game*—rallied around him. They wanted a showdown. They wanted blood.

On the flip side, Middle East violence escalated. They, too, wanted a showdown and were cheering on Grimes.

Behind the scenes, Cal's team had been given orders. The intel was solid. The team prepped and readied to go.

But something had gone wrong. If Bianca was right, Senator Halston had leaked the information and somehow it had gotten back to Grimes.

Three good men were dead. Cal was out of a job. Bianca was being shot at.

What the fuck was going on?

The storm had cleared out of the area but Cal could see the system a few miles ahead of them to the north. He juiced the engine and felt the boat strain under his direction. *The Love Boat* wasn't even up to twenty-five knots, but then again, from what the previous owner had told him, she hadn't been on the open water in ten years.

At this rate, Tephra or whoever was after them, could swim faster than they were traveling. Being on open water had advantages, but not if the boat wasn't seaworthy.

Tephra. No way was he an assassin. The man was an absolute god in the SEAL world, a loyal soldier through and through.

Bianca had intel Cal didn't on many things inside the government, but she had to be wrong on this. If Tephra were alive, why keep it a secret?

Had something gone wrong on his last mission? Was there a reason the man needed to stay MIA?

Cal needed more information. He suspected Bianca had it. He didn't want to leave the deck for long, though, and didn't want her anywhere in plain sight. He'd hug the coastline for now and not risk her being spotted or shot at again.

For a while, it was enough to simply drive the boat and watch the water and the ever-darkening horizon. Although the boat wasn't speedy, they were catching up to the storm. He might have to slow down or find a spot to dock if the storm didn't move inland soon.

Surprisingly, Bianca followed instructions and stayed below deck. While he should be relieved that she'd listened to him, he actually felt a twinge of worry. She never did what she was told. Maybe she really was in shock and he should go check on her.

He slowed the boat and switched on the autopilot again.

Maggie followed him below deck. The cabin was dark after he'd hung the T-shirt over the broken window, but the fabric blew out here and there as the breeze caught it, sprinkling light over the bunk bed. Bianca lay under the covers, her eyes closed.

She'd removed her ponytail holder and her hair tangled on the pillow. Her white dress shirt lay on the bench seat, blood splashes in multiple spots. Cal moved closer to the bed, watching the rise and fall of her chest. Her breathing was even, not too shallow, not too deep.

She'd replaced the white shirt with one of his standard gray T-shirts and the sight of her wearing it brought back memories of their lazy weekends together. Times like those had been few and far between, making the memories richer. She'd always slept in his T-shirts, claiming they were softer than any of her pajamas.

He reached out and touched her hand on top of the blanket. *Warm.* The shirt-curtain blew open again and he could see her cheeks were flushed from sleep. Her lips, parting on a sigh, were rosy.

No signs of shock. Just to be sure, he lightly slipped two fingers to the inside of her wrist and found her pulse. While her wrist was tiny, her pulse was strong and steady. Closing his eyes, he counted the tiny beats under her skin.

Even after he was sure she was fine, he let his fingers linger on her skin. He stroked the tiny bones on the inside of her wrist, remembering how she loved to be kissed there.

"Cal?" Her voice was sleepy, her eyelids half-closed.

The gray of his shirt made her blue eyes brighter when the light hit them. "Yeah, B"

"Is everything okay?"

"Fine. I was just checking on you."

Maggie pushed her nose into Bianca's face and she patted the dog's head, barely avoiding a dog kiss. "I haven't slept in days. Too scared." She gave a half-hearted chuckle and ran a hand over her face, flinching when she rubbed against the bandage on her cheek. "It felt good to curl up and take a nap."

In my shirt. In my bed.

Cal patted her hip. "Go back to sleep. You're safe."

She met his gaze, eyelids still at half-mast. "Will you fix the camera?"

"The camera?"

"It must have fallen over in the storm." She drew out her phone from under the pillow. "I'd feel better if I could see you when you're up there."

The phone. *Dammit.* He snatched it from her hand. "This thing has GPS. Someone could be tracking you. We have to destroy it."

"No, wait!" She sat up and grabbed it from him. "I've disabled the GPS and made the phone untraceable."

Seeing the skepticism in his eyes, she said, "Trust me. Anyone tracing the phone believes I'm in downtown San Diego right now." She looked down and cringed. "Crap. Another missed call from Coop."

"Coop?"

"My taskforce boss, Cooper Harris. I was supposed to be at a meeting at ten. He won't be happy I missed it."

She started to dial and Cal once again lifted the phone from her hands. "No communication. None."

"But I—"

"None, Bianca." He held it out of her reach. "Not until I figure this mess out."

She glanced up at the screen and let out a sigh. "Looks like service is pretty limited and I assume you disconnected your Wi-Fi so I can't access the camera anyway."

He looked at the phone, and sure enough, only one bar was lit. "We're off the grid until further notice."

"Okay, okay." She wiggled her fingers at the phone. "I promise not to call anyone. Can I have my phone back?"

"What for?"

"My life is on that phone."

Giving her back the phone was a bad idea, but she gave him a forlorn look, and like usual, he caved. "I'm not kidding about the communication. Service or no service, you are not to text, call, email, or surf the net. Got it?"

She gave a false salute. "Sir, yes, sir."

CHAPTER EIGHT

Engine noise woke her. The boat was downshifting. Were they docking?

Shadows engulfed the cabin. A check of her phone showed she'd been out for nearly three hours.

Groaning, Bianca slid back down into the warm covers that smelled like salt, humidity, and Cal—warm and comforting, like her favorite blanket at home. Which made sense since Cal always stole the blankets when he was home and wound himself in them.

She closed her eyes for a second and smiled. The hum of *The Love Boat*'s engine had lulled her to sleep. A deep sleep she'd desperately needed after the previous days of paranoia and anxiety had kept her fight-or-flight mode fully engaged. How did Cal and men like his SEAL unit live like that on missions?

Her stomach growled, and beside the bed, Maggie's tail thumped against the floor. "Hi, girl."

The Lab licked Bianca's cheek. Dog breath flooded her nose. Shifting away, Bianca patted the dog's head. As she sat up, the boat angled clockwise and continued to decelerate. She stuck out a hand to stabilize herself and the boat bumped against something, jarring her.

It was the first time she'd been on a boat, but she knew they were definitely coming to a stop. Rising up on her knees, she brushed Cal's shirt aside to peer outside.

Water, cloudy skies, a long dock that led to shore, and a huge beach house that rose several stories in the air.

Large, reflective windows stared back at her, the low-hanging clouds seemingly perched on the high roof peak.

The engine died. Bianca scrambled off the bunk bed, shoving her phone into her briefcase. They'd stopped for a reason, and she wanted to be ready to disembark if necessary.

Where are we?

She grabbed her dress shirt, still caked with blood, and shoved it in her briefcase with the phone. Probably wise not to wear it in public, but it was the only change of clothes she had unless she wanted to confiscate more T-shirts from Cal. Not a terrible idea, but from the stash she'd taken the current one, she'd noted he didn't have any to spare.

The cotton of the shirt she was wearing was soft, like it had been worn a hundred times. Maybe it had. Like the sheets, it smelled faintly like Cal and a lot like good old laundry detergent.

Need rushed through her, hot and desperate. Besides her career, Cal was all she had in the world. She'd almost lost him to Grimes. Still might lose him to Tephra. Even if they succeeded in figuring out why she'd become a target of the government and put a stop to it, the divorce would sever their relationship. She rubbed a hand across the fabric at her stomach, willing the sudden cramp there to subside. *Emotions aren't productive.* She had to shut them down.

Though soft, Cal's footsteps overhead seemed hurried as he crossed from side to side. *Tying off the boat.* She itched to go up there and see what she could do to help, but knew better. He'd only yell at her to stay below.

Waiting wasn't her strong suit. Never had been. Her body craved movement, her flight mechanism still engaged. Her mind craved some piece of information, some tidbit of knowledge that would bring this disastrous situation to an end. She'd always lived in her head, her brain needing constant stimulation. While it made her a highly successful analyst, it made for a lonely life. She was far more suited to books, data, and research than to real life.

Far more comfortable sitting behind a computer screen than dealing with an assassin with a hit out on her.

Maggie went to the bottom of the stairs and peered up, expecting Cal. Bianca finger-combed her hair into a fresh ponytail and waited.

A few seconds later, he appeared, his short hair glistening with rain, a blast jacket covering his upper body. "Ready?" he said, his eyes scanning the T-shirt and her briefcase.

Ready for what? She could only imagine. "Where are we?"

He crossed to the bed and tugged out the drawer below it. Shirts were tossed back and forth until he withdrew a sweatshirt. He tossed it to her and she caught it in midair. "Put this on."

She set the briefcase on the table, then drew on the sweatshirt. As she pulled her ponytail out of the neckline, he handed her a ball cap. "This too," he said.

To protect her hair or as a disguise? "Is someone following us?"

"No." He started for the stairs and patted his leg for the dog to follow. "But we can't be too careful."

True. Every city, state, and federal institution had cameras, and video surveillance was no longer limited to government and businesses. Home security was a booming market and most people had a camera on their phone.

From the ground up to the satellites in space, someone somewhere was snapping images and taking videos of everything from ant colonies to major international crises.

"Keep your head down," Cal instructed as he climbed out of the cabin.

Bianca did, following close behind him. "Can I have that Glock back?"

Was that a chuckle she heard? She couldn't be sure as they

rose to the deck, rain falling lightly and the waves of the water lapping gently against the sides of the boat.

He took her hand and helped her cross from the boat onto the dock. It was designed with two slips for boats. Cal's sat in one, the other empty. Did that mean the owners of the house were gone?

She tried to keep her head down, but she needed to get a look at her surroundings. Tilting the brim of the hat farther down, she lifted her chin slightly to peer from underneath it.

Maggie jumped from the boat and sprinted down the dock toward the house, letting go of a joyful-sounding bark. Had the dog been here before?

Cal moved beside Bianca, his firm hand going around her elbow. "This way."

Like there was any other?

The long, wooden dock reminded her of a gang plank on a pirate's boat. Except she wouldn't be forced to jump into the ocean at the end, she'd be forced to go back on dry land.

Walk the plank. Tephra's out there somewhere waiting for you.

Her throat tightened. Her feet refused to move. She didn't want to stay on *The Love Boat* forever, hated being on the water, but the safety and simplicity of it beckoned to her.

"B?" Cal's voice was quiet but urgent in her ear. His hand released her elbow and slid around to the small of her back. "We need to move."

Move. Right. Bianca forced her rubbery legs to walk. The touch of Cal's hand on her lower back was light. His gaze swept the area, his other hand hidden under his jacket, holding a gun at the ready, no doubt.

Houses dotted the beach, each with a sizable yard so none were right on top of the other. Some were larger than others, all set back from the sand and water.

Now that her legs were cooperating, she and Cal hustled down the gangplank and hit land. Maggie was already waiting up near the house, wagging her tail and panting like usual.

Bianca's feet sank in the sand, tiny grains sneaking into her shoes. She and Cal went over a slight incline, passing clumps of tall, stiff, beach grasses, and into the green, well-manicured lawn in direct contrast to the wild, untamed beach.

A few yards in sat an infinity pool and between that and the house's patio was a lap pool. Cal guided her around both, checking over his shoulder and keeping an eye on their surroundings as he led her to the back door.

Or was it the front?

Depended, she guessed, on whether you considered the beach your front yard or your back.

"Nice place. Whose is it?" Bianca asked again. For some stupid reason, her teeth wanted to chatter like they had on the boat. Her insides were shaking as well and she clamped down on her jaw, wondering how she could be cold when she was sweating under Cal's sweatshirt.

"Remember Emit Petit?" Cal was looking at a keypad next to the door.

A face from her memory surfaced. "The kid you used to skateboard all over the neighborhood with? The one who broke his femur in three places the summer we were eight?"

He punched some numbers and nodded. "Marlene is with Doctors Without Borders now. She and a couple of her crew got mixed up with some kidnappers last year. You didn't know?"

Marlene was Emit's older sister. "No."

"And here I thought you called all the team's missions from what you said earlier."

"I only have say in those involving high-ranking terrorists." Ferns grew in large pots flanking each side of the double doors. "Didn't Emit go in the Navy like you? I remember he wanted to fly jets or something."

The light on the panel went from red to green, and Bianca heard a quiet click of the lock. "He passed all the tests but one. Every time he was under a couple Gs of pressure, he'd throw up. Thought he'd try SEAL training, but that didn't work out either. He rang out after day two."

"So this is his place?"

Cal opened the impressive wrought iron French doors, holding one side wide for her and Maggie to enter. "One of Emit's ways of saying thank you for his sister's safe return."

"He gave you the combination to his beach house?"

"It's his vacation home. Said I could use it anytime. Never expected to need it."

The inside was as impressive as the outside, the foyer a giant room with a two-story ceiling, dark hardwood floors, a crystal chandelier of swirling blown glass, and a beautiful wrought-iron staircase that curled up to the second floor. Underneath it was an ocean blue wall of cascading water.

Bianca cleaned the raindrops off her glasses, scanning the beautiful interior again once she had them on. It was tasteful and peaceful and didn't match the memory of Emit in her head.

Cal shut the door and played with the security system. Maggie shook water off her fur and trotted around, sniffing at various pieces of furniture. Bianca removed her shoes and tried to brush off the sand sticking to her feet.

The open living space held two expensive Italian leather couches facing each other in front of a large stone fireplace. Two chairs were positioned nearby in a slightly separate area with an antique side table and floor lamp. The art on the walls—mostly seascapes—looked original. Who knew the scrawny kid with a mop of dirty-blond hair and freckles would grow up to have such nice taste?

Cal was removing his blast jacket. Bianca saw a gun tucked into his waistband as he raised his arms to get the jacket over his head and his shirt rode up on his stomach.

"I didn't realize you and Emit had stayed in touch."

"We hadn't until his sister ended up in trouble." Cal motioned her away from the front windows. "I couldn't exactly take you to a friend's house or anyone you or I have stayed in touch with over the years. If the idiot shooting at you is smart, he'll have every one of them flagged."

Just like the way she had with Cal, leading Tephra right to his doorstep. "Take off your shoes."

He stopped, looked down at his sneakers and back up at her. "What?"

"You're tracking sand and water all over the floor."

He did a half eye roll, losing the shoes and looking at her. "Happy?"

"How did you know Emit wouldn't be here?"

"He's in risk management and doing a gig for Blue Chip Casinos. They have an international poker tournament in London this week. Figured he'd be out of town."

Apparently, Cal had figured right. "Since when do you know about poker tournaments in London?"

"I know a few things that might surprise you."

The foyer was open all the way to the front and he walked past the staircase and another antique, this one a hall table under a large framed mirror on the north wall, to get to it. He checked the door and the windows beside it before seeming convinced everything was secure.

He headed for the kitchen and Bianca followed, not sure what she should do.

The dark floors gave way to creamy travertine. The cabinets were a pretty cherry color and the marble countertops had swirls of a rich brown, white, and a hint of the same cherry color. Muted light bounced off the gleaming stainless steel appliances and four oblong pendant lamps hung from the ceiling over the breakfast bar.

Cal went right to the side-by-side refrigerator and pulled both doors open, scanning the contents. "No fresh milk or fruit, but"—he lifted a bottle of yellow mustard from the door and showed it to her with a grin—"plenty of beer and condiments."

Beer and mustard. *Yum, yum.*

Bianca opened a couple of cabinets, pulling out crackers, cereal, and a box of pancake mix. "All is not lost."

"Cool." Cal withdrew a couple of bottled waters from the fridge and set them on the counter. "We have food, water, and a roof over our heads for the next few hours. We can sort out what's going on and make a plan."

A few hours? Then where would they go? Like Cal had said, they couldn't exactly go to friends or family. Tephra would be watching them, and who could they trust in government?

At this point, no one.

"I'm going to check upstairs." Cal pointed at the odd menagerie of food she'd found in the cabinets. "Help yourself to some lunch."

Bianca hugged herself and leaned back against the counter. Cal's footsteps grew distant as he climbed the stairs to the second floor. Lunch seemed like a mundane thing to think about when her life was in serious jeopardy.

Then again, it might be her last meal.

Forcing herself to move and do something, *anything*, to take her mind off of her predicament, she searched the cabinets for a skillet and went to work making pancakes.

CHAPTER NINE

After double checking they were indeed alone in the house and everything was secure upstairs, Cal stood near the master bedroom's patio doors. They went out on a second-story deck that looked out over the ocean.

Downstairs, he heard the distant, homey sounds of Bianca moving around in the kitchen. Clanging pots, running water.

They couldn't stay on the run forever. At some point, he had to get to the bottom of what was going on. He'd had time to think on the boat, but he still had more questions than answers. For the life of him, there was no way he could wrap his brain around the idea that Rory Tephra was alive and well and doing wet jobs for the CIA.

On the flip side, whoever had come after Bianca was good. Prepared, quick, dangerous.

Ground zero. I need to find out where this all started before I can figure out where it's going.

But first, he needed backup.

Inside the master bedroom's walk-in closet, he searched for the satellite phone he knew Emit had hidden under a trap door in the floor. After moving some shoes and lifting a corner of carpeting, sure enough, there it was.

Making sure Bianca was still busy downstairs, Cal drew out the phone and punched in the phone number to Rock Star Solutions, Emit's private division of his risk management business. The high-risk division dealing with protection services.

Cal hadn't been entirely truthful with Bianca. He and Emit had stayed in touch over the years, Cal referring a few good men Emit's way for employment with RSS. SEALs who'd left the teams but still had the training and valuable skills his old friend needed to keep high-risk targets and their loved ones protected from the crazies wanting to do them harm.

Ironic that Emit had needed Cal's team to rescue his sister, but Marlene had always refused to use her brother's services. After her ordeal with the kidnappers, she still hadn't returned to Doctors Without Borders, but Cal bet when she did, she took one of Emit's bodyguards with her.

The call was answered on the first ring. "Rock Star Specialty Services," a woman answered, cheerful but professional. Her voice was clear and crisp and held no accent. "How may I direct your call?"

Emit had told Cal if he was ever in need of anything to call. Cal had laughed about it. Him needing protection? That would never happen. Sure there were plenty of nuts out there who wanted to take him out, either for revenge or simple sport, but he'd never worried about them.

Now, he wasn't an active SEAL. Maybe he never would be again. He could protect Bianca better than anyone else, but only if he knew who the enemy was, how many, and what their mode of operation was.

As it stood, he wasn't certain about anything. "I need to speak directly to Liber, please."

Emit had always had a thing for Roman deities and hard rock bands. Liber was the Roman god of freedom, a name Emit had picked as a code word for himself...the protector of freedom.

The woman didn't hesitate. "Are you in danger?"

"Someone with me is."

"Is it imminent?"

He sure hoped not. "Not at the moment, no, but it could become that way soon."

"Are you on a secure line?"

"Yes."

"Name and problem?"

"Cal. An assassin is after my wife."

The woman seemed to take this information in stride. "Please hold. Liber is out of the country, so this may take several minutes. Please do not hang up unless your life is in immediate danger and you must take cover. Liber will not be able to call you back."

"I understand."

The phone made several clicking noises as he was put on hold. Soft music played in the background. Cal eased toward the closet door, heard Bianca continuing to bang things around in the kitchen, and relaxed for a moment. He sat on the floor and rubbed his eyes, listening to the soothing music and hoping he was doing the right thing.

A minute passed, then another. Cal had been SEAL Team Seven's leader for a reason. He knew when he needed a unit, or a friend with the right resources, to help him achieve a successful mission. This was definitely one of those times.

Another click and Emit came on the line. "Cal? Is B okay?"

The sound of his old friend's voice reassured him. "She has a cut on her cheek from a bullet and she's freaked out, but she's okay."

"Are you sure you're on a secure line?"

"I'm on your sat phone at the vacation house. It better be secure."

"You're at the house?" He chuckled. "I told you you'd need my help some day."

"I'm in deep shit here, Emit. The guy after Bianca is Rory Tephra."

A pause. "You're losing it, man. Tephra's MIA, probably dead."

"Something is fishy about this whole thing. I don't know who or what to believe, and after what happened in Afghanistan, I don't have many friends."

"Sit tight. I'll have an extraction team at the house in forty-five minutes, maybe less. They'll take you to ground and I'll hop on a plane and get back there as fast as possible. We'll figure this out."

Forty-five minutes. Cal bent his knees and put his back against the closet door. "And if the assassin shows up before then?"

"Get Bianca out and we'll regroup on the fly. There's a go bag under the floor where you found the phone. Disposable cell phones, two handguns, and some other security hardware that will come in handy. Call me from the road and I'll have the extraction team meet you wherever you are."

It wasn't ideal, but it was better than nothing. "I need wheels."

"South end of the street in the big yellow A-frame is a guy named Means. Fighter pilot who works for me freelance on occasion. Tell him I sent you. He'll find you something."

"I don't have that kind of money on me."

"There's cash in the bag, but you won't need it. Means will fix you up and charge it to me. Trust me, buddy. I got your back."

Cal hung his head between his bent knees for a moment and breathed a heavy sigh. "Thanks, Emit. I owe you."

"You rescued my sister. This is the least I can do." He let that sink in, then said, "Stay safe. I'll see you in approximately ten hours."

The line went dead. Cal replaced the phone and drew out the go bag. Exactly like Emit had said, there were phones, guns, and cash.

Cal replaced the floorboard and carpet, took the bag, and headed downstairs, the smell of something warm and familiar filling his nose. The scent reminded him of his stepmother's kitchen, where something had always been cooking. His mouth watered.

He stashed the bag under a couch cushion in the living room, deciding it would be easier to tell Bianca about the extraction team and his plan after he'd eaten.

Bianca stood at the stove, humming, a spatula in one hand, the other on her hip. She was barefoot and had tied an apron around her waist. It emphasized her curvy bottom and Cal's mouth watered for a different reason.

He hadn't eaten all day, hadn't been hungry until now.

He wanted to slip up behind her and wrap his arms around her, nuzzle her neck, like he used to do when they were newlyweds. She'd always been a fairly good cook, not as good as his stepmom, but almost. Delene had come into Cal's life at thirteen—a hard age to accept a new mother. Delene had been good to Bianca though, and she'd spent hours teaching Bianca all her recipes. Cal had grown to love and respect his stepmom because of how much Bianca loved her.

Bianca now glanced over her shoulder at him. "Hey, I made pancakes. They're not great since I didn't have milk or eggs, but I did find butter that hadn't expired, the real stuff, and threw a couple tablespoons of that in with a dash of vanilla."

She used the spatula to pile a couple on a plate and set the plate on the breakfast bar. Maggie stood sentry nearby, wagging her tail at every move Bianca made, patiently waiting for her own pancake.

This was how it should have been with them. Easy. Normal. A big, fancy house, a couple of kids, a dog. *What the hell happened to us?*

Bianca glanced at him. "Cal?"

"Yeah." He sat in one of the chairs, grabbed the syrup she'd set out and drowned the pancakes in it. As he dug in, the first bite of maple, vanilla, and butter exploding in his mouth, Bianca returned to the stove, her back to him once more.

Regardless of the lack of ingredients, the pancakes were delicious. He watched as she poured more batter, cocked her hip to the side, and rested her right foot against her left ankle. Her purple toenails were dark against her fair skin. Strands of hair had, as per normal, escaped her ponytail and hung down the back of her neck. She'd removed the sweatshirt but still wore his T-shirt, the bottom edge of it drifting just under her butt cheeks.

She flipped the cakes in the skillet, turned to look at him. "What's the verdict?"

"They're delicious," he said around a mouthful.

The right side of her mouth quirked slightly and she turned back around.

"Bianca?"

"Hmm?"

"Why is someone trying to kill you?"

She glanced at him, this time with a look that said she thought he was dense. "Because I know Senator Halston leaked the information about your mission. It's his fault the mission was a failure and three Navy SEALs died."

"Has to be more to it than that."

Her brows dipped and she tapped her finger against the handle of the skillet. "At first, I thought so, too, but what? I mean, I know a lot of highly-classified information, super-secret stuff, but so does my boss. Doesn't mean we should be targets for an assassin."

Assassin. The word set him on edge. "What about the other blue elephant? You said she died in a car accident six months ago. You don't think it was an accident, do you?"

"She didn't have anything to do with Grimes or the Middle East sector. She worked the Korean and South American sectors. I couldn't find any correlation."

She turned back and began flipping pancakes. "On the other hand, I may be the only person outside of Halston and the man who called him who knows about this. If someone wants to cover up Halston's epic fail, I'm easily expendable."

"You're sure this doesn't have something to do with the taskforce?"

"The taskforce?"

"Your group investigates gunrunners and drug smugglers, right? Criminals who hold grudges and have no qualms taking people out?"

She turned down the burner. "I'm not an undercover agent, Cal. I gather information and analyze it for the taskforce, that's all. None of the criminals we investigate have a clue who I am or that I work for the SCVC."

"You're sure."

"Positive." She checked for doneness, then flipped two pancakes onto another plate. "You ready for more?"

He was. "You going to eat any?"

She refilled his stack. "There's plenty."

He forked another bite into his mouth and chewed as his brain worked over the problem. A contented silence threatened to make him forget what a screwed-up situation this was. "You're sure this is related to Halston and my mission?"

Finished with the last batch, she made a plate for herself and came to sit beside him. Her bare arm grazed his and her knee bumped into his thigh as she wiggled into place on the adjacent barstool. The homey smell of a decent breakfast mixed with her familiar scent.

Close. Too close. After all these months, it was hell being this close to her and not being able to touch her the way he wanted to.

Clearing the sudden tightness in his throat, he slid the syrup in front of her and hauled ass to the cabinets to find a glass and fill it with water.

He chugged it, set the glass down and turned back to her.

She was drowning her stack with syrup. "This is the real stuff. I haven't had real maple syrup since that trip we took to Vermont. Remember that?"

Vermont. One of their few vacations together. He'd wanted to stay in a fancy hotel. She'd insisted on a tiny bed and breakfast nestled at the base of a mountain. The views had been gorgeous, especially the view of her naked in the big, king size bed while he fed her pancakes soaked in world-class syrup. "B, focus. Are you sure?"

A soft sigh issued from her lips. "Give me a minute to enjoy my food. I've done nothing but think about this since I heard that phone call. I've gone over every scenario, every angle, every possibility." As she chewed and swallowed the first bite, she glanced up and looked him in the eyes. "I've analyzed every angle. This is about Operation Warfighter and Senator Halston. I'm sure."

Cal returned to his seat, knowing it was a bad idea to get that close to her again. His stomach was pleasantly full. No one was shooting at them. The extraction team was on its way. Everything about her reminded him of home.

A drop of syrup was stuck on her bottom lip. Cal wanted to lean over and lick it off. Instead he gripped his water glass tighter and gave himself the same advice he'd given her. *Focus.*

She used her fork to cut another bite off her stack and stared at the layers for a second. "So what do we do now?"

Sit tight, Emit had said, but once Cal was sure Bianca was safe, he was going to the source of her information. "Where's Halston?"

She gave him a quizzical look. "He's stumping for the president here in California. The last big push before the election."

"Where exactly? Do you know?"

"Today was San Francisco. Tomorrow, Sacramento. Ten wineries are hosting him on a wine tasting tour."

Senator Halston was going on with life while Cal's men—his friends—were dead and buried.

The breakfast he'd just enjoyed turned sour in his stomach. Rising from the stool, he fought the demons always riding his back these days and headed for the living room to clear his head.

"Cal?" Bianca called.

He stopped but kept his eyes glued to the fireplace.

"You never answered me," she said. "What do we do now?"

"Sit tight." He swallowed the hard lump in his throat and forced himself to answer. "I'm going to get us some wheels."

CHAPTER TEN

Bianca felt like a snoop.

The upstairs nursery was decorated in blue. Crayon-bright letters on the far wall spelled out *Austin* over the crib. Cal had left, telling Bianca to clean up and pack some food. They'd be taking a road trip to Sacramento, a long drive and they wouldn't be making pit stops. He'd left to find them transportation.

He was hiding something from her. Not the usual secrets they kept from each other. No, this was something else.

But she hadn't pushed him about it before he snuck out, instead hustling through the shower. She hated the idea of using a stranger's soap and shampoo and leaving her used washcloth and towel behind, but knowing it might be a long time before she had access to her own bathroom again or any bathroom with a shower even, she'd done it anyway.

Cal had once again handed her the Glock before he'd left and she'd kept it in easy reach. At that moment, it was secured in the waistband of her pants at the small of her back. A terrible place for a gun, it was, however, the best place she had outside of her hand.

Maggie lay in the hallway fast asleep. *My own personal security system.* With the dog so relaxed, Bianca relaxed a bit too.

Her feet took her from her voyeuristic stance in the hallway across the threshold of the room. She hadn't meant to stop—she still needed to find some food and a cooler for the road trip—

but the nursery had caught her eye and she couldn't help pausing to look at the cheerful colors, rocking chair in the corner, and scattered toys.

A white dresser held a table lamp with a train stitched on its shade. A silver picture frame with a photo of a baby dressed in a shirt with the Dodgers' logo on the breast sat next to it. Her fingers brushed over the child's face in the photo. *So small and innocent.*

The ache of loss cut through her belly like a white-hot knife. Tears pressed into the corners of her eyes. She blinked and fought against the compression suddenly around her chest.

Two babies, lost.

One boy.

One girl.

Unlike Emit's wife, neither of Bianca's pregnancies had made it full term, and even after all this time, the grief and the guilt lit her up daily.

Prom their senior year of high school, Cal had gotten her pregnant. She was such a cliché. Her life had spun into chaos after that.

Her mother had killed herself, and Bianca had spent a good deal of time finishing her senior year while proving to the judge and social services that she'd been supporting herself and her mother for years.

And six weeks after prom, that perfect night, Cal's dreams of going to college on a swim scholarship had gone up in flames as Bianca broke the news to him that she was pregnant. He gave up all of his extra-curriculars and got an after-school job.

A few weeks after that, she miscarried. For once in her life, her emotions took control and she managed to ruin the only good relationship she'd ever had, pushing Cal away the night before graduation. He'd been hurting, too, but she could barely handle her own pain and depression.

Worse, she'd felt relief. Like many teenage girls, she hadn't been ready for the responsibilities of a baby. She lay awake every night fearing she'd turn out like her mother, neglecting, or worse, abusing her own child. She'd also felt relief over the fact her mother was gone.

But the relief had been drowned out by guilt. Cal had wanted to get married anyway, but she'd refused, fighting with him on purpose to make sure he left and never looked back. He deserved better. Deserved someone who *was* better.

A vicious cycle that had nearly wiped out any hope for a future, because when Cal *did* leave and sign up for the Navy, the abject loneliness his absence created nearly buried her.

Eight years later, things were different. She and Cal were married and had put the worst behind them. They were older, wiser, and ready for a family.

Or so she thought.

Tears threatened again and she blinked them away. In the past few hours, she'd been on the verge of tears multiple times. What was happening to her?

In the next room, the phone rang, making her jump. *Stop daydreaming. Go get some food packed.*

Emotions once more in check, she fled the nursery and went downstairs. Maggie woke and followed. The phone continued to blare. Who had a landline these days? Especially at a vacation home they probably only visited a few times a year?

In the kitchen, Bianca ignored the ringing and found some fabric grocery bags. The phone stopped, the answering machine kicking in.

She was filling a bag with unopened boxes of crackers when the answering machine's message stopped and the beep sounded. Silence followed, then the distinct click of the call disconnecting.

Bianca stared at the kitchen's extension mounted on the wall. Telemarketer? Wrong number? Odds were one or the other.

So why did she suddenly feel like someone had invaded the house?

Bianca fingered the gun at her back and glanced at Maggie. The dog sat watching her, no sign she shared any concerns over the phone call. Bianca crept to the side of the window over the sink and cautiously peaked out. The landscaped front of the house, a narrow street, and double-wide driveway met her eyes. The street was lined with houses and what appeared to be a five-story condominium unit.

A woman was walking a dog on the nearby bike path. Two houses down, someone was getting a furniture delivery.

No Cal, but nothing suspicious, either.

Where had he gone? He couldn't buy or rent a car without leaving a trail, and Bianca knew that was the last thing he'd do.

As a Navy SEAL, he had extensive training in the art of evading the enemy. He'd led his team into a myriad of foreign countries, taking out terrorists, rescuing Americans, and keeping the peace in a world bent on war. A real live hero who never wanted glory, only justice.

Few Americans knew about his successes or the long list of threats Cal and his platoon had disposed of. But Bianca knew. It was one of the only reasons she slept soundly at night...knowing Cal was out there protecting her and the United States. Even without their extensive history, she would have considered him one of the few men in the whole world who could help her. *With* their history, she knew he was the only man she *wanted* to help her.

Shrugging off her nerves, she moved back into the main area of the kitchen, locating a pantry behind a false cabinet face. The shelves were stocked with a large assortment of nonperishables, mostly kid-friendly foods. Cookies, graham crackers, and cans of Chef Boyardee. She smiled, wondering if the canned pasta meals were for Emit's children or him. He'd practically lived on raviolis for years.

Cans were out; they were too heavy. The shelf to her left held boxes of prepackaged cupcakes and crème-filled goodies. There were two boxes of Pop-tarts. All the expiration dates were in a few weeks, and since there was no telling when Emit and his family were coming back—and she never could waste a good chocolate cupcake or box of Pop-tarts—she packed several of the boxes into a separate bag.

Water was next. The pantry had cases of bottled water next to stacks of soda and sports drinks. On the floor in the corner was a white Styrofoam cooler. Bianca put a dozen bottles of water into it.

Heavy, but water was essential.

The ice maker in the freezer had been shut off, so there was no ice for the cooler. There were several cold packs, so she took those and put them in with the bottles.

Her phone buzzed on the kitchen counter, where she'd left it, with an incoming text. The touch screen showed a message from a number she didn't recognize.

It also showed she'd missed two calls and three texts. Cooper, Ronni, and the taskforce's tech guru, Bobby Dyer, had tried to contact her. On top of that, the FBI director that headed the taskforce, Director Dupé had also called. She was definitely in deep shit.

Need to contact them. Let them know I'm all right before they put out an All-Points Bulletin.

But she wasn't all right. And Cal had said she wasn't to contact anyone for any reason.

There was one outlier. A number she didn't recognize that had left a text. She twirled the phone on the counter for a moment, watching the sparkly purple case as it caught the late-morning light. "What do you think, Maggie?" she asked the dog. "Should I read it?"

Maggie perked her ears and gave a short bark. Good enough.

Bianca opened the text. *Be ready to move in fifteen. C.*

Cal. He didn't have a cell phone but must have scored a disposable one.

She lived on her phone and had tricked it out to handle just about everything in her life she could. Without thinking, she started to text him back, then caught herself. The phone was encrypted and had a variety of firewalls and security, but nothing was fail-proof. She had no idea who had been trailing her or how sophisticated their tracking abilities were. After all the things she'd heard about and seen in the halls of the NSA, she knew nothing was impossible when it came to tracking someone down and learning everything about them.

The thought made her shudder. No contacting anyone. That's what Cal had said and he was right. Even if he was using a phone he'd just picked up, and no one could trace that, it was better not to chance a reply because someone *could* be tracing her outgoing communications.

Slipping the phone into a pocket, she thought about ways to contact Cooper instead. If she didn't make contact soon with a believable, if false, story, the taskforce and their leader would go looking for her, and that would add to her and Cal's problems.

She snapped her fingers. Upstairs, she'd noticed a laptop in the office. No one knew she was here, and Emit's computer couldn't be traced to her. She could use the laptop to send a message to Cooper saying she was sick and needed a few days off. If Tephra was tracking any of Cooper's transmissions— phone, email, texts—and was able to follow the IP address back to this address, he'd hit a dead end. Bianca would be long gone with Cal, on her way to Sacramento, and there was no one here to be in danger from her visit.

On the kitchen wall, the landline rang again. *Great.*

As it continued to blare, Bianca grabbed two of the bags she'd loaded with food and hustled them out of the kitchen to set them by the door leading to the front driveway. She went back for the cooler of water, Maggie following on her heels, tail wagging.

The answering machine clicked on. This time when the message was done, the caller spoke.

"Cal Reese," a man's gravelly voice said. "Seems like the

rumors are true. You're almost the caliber of SEAL I was."

Bianca froze in mid-step. The voice was American, and carried a slight Boston clip. She'd never heard it before but didn't need her memory to tell her who the caller was. Her analytical brain knew.

Rory Tephra.

Oh God. How had he found them?

"Pick up the phone, Reese."

Bianca's fingers trembled as she reached for the island's counter to steady herself. *I'm going to die.*

Her hand found the Glock and she pulled it out of her waistband. *But not without a fight.*

"You're not an easy man to track down," Tephra said. "No Facebook account, no cell phone, no credit cards. Hell, you don't even own a goddamn car. Interesting. I suppose you're a paranoid bastard like me."

Here, the man laughed, like this was all good fun.

Next to Bianca's leg, Maggie whined.

"So here's the deal, Reese. I got a job to do. A job involving your old lady. I know your character well enough to know you're going to get in the way of that, so take this as a courtesy call. You get in my way, you'll end up swimming with the fish. Nothing personal. I'm doing my duty to our country."

Duty? How was it that killing her was an honorable thing?

Righteous anger swelled in Bianca's chest. With her free hand, she grabbed the handset off the wall, lowered her voice and spoke. "Why are you after me?"

There was a slight pause from the other end. "Well, well. The object of my affection. Hello, sweetheart." She heard the smile in his voice. "How's the cheek?"

She needed answers, and although it scared the beejesus out of her to talk to the assassin bent on killing her, he was the one person who had those answers.

Keep your voice calm. Don't let him know you're shaking like a leaf. "Who hired you?"

"Aww, now, come on. You know I'm not at liberty to say. But look, since you're the wife of a fellow SEAL, I'll keep it simple. Walk outside to the boat dock and I'll make it a quick and merciful death."

She slapped a hand over the phone's receiver and pinched her eyes shut. *Do. Not. Hyperventilate!*

Run, all her instincts screamed. She wanted to. Fear was a powerful motivator.

Yet, deep down inside, a fresh rush of anger stabbed at her, making her want to rip the phone from the wall. She was about to die and she didn't even know why.

Holding the phone out away from her face for a second, she took a couple of deep, shaky breaths, her heart racing. Her right hand squeezed the Glock hard enough to turn her knuckles white. *Where is Cal?*

Didn't matter. He wasn't here and Tephra was.

Bringing the phone back to her mouth, she crouched near the refrigerator, keeping clear of the windows. Maggie watched her with a curious look and Bianca steeled her nerves. "Go to hell, Tephra."

"Now see." He chuckled again, a deep, raw sound that made the hairs on Bianca's neck rise. "They told me you had some fire in you. That you were smarter than me and you'd be a hard mark to hunt down. You know what I told 'em? That if you were so smart, you'd realize the futility of running. You know there's nowhere you can go that I won't find you, right?"

Taunting her was a cheap ploy. She refused to fall for it.

Use it. Make him lose the bravado and he'll lose his control. The more he tries to upset you, the calmer you need to become.

Swallowing hard, she forced herself to sound confident. "Kudos to you, Rory." Negotiations 101: use their name and make it personal. "You must be even better at wet work than the CIA's top secret files claim. How did you find me?"

Another slight pause. Was he analyzing her like she was him? *You bet he is.* "You may be smart, but you don't understand men like me. Men like Cal Reese. At least he can appreciate Grace and what it takes for me to shoot a moving target at a long distance. Where is he? Put him on the phone."

"Who's Grace?"

"My weapon."

He'd named his rifle? Was that normal for snipers or was Tephra a fruit cake? She'd have to ask Cal.

If she survived this encounter.

I'm not *going to die.* "What does Grace have to do with tracking me to this house?"

A snort. "And here I thought you were smart."

She *was* smart. Tephra thought Cal was inside the house with her. If he'd been watching the place for any length of time, he would have spotted Cal leaving.

Unless Tephra hadn't seen him. Cal was one damn good SEAL. A pure ninja if he wanted to be. Either that, or Tephra had just arrived.

Which meant he hadn't kept eyes on them the whole trip, and since he was only making contact now, she was sure that was correct. He'd only arrived.

If so, he had to have tracked them somehow.

A tracer. On the boat or on her?

Grace. A gun. A bullet.

The bullet. The one that left its calling card on her cheek and embedded itself in the wall of *The Love Boat.*

The memory of Cal digging the bullet out of the paneling flashed through her mind. Cal's confusion. "You used a smart bullet," she said into the phone.

Bianca had known a guy, Winston, who'd been on a team that had developed two types of micro-transmitting tracking bullets. While the general public didn't have access to them, and there were plenty of people fighting against their use by law enforcement, there were multiple government entities already using the specialized bullets—CIA, NSA, and several special units the DoD ran under the radar.

"Ding, ding, ding. We have a winner!" His smugness grated on her nerves. "If they miss the target—and mind you, I've only missed three times in my career, you included—they leave behind a micro-transmitter that gives out a pulse. I even have an app for it. Oh, wait, you developed the app, didn't you, Ms. Marx? Handy, I must say."

She lowered the phone headset so he wouldn't hear her swear under her breath. One of her first jobs for the NSA was to design an app agents could use in the field to locate the tiny transmitters placed inside smart bullets. Why hadn't she paid more attention to that damn bullet Cal had removed from the paneling?

She'd never seen the real thing up close and personal, only diagrams, so she might not have noticed any difference. Her skills had been focused on the technology behind the ammunition at the time she'd developed the app.

Some micro-transmitters stayed inside the bullets, others were ejected upon impact. The micro-transmitter inside the bullet Tephra had used must have disengaged from the casing when it hit the paneling, a tiny fish hook device embedding the miniscule tracker into the wall.

Bianca banged her head back into the fridge. Nothing like arming the assassin trying to kill you with a handy tracking device complete with a GPS app for his phone. "I'm glad you appreciate my hard work," she lied.

Maggie's head whipped around to look at something Bianca couldn't see in the living room. The dog's ears pricked, her focus intense on...what? The door? She stood alert but not barking, her head tilted slightly.

Cal.

Bianca rose, but stayed low in a crouch. She needed to warn him and distract Tephra. But how?

"Yes, well," Tephra's voice sounded slightly muffled. "Why don't you come on out now? I need to wrap this up."

Setting down the landline's handset on the breakfast bar,

Bianca fished out her cell phone. *Stall.* She raised her voice slightly and spoke to the landline. "You think I'm going to walk out of this house willingly and let you kill me?"

Maggie's tail went up but didn't wag. Bianca inched past the breakfast bar and tried to see over the dog's back. Gun at the ready, she scanned what she could see of the living room, the patio windows that showed the beach, the long wooden dock, and the ocean. Craning her neck, she squinted around Maggie's big, black head. A small, nondescript fishing boat had pulled up behind *The Love Boat.*

"Less messy," Tephra said. "The government doesn't like messes on US soil. Harder to clean up."

Bianca found Cal's last text and hit reply. But she couldn't type with the gun in her hand.

She slid back over to the handset, and put her face close to it as she set down the gun and typed: *T is here! What do you want me to do?* At the same time, she said, "Harder to *cover* up, you mean."

"Same thing," he replied, then paused. "Your husband isn't there, is he? You're all alone."

Bianca picked up the Glock and stared at her cell phone's screen, willing Cal to respond. She kept her mouth close to the handset and took a steadying breath. "Doesn't matter. I'm not coming out. If you want me, you'll have to come and get me."

Silence and then that awful annoying chuckle. "Suit yourself."

The line went dead.

Bianca gritted her teeth. *Stupid!* Instead of baiting him, she should have kept him talking. She didn't know any more now than she had two minutes ago.

Maggie let out a *woof* and started to run. She couldn't get traction, nails clicking on the floor as her feet slid around underneath her. Bianca lunged for the dog's collar, missed, dropping her cell phone. "Maggie!"

Too late. The dumb dog shot away from Bianca's hands, one

of her feet sending Bianca's cell phone across the floor to the opposite wall as she shot forward toward the door.

Bianca glanced at the double-wide doors, saw nothing from her position on her knees. Maggie was going crazy now, barking and pawing at the doors. Bianca knew little about dogs. Was that an aggressive, *don't mess with me* bark or a *welcome back, Master, let me lick your face* bark?

Against the far wall, her phone vibrated with an incoming call. From her position at the edge of the kitchen floor, there was no way Bianca could see what the screen said.

The only way to get to the phone was to belly crawl across the floor. If she did, she'd be in plain sight of the patio doors, making herself a slow-moving target. Better to stay on her feet and run. She could only hope Tephra didn't take a shot through those patio doors. Maybe he wouldn't...that would be one big mess for sure.

Maggie stopped barking and went from window to window, trying to see out. Whoever had been at the door had moved.

"Get away from the windows, Maggie," Bianca said under her breath. Her phone continued to vibrate. *Call, not text.* She needed to answer. Cal was probably shitting bricks.

Not only that, the screen lighting up was like a bulls-eye for anyone trying to find her inside the house.

Maggie scampered back to Bianca's side, licking her face and whining. "Go get my phone, Maggie," Bianca said softly, pointing the dog in the direction of the phone. "Like you did before."

Maggie sat down and panted in her face.

"Phone." Bianca pointed and gave the dog a slight nudge. "Go get the phone."

Maggie cocked her head sideways as if Bianca spoke in an alien dialect.

She's a dog, idiot. Of course she doesn't understand you.

Besides, some part of Bianca didn't like sending the dog into the line of sight of a maniac with a gun. She patted the dog's soft head and laid her forehead against it for a moment. Her heart slammed against her ribs like a trapped bird inside her chest. "Never mind," she whispered. "My phone, my bad guy. I'll do it."

Scanning what she could see from her vantage point, Bianca duck-walked to the sofa, keeping low. She couldn't see enough, so she raised her head ever so slightly, gun at the ready, to peer over the back.

Sea grass clumps blew in the wind. In the distance, the ocean waves rolled up to the beach and subsided.

Maggie trailed along, wagging her tail but remaining quiet. Bianca held her breath, listening and waiting. When nothing happened—no windows broke, no bullets came whizzing at her face—she let out the breath. Nervous energy burned in her veins and she couldn't help the half-hysterical, half-relieved laugh that forced itself up her throat.

She didn't know much about assassins, but she did know they were patient. Tephra probably had her in his scope's sight already, but maybe not. Maybe he was still setting up Grace, or making a plan to enter the house and shoot her up close and personal.

Execution style. No broken glass, no bullets embedded in the walls or accidently hitting the vase on the coffee table and shattering it.

Much less messy.

Except, he didn't know Bianca had her own gun. And the dog. She wouldn't put Maggie in danger, but Maggie's instincts might keep Bianca alive for another day.

Her wrist grew tired of holding the Glock. She ignored the ache. Keeping the gun in position, she eyed the phone. She wasn't Cal, wasn't a SEAL by any stretch, but thanks to an abusive mother, a SEAL for a husband who took personal defense training to a new level, and a job that required even office grunts to know the ins and outs of a survival course, she wasn't a helpless maiden either.

One, two, three... She lunged for the cell phone. Halfway there, she went down on one hip to slide by the purple plastic, letting her momentum carry her past the phone, her left hand grabbing it as she kept the Glock semi-trained on the door.

Maggie barked and ran after her, a game. Bianca ended up with her back against the stairway, the wrought iron bars and wooden treads providing only a skeleton of cover.

Not enough.

Acting once again like a fast-action movie star, Bianca gained her feet, and keeping low, made a dash back to the security of the kitchen island. She and Maggie fell into a tangled heap at the base of the breakfast bar, Bianca releasing another anxious laugh as she fended off Maggie's playful face licks. They'd succeeded without a shot being fired.

Her glasses were askew. They hit the floor as Maggie's excited ministrations knocked them off her face. "Sit, girl," she said, fumbling to replace the glasses and look at the cell phone's screen.

The dog did as instructed, a drop of drool hitting the screen as she panted over it.

The call had gone to voicemail, but it hadn't been from Cal. Bianca hung her head. *Cooper.* He was persistent, that was for sure.

Tephra already knew where she was, so keeping her location a secret was a moot point. Cal wasn't back and hadn't responded to her text. When he did show up, he'd walk into an ambush. Would Tephra kill her and disappear? Or would he decide to take out Cal, too, assuming he knew too much?

Tephra's kills always looked like suicides or accidents. Either that, or the target simply disappeared, never to be seen again. If he'd gotten to her sooner, he might have made her disappear. Now, he had Cal to worry about.

Murder-suicide. If she were him, that's what she'd make it look like. The images played out in her mind. She and Cal were in the middle of a divorce. They'd argued, he shot her, then turned the gun on himself. Neat and convenient.

Damn. No way could she let Tephra get away with that.

Her hands shook and she set down the phone, using Cal's T-shirt to wipe away sweat from her forehead. Queasiness ricocheted around in her stomach, the morning's pancakes backing up in her throat.

The house had a high-end security system. It would take Tephra time to bypass it. Since he didn't like messes, she guessed he wouldn't want to trigger the alarm and send police their way. The time it took him to work on that, she needed to come up with a plan.

Booby-traps? She knew nothing about making them outside of the silly stuff she'd seen in *Home Alone.* She doubted in real life if any of those would work.

The ache in her wrist had turned into full-fledged burning. Off to her left, she heard the faint beep of the security system. Maggie's ears rose and she stood. Bianca peeked around the corner, checking the door that faced the street. She didn't see anyone through the frosted pane of glass in the transom, but saw the green light blink. Someone had punched in the code.

Cal. He was back. Had to be him from the way Maggie's tail was wagging. The dog ignored the door across from the breakfast bar, though, and sprinted for the living room, leaving Bianca behind.

Yep, had to be Cal. Relief swamped her. Her shoulders slumped and her hand nearly dropped the Glock.

Pull it together. You're not out of the woods yet.

Gaining her feet, she edged past the refrigerator and leaned out enough to see the double doors facing the beach. Through the patio window, she could see Tephra's boat still bobbing out on the water. Her phone buzzed and she ran back to grab it off the floor.

Not again. Cooper's persistence had bled into the neurotic

arena. He was obviously extremely concerned or extremely pissed.

She had to tell him what was going on, for his sake, as well as hers. She and Cal needed help. She wasn't sure just how far north up the coast they'd traveled, and she knew Cooper couldn't get there in time, but he'd know some way to help them.

Punching the button, she went back to her lookout spot. Why hadn't Cal come through the door yet? "Agent Harris," she said just above a whisper, "Please don't say anything, just listen. I don't have much time."

Maggie was scratching at the bottom of the double doors. Bianca's nerves went on high alert as she stared, gripping the Glock, and pointing it at the doors. "I'm north of San Diego in a house owned by Emit Petit. Not sure of the exact location, but I'm in trouble. There's a man trying to kill me and…"

Behind her, she heard a pop and then a squeak…the kitchen door. She whirled around and gasped.

A man with graying red hair and a large nose stood in the doorway. A black leather vest hung on his frame, showing bare arms and heavy tats. His jeans were dark, held up by a big belt buckle. His motorcycle boots were covered in dust.

In his hand was a nasty, black handgun with a silencer on the end. "Hello, sweetheart," Rory Tephra said.

Bianca dropped her phone.

CHAPTER ELEVEN

"Agent Marx?" Cooper said into the phone. From the other end came a clattering noise—she'd dropped her cell. "Bianca!"

The marina buzzed with activity. Two police cars, an ambulance, a bunch of spectators. A pair of EMTs guided a gurney toward their vehicle, a white sheet covering a body discovered dead in a nearby boat.

Across from Cooper sat Bobby in his wheelchair, his dark eyes boring into Cooper while a white cord hung from an earbud in his ear. The computer guru was listening in on the conversation Cooper was having with Bianca from his trusty jacked-up laptop from which he did all his spying.

Or the *non*-conversation Cooper was having with her as it was. Cooper gripped the phone. Bianca had disappeared and left him hanging. Not like her at all. If anything, since she'd joined the taskforce, she'd been anal about her job, working eighteen-hour days, and going above and beyond on every case he'd handed her.

She hadn't shown up for a meeting this morning, hadn't answered repeated calls and texts. Not only from him but from the other taskforce members as well. The last contact had been shortly after 0800 hours with Ronni, his lead FBI undercover operative.

Cooper wasn't a worrier. He did however have a gut feeling that Bianca was in trouble.

Bobby had traced her phone to the Starbucks down the road

from her apartment. The manager inside claimed Bianca was a regular but hadn't shown up that morning for her daily chai tea latte. He'd seen her in the parking lot, leaving her car to get into a cab.

At the news, Cooper's gut feeling had turned into full-blown concern.

Agents like Ronni and his right-hand man, Thomas, often broke routine and didn't always report in on a regular basis. Came with their jobs as undercover operatives. Bianca Marx wasn't an operative. She was a brainiac with obsessive work habits. He could set his watch by her.

At least she'd answered her phone this time, but the story that had issued from her mouth was so crazy, he wondered if she'd been drinking. "Agent Marx, what is going on?"

In the background, a dog barked, a man grunted, then a loud blast rang out. The noise seemed to explode close to Cooper's ear and he jerked the phone away.

"Was that a gun shot?" Bobby said.

Sure sounded like it, but before Cooper could get his phone back to his ear and try to find out, another noise came through the speaker…a crunching sound. The line went dead.

"Goddammit," he swore under his breath, hitting the redial button.

Thomas half-jogged, half-walked from the marina's office and headed their way. Humidity was high and sweat glistened on the kid's tan forehead.

Bobby pulled the earbuds from his ear and began furiously typing on his laptop. "Searching for Emit Petit in Southern Cali."

Who the hell was Emit Petit and why was Bianca at his house? "Did she honestly say someone was trying to kill her?"

Bobby glanced up, met Cooper's eyes. "You heard correctly."

Shit.

Thomas stopped next to Cooper's side and read from a small notebook in his hand. "According to the manager, Cal Reese worked here and lived on a boat docked in slip thirteen." He pointed to the last slip along the dock. "Guy saw a blond female that fits Bianca's description talking to Cal around 0800 hours and go on his boat. Never saw her leave, but once the storm came in, he claims he was busy fielding calls and might have missed her exiting. He did catch a glimpse of Cal going on that boat"—Thomas pointed to a dingy houseboat a couple of slips closer to them—"belonging to one Gus Molier, a long-time tenant here at the marina, and leave a minute later. Molier is the guy they hauled out on the gurney."

Bianca's cell phone rang. Once, twice, three times. Cooper set his jaw.

"EMTs say Molier's neck was broken," Thomas said.

Bobby stopped typing and pinned Thomas with a look. "Tell me the guy took a fall and broke it himself."

Thomas shook his head. "No official ruling yet, but Molier was lying in bed. A friend came to meet him for breakfast and found him."

"You don't break your neck lying in bed," Bobby said.

That left murder.

Not many men could kill a person by breaking their neck. A SEAL could.

Cooper knew everything about his taskforce members. Things they didn't know he knew. Even though Bianca never spoke about her personal life, he knew she was in the middle of a divorce and her Navy SEAL husband had recently returned to the States holding his ass and not much else after a blown mission.

SEALs had enormous mental, physical, and emotional reserves, but they were still human. Had Cal Reese snapped, and say, oh, killed his neighbor and kidnapped his soon-to-be ex-wife?

Bianca's phone went to voicemail. Again. Cooper nearly threw his own phone across the marina.

When she hadn't answered multiple calls and texts earlier

that day, he'd had no choice but to hunt down Cal Reese. Except upon arrival, he and the SCVC Taskforce had found this mess.

"Got 'em," Bobby said, staring at his screen. "Emit Petit. Lives and works in L.A. Has a second home on the beach a few miles south of there."

L.A. was a solid two hours north without traffic. Cooper disconnected and pocketed the phone. "Call the local cops and have them send cars to both addresses immediately. Get the Coast Guard searching for Reese's boat. Warn all of them that they may be dealing with a volatile military-trained expert." He motioned at Thomas. "You're with me."

Thomas nodded and headed for Cooper's SUV. Bobby was already dialing his phone. "You want an APB for Reese?"

There's a man trying to kill me... "You bet your ass I do. If they locate him, they are to hold him until I get there."

Bobby's wheelchair hummed to life. "Coop, hold up. There's something you should know."

Cooper stopped and turned back. "What?"

"It's Reese. My source inside the DoD says he's got PTSD. Could be dangerous. His superiors believe he's responsible for the deaths of three men during his last mission. There's a military investigation going on."

The day just got better and better. "Find that bastard."

"Coop!" Bobby stopped him again. "I know what you're thinking, but don't go off half-cocked. It sounds like Bianca got on his boat willingly, and you have no proof that she's still with him, or that he murdered Molier."

He didn't have proof, but he had his gut, and his gut said that was definitely a gunshot he'd heard on the other end. "She might already be dead, Bobby."

His friend's expression darkened. He shut his laptop and engaged his wheelchair, following Thomas to Cooper's SUV. Bobby had great respect for the NSA agent and her enormous brain. "You're going to need me. I'm coming with you."

Bianca's phone lay semi-crushed on the kitchen floor. Several sorry, weak buzzing sounds had come from it before it died completely.

She'd fired the Glock, aiming straight for Tephra as he went to crush the phone with his booted foot. She'd seen by the shocked expression on his face, he hadn't expected her to be armed. Too bad her aim was so bad, she couldn't hit the broad side of a barn.

Or a man.

He'd raised his hands as if to surrender at the exact same moment she'd pulled the trigger. His boot was already on its way down to smash her phone, the bullet nicking his upper left arm and sending him spinning sideways.

He hit the breakfast bar, falling as she pulled the trigger again and the second bullet went screaming across the few feet of space between them and landed in the wall above the stove.

He'd laughed—*laughed*—and hid behind the cover of the bar. "I just want to talk, sweetheart. I have something important to tell you and I can't unless you and I are face-to-face. There are people watching both of us, monitoring our every phone call, our every move."

Talk? Bianca's ears rang from the gunshots. She must have heard him wrong.

Maggie, bless her doggie heart, attacked him, the sound of his laughter dying in his throat and morphing into a howl of pain. Holding the gun with both hands, Bianca moved around the end of the bar to see him.

Maggie had sunk her teeth into his right calf and was holding on for dear life. Tephra tried to hit her nose with a fist, missed, and hit her in her ear instead. The dog didn't even flinch.

But then Tephra raised his eyes and saw Bianca standing there with the Glock trained on his chest. "You won't shoot me in cold blood," he said.

A trickle of sweat ran down the back of her neck. She firmed her hands on the gun. "Already did."

His shoulder was bleeding, a steady stream running from the open wound, down his arm, dripping off his elbow onto the floor.

He raised a finger and touched his cheek. "Tit for tat, then, eh, love? You and your dog have gotten me good, but hold up a minute. I didn't come in here to harm you."

Right. Where was his other hand? Realization dawned…he was going for a gun. The taunting was just a distraction.

"Maggie!" she yelled, but Tephra moved faster than she expected.

"Stop! I'm not going to…"

She fired, he dodged, the rest of his sentence lost to her as she was hit by a moving train.

Or a tanker.

Or maybe a force of nature.

Big arms went around her, taking her to the ground and knocking the air from her lungs. *Déjà vu.* She couldn't be sure what happened, but she found herself on the floor as gunshots rang out and she fought to breathe.

The weight that sent her sprawling and now covered her wasn't any of the things she'd imagined. Cal lay on top of her, firing a big, black gun right through the bar's cabinetry. The next thing she knew, he was rolling both of them away from the bar, gaining his feet and dragging her up with him.

He grabbed her arm and hauled her out of the kitchen, running through the living room and to the set of double doors that led to the beach.

Tephra yelled; Maggie barked. She and Cal hit the door. He threw it open but she looked back and called for the dog. "Maggie!"

The dog came bounding after them as Cal shoved Bianca through the opening and forced her to crouch against the house. One hand gripped the back of her head as he put his mouth to her ear. "Stay low and get to the street." His cheek brushed hers, his warm breath tickling her ear. "Two blocks down is an old yellow Chevelle. That's our car. Get in it and stay low."

"What about you?"

"This ends here." He pushed her to her feet and nudged her to run. "I'll catch up in a minute."

"I need my phone."

"What?" He looked at her like she was daft.

"There's sensitive information on that phone that Tephra could retrieve. I'm talking national security stuff, Cal. I need that phone. It's on the kitchen floor."

"Why would you be stupid enough to keep top secret info on your goddamn phone?"

The words stung, but she knew none of this made sense to him and there was no time to explain. "Don't let him get his hands on that phone."

The light shifted in his eyes. An indeterminate, subtle change. *Understanding.* "What did you do, Bianca?"

Before she could answer, his face hardened. "Go. Get out of here."

She didn't want to leave him, but he turned ready to leave her. Grabbing him by the arm, she tugged him back and kissed him. Right square on the lips. He'd been her hero since she was a gawky seven-year-old, and he still was.

He drew back, surprise on his face, eyes searching hers. Then he grabbed her by the back of the head and pulled her in for another kiss. She didn't resist, even though her logical brain told her it was foolhardy to be kissing at a time like this.

His lips were warm and firm, pressing against her in slow, but oh, so familiar caress. Instinctively, she closed her eyes. Her heart, already racing, skipped a beat, and an aching sensation throbbed inside her chest. All she wanted to do was throw her arms around Cal's neck and never let him go.

But this was real life. This was Cal, Mr. Navy SEAL. No matter how good the kiss felt, no matter how long it had been since they'd had such a heated, sexy mingling of their lips, he wasn't swept away by it like she was.

He broke the kiss and stroked his thumb across her jaw. "I'll get the phone," he said, his voice a touch ragged. The next second, he disappeared into the house, the sound of the deadbolt clicking into place.

CHAPTER TWELVE

He was alone in a house with a killer.

Cover wasn't hard to find with the oversized, expensive furniture, but the open-concept layout was hardly ideal. Cal scooted next to a tall, solid antique armoire that gave him a decent hiding place and went still. The heavy wood of the piece was probably the only item in the room that would stop a small caliber bullet.

His H&K felt solid in his hand. The house seemed too quiet now in the aftermath of the altercation. The sun was sinking low in the West, golden light shining brightly through the picturesque windows and highlighting cherry undertones in the hardwood floors.

Cal wasn't sure why the man hadn't taken a shot at him as he'd hustled B out the door. He'd made sure his body was a wall between her and the assassin, making himself a perfect target.

A normal person might believe from the stillness in the house that the intruder had left. Cal's finely-tuned senses told him differently. No matter how quiet, how stealthy another human being could be, he could sense them. Their very presence gave off energy—a subtle pressure to the air—and combined with the fight or flight mechanism in their brains, they left an impression like a ghost. Hard to see or hear, but there all the same.

Cal waited.

"You are certainly complicating things," the man called from the kitchen a few minutes later. "I know I scared her with all that talk about killing her, but that was for Uncle Sam's ears. Can't be too careful. They're listening, you know. Watching me. Watching you. I have to make it look good. Truth is, I only want to talk to your wife, not kill her."

Was this Rory Tephra? Cal had seen pictures of the man from his SEAL days, but the brief glimpse he'd caught of him in the kitchen didn't match up to the image in Cal's memory.

"Is that why you shot at her? Newsflash: women don't feel like talking after a bullet grazes their cheek."

The man's voice echoed with pride off the kitchen's high ceilings. "If I'd wanted her dead, Reese, I wouldn't have missed that shot and you know it."

But he *had* missed—barely, and because of Maggie. "What game are you playing?"

"A serious one. Marx is not the only target on this mission."

"Gus Molier was a target?"

"Who?"

"My marina neighbor, you bastard. Why'd you have to kill him?"

A pause. "His real name was Colin Mills. A slick little assassin known for his serial killer tendencies. He doesn't shoot his target—he kidnaps them, does his torture shit, and dumps their body in the ocean. He's the go-to man for the Russians, but I've heard the Chinese have hired him a time or two. Good thing I showed up when I did, or you might have been fish food."

What is he talking about? Gus wouldn't hurt a fly.

This man was psychotic. And injured. Was he buying time with this conversation? Cal listened closely for any sounds he was moving around, trying to stem his bleeding shoulder or escape out the kitchen door.

He heard nothing except the hum of the fridge. Through the silence, the faint high pitch of a police siren alerted him to approaching trouble.

"Enough of the bullshit," he called. "Who are you and what do you want?"

"You know who I am." The siren grew louder. The man issued a heavy sigh and Cal heard shuffling. "Seriously? You called 911? What kind of SEAL are you, Reese?"

"I didn't call anyone."

The slightest squeak of rubber on tile. "Well, unfortunately, there's no time to explain now, tadpole. I gotta run."

"Wait!" Cal peeked out from the armoire, gun raised. No one. *Where did he go?*

Cal crept forward, past the fireplace and toward the kitchen archway.

The door stood open, the kitchen empty. From the outside, the siren grew louder, a second one adding to the cacophony.

Blood droplets made a path across the floor from the island to the door. Cal glanced at the spot where Bianca's crushed phone had been.

Gone.

Whatever had been on that phone was now in the hands of the psycho.

The first police car arrived, skidding into the drive. *Time to go.* Cal started backing out the other way, praying Bianca had made it to the car and was safe. His gaze swept across the island and caught sight of a piece of paper on the countertop. Had that been there before?

Car doors slammed outside. No time to look. He shoved the paper in his pocket and high-tailed it.

CHAPTER THIRTEEN

The shaking started the moment she saw Cal.

Hold it together.

Exactly what she *had* been doing, huddled behind the wheel of the car with Maggie as police cars streamed by and dozens of onlookers followed. Holding her breath, trying not to let her mind run wild with possible scenarios. That lightheaded feeling had returned and a weird ringing had set up camp between her ears.

Seeing Cal, safe and unharmed, sent a wave of relief coursing through her system. Through the windshield, his gaze locked on hers. Her frozen lungs gulped oxygen and a smile broke over her face. Her lips still remembered the warm imprint his had left behind.

He didn't smile back.

Maggie, in the passenger seat with her head out the window, wagged her tail furiously in Bianca's face. Bianca couldn't blame the dog. She knew the feeling.

She started the engine. Cal approached the driver's side, eyes scanning the area. "Move over."

His voice was grim. Bianca started to protest that she would drive, but the next second, he opened her door, leaned down, and forcefully shoved her across the bench seat.

"Hey!"

The dog danced over her lap and greeted Cal. He patted her head and slipped into the driver's seat, putting the car in gear at the same time. Before he even shut the car door, they were moving.

Fast.

Bianca hastily snapped on her seat belt, doing her best to keep Maggie from slamming into the dashboard as Cal took a sudden left. She wanted to throw her arms around him, hold him tight for a minute to reassure herself he was there and he was okay. The tight set of his jaw and his quick movements as he dodged around people and other vehicles told her now wasn't the time.

She kept quiet, biting the inside of her cheek for a couple of miles until they located the highway. Maggie climbed into Bianca's lap and stuck her head out the window, and although Bianca protested, she let the dog stay. Dog smell filled her nostrils, but as they increased speed, the wind flowing through the car lessened it, and the feel of Maggie's strong, solid body, half in, half out of her lap, was reassuring.

I'm not a dog person, she reminded herself, *except maybe for this one.*

The Chevelle continued to eat up the highway and still Cal said nothing. *Typical.*

The boy who'd seduced her with nonstop talk in high school about his dreams and their bright future together had turned into the man who wouldn't communicate. During their marriage, he'd become more and more withdrawn, his mind always on the next training operation or mission. She'd understood he couldn't discuss his job, but it had gotten so bad, he wouldn't engage in even a simple conversation about the weather.

He doesn't know what to say to you.

Petting Maggie's side, Bianca divided her attention between the side-view mirror and straight ahead. The sun was setting on Cal's left, the peach-colored orb of hydrogen and helium hovering ever lower over the Pacific and taking its heat and light with it.

On her right, shadows grew larger, inching ever closer. Cal was thinking—always thinking—but she couldn't stand the silence any longer. "What happened back there?"

No response. A muscle jumped in Cal's jaw. *Uh-oh.* "Did you kill him?"

Silence. Then, "No."

Bianca didn't know whether to be relieved or not. Killing Tephra wouldn't stop whoever was after her. They'd simply send another assassin to do the job. "Did the police arrest him?"

"No."

At least Cal was answering her questions, even if his answers could use some elaboration.

If you don't want yes and no answers, ask a better question. "Why were they there? Who called them?"

"Neighbors probably heard you fire your gun."

"Oh. How did you get the car?"

His jaw worked slightly as if he were grinding his teeth. "Traded the boat for it."

"The boat? What about my briefcase? What about your closet full of guns?"

He glanced sideways at her, back to the road. "Your briefcase and a couple of guns are in the trunk."

She waggled her fingers at him. "Can I have my phone?"

The muscle jumped in his jaw again, and this time, he didn't answer even after she waited several seconds.

Double *uh-oh.* "Tell me you got my phone."

Cal shot her a menacing look. "He took it."

"What?" As the realization sunk in, she laid her forehead against Maggie's shoulder. "Why the hell would Tephra take my broken phone?"

"Maybe because you had top secret info on it?"

His voice had turned sarcastic. She couldn't tell him the truth—there was no top secret information. A few funky apps she'd designed, yes, but the reason she wanted the phone back was because of the photos.

The last happy time she'd had with Cal was recorded in a series of pictures on that phone. Earlier that year, they'd taken a weekend trip to northern California to watch migrating whales. Cal hadn't wanted to go, but she convinced him a weekend getaway would be good for them. He hadn't known, but it was her last ditch effort to save their marriage. They'd spent their days on a boat—her least favorite place in the world—watching for whales. Their nights were spent enjoying fresh seafood and good wines.

Cal had relaxed. She knew he would on the water. They'd laughed and talked and made love a dozen times in a few days.

She'd taken shots of Cal and the whales. Her favorite, though, was one taken by a friendly passenger who'd offered to get both of them in the picture. Cal had enclosed Bianca in his arms and leaned his head against hers. At the moment the woman snapped the photo, a whale breached the water behind them, as if it wanted its picture taken too.

The last happy time we'll ever share. Gone.

Cal wouldn't have understood. He would have rolled his eyes and shook his head. That's why she'd told him she had information on her phone that could endanger national security. She'd known if she told him the truth, he wouldn't make an effort to get the phone.

Now it was too late.

"Is that why he was after you, B? Did you steal security secrets?"

"You think I'm a traitor?"

He locked eyes with her for half a second, shook his head and looked away. "I know you're not telling me everything. Same as usual."

Turning her head so Cal couldn't see her face, Bianca watched the darkening landscape roll by as a tear slipped down her cheek.

CHAPTER FOURTEEN

Cooper spotted Ronni rushing toward him even before he was out of his vehicle. The block of expensive beachfront properties was jammed with police cars, CSI techs, and onlookers.

Ronni and Nelson Cruz, an ICE agent with the taskforce, had been keeping surveillance on a bus driver suspected of moving drugs and fake Gucci bags near Huntington Beach. They'd arrived at the house an hour before Cooper and his merry band of Thomas and Bobby, but had run into a wall of law enforcement wanting to protect their territory.

"Talk to me, Punto," Cooper said as Ronni met him halfway to the yellow tape cordoning off the house and sidewalk. Thomas was helping Bobby out of the SUV. "Did Dupé get you access to anything?"

The two-story house loomed behind her, an expensive place with blue-grey siding and white trim. "The director's call was not well received." She kept her voice low and her eyes on the surrounding crowd. "But I got the sergeant in charge, Ethridge, to pony up a few details."

She waited for Thomas and Bobby to catch up with them before leading the three of them away from a cluster of folks gathered at the edges of the yard. A police officer guarded the front door, holding it open for a CSI tech to enter.

Ronni took the sidewalk to the side yard and led them around back to another officer keeping watch over the boat dock. He seemed to recognize her, but held up a hand to stop them all the same.

Cooper flashed his badge, as did Thomas and Bobby. The cop nodded once and lifted the yellow tape to allow them to pass.

Ronni continued walking, taking them to the boardwalk that led to the dock. There, she stopped and pointed at a small house boat that had seen better days. "Guess who owns this boat?"

"Reese?"

"A guy showed up about twenty minutes ago saying it was his. When Ethridge questioned him, the guy said a man fitting Reese's description sold it to him in exchange for a pale yellow 1969 Chevelle."

Thomas scanned the boat. "Even without seeing the car, I'd say Reese got the better deal."

"Ethridge already put out an APB on the car."

Cooper didn't really give a damn about Reese. "Was Agent Marx here?"

Ronni nodded. "The next-door neighbor reported she heard gunshots and saw a woman fitting Bianca's description leaving the house with a large, black dog shortly afterward. The woman and dog headed north on foot. They were in a hurry."

Bianca was alive. Alive was good. "The neighbor didn't see Reese?"

"No, but she did see a second boat in the slip and a man boarding it after the woman and dog took off. Said he was in a hurry to leave as well."

"Reese?" Bobby asked.

"She didn't get a good look at him except from the back, but estimated he was under six foot and weighed one-eighty. She also said she thought he was in his mid- to late-forties—his hair had streaks of gray in it. I showed her the photo of Cal Reese Bobby sent to my phone. It wasn't him."

Two boats, a second man. Bianca leaving the house on her own. Cooper's brain spewed out scenarios, none of which he

MISTY EVANS

particularly liked. Was Reese involved in something bad and Bianca was now caught in it? "Who fired the shots?"

"We don't know." Ronni led them to the glass doors, explaining about the security system and how there was no forced entry. No locks or windows had been broken. Whoever entered knew the security code.

Bobby has his tablet out. He glanced up at Cooper. "Got a hit on Emit Petit. He was a childhood friend of Cal's and Bianca's."

"Both of them?" Thomas asked.

"They grew up together in Oceanside," Bobby said, continuing to read his screen. "Lived in the same neighborhood and went to the same school."

Bobby's brows lowered and he frowned. "My source at the Defense Department won't go on record, but he says it's possible one of SEAL Team Seven's missions last year was to rescue Petit's sister from a kidnapper."

"So Cal and Bianca came here for what?" Thomas asked. "A second honeymoon?"

"There's blood splatter in the kitchen," Ronni said. "I haven't gained access yet, but I know they also found bullet casings."

Cooper's hands balled into fists. His taskforce members were like family. The thought of one of them being injured made him want to punch something. "Is it Bianca's blood?"

Ronni's eyes were sad as they met his. "We don't know yet. CSI is working on it. I asked the witness if she thought either of the people she saw were injured. She said the man was holding his shoulder and there might have been blood on his arms. She wasn't sure."

He looked out at the boat. "We have a dead body back at the marina, a missing agent, a mystery man with a second boat, and a SEAL with PTSD. Theories?"

Cooper's team all stared back at him, no one saying a word.

"That's what I thought." He needed to see the inside of the house and talk to Ethridge. He probably should check out the boat as well.

114

Waste of time. A trained SEAL wouldn't leave clues. "Ronni, you and Bobby stay here, check out the house and the boat. Update us on anything new. Thomas, let's roll."

"Where are we going, boss?" Thomas hustled to keep up with him.

Being on the move—doing something—eased the tightness in his fists. "To hunt down a pale yellow '69 Chevelle."

CHAPTER FIFTEEN

Three hours later

The last time Bianca's head had been in his lap, he'd been a happy camper. Now, Cal was anything but.

Not entirely true. Driving through the cool fall night, Bianca and Maggie with him, both safe and sound, had a strange effect on him. He wasn't the lone wolf type, wasn't into solitude and finding his Zen. Yet, right at that moment, he felt calmer and more clearheaded than he had in weeks.

He should have found the nearest FBI office and dumped Bianca's butt off there. Whatever she'd done, whatever information she'd stolen, was not his problem. But when had he ever turned his back on her?

FUCK. Foolish. Unwise. Careless. Kowtowed. His acronym for life with Bianca. When it came to her, he was all of those things. In other words, fucked.

He glanced down at her sleeping face nestled in the V of his crotch. Her hair was tousled, spread out over his legs, her dark lashes blending into the shadows under her eyes.

Beautiful. All high cheekbones and smooth, porcelain skin, even in the yellowy glow from the dashboard. She wore squat for makeup, which always made her look younger than she was, and she refused to get contacts, wearing her glasses like a shield. Hiding her emotions.

The current pair of heavy, purple frames had fallen off an

hour ago, and he'd set them on the dash. Now, he gently brushed several strands of hair off her cheek. At his light touch, her full lips parted. She said something in her sleep, the sexy sound, and her warm breath, doing a number on his groin.

Had he really kissed her back at the beach house? Technically, she'd kissed him. Hers was sort of an impulsive, hyped-up, adrenaline-driven quickie on his mouth. His, however, had been more calculated. Premeditated. He'd wanted to kiss her and kick her in the butt at the same time since she'd shown up at *The Love Boat.*

But mostly kiss her.

FUCKed. Yes, indeed. She'd ripped his heart out filing for divorce and he still wanted to kiss her.

His backside had grown numb from sitting so long but he dared not move, lest he wake her. She was easier to get along with when she was sleeping, and it was easier on him to admire her beauty and remember how things used to be between them.

Earlier, he'd stopped at a convenience store north of L.A. to gas up and grab some snacks. Bianca had led Maggie to a nearby patch of grass to pee. Bianca's eyes, her whole demeanor, had been cheerless and strung out. Cal had tried to harden his heart, tell himself there was nothing he could do for her, but she'd looked at him with those eyes—the ones that wrecked him every time—and instead of driving her directly to the Feds and letting them deal with her, he was on this back road with her and the dog, wondering what the hell he'd gotten himself into.

Since the moment he'd burst into Emit's kitchen and saw her standing over the man on the floor with the Glock in her hand, he'd been trying to reconcile the geeky girl he'd been in love with since second grade with the woman warrior she'd become. She was still a geek, but circumstances had hardened her, changed her. It took a lot to bring out the tiger in Bianca, but when push came to shove, she had the resolve and tenacity to accept whatever challenge was handed to her and come out swinging.

But shooting a man? If he hadn't seen the wound in the man's shoulder, seen the blood, he wouldn't have believed it.

She'd only injured him, not killed him. Was it for lack of skill or on purpose? How had she gotten the upper hand against a trained assassin?

Cal glanced in his rearview. No one was following them. He'd stayed off the major interstates and taken the scenic route wherever possible, avoiding larger cities and their police forces. He still hadn't touched base with Emit... Was it coincidence that the assassin had shown up right after Cal placed that call to his friend?

An all-night news station played softly in the background. There had been no breaking stories about a dead body at Culver's Marina or a shootout at Emit's place. That only meant law enforcement was keeping things quiet. Why?

Because of Bianca. An NSA agent on the loose was a dangerous weapon.

Cal had replayed his conversation with Rory Tephra in his head a hundred times as he drove through the night. At first, he'd tried to talk himself out of believing it was the MIA SEAL, but Rory's words had convinced him.

You know who I am.

Gotta run, tadpole.

SEALs were frogmen. The older ones often called the younger ones—the rookies—tadpoles.

I only want to talk to your wife.

Marx is not the only target on this mission.

Tephra hadn't lied; Cal was sure of it. From confessing he didn't actually want to kill Bianca to implying the mission was bigger than taking out a nerdy NSA agent, it all added up. Bianca hadn't gotten the drop on Tephra because she was a skilled operative hiding behind her geeky persona. No, Tephra honestly wanted to talk to her, not kill her. Only, he hadn't expected her to fight back.

If only Cal had had time to ask more questions. The note

from the breakfast bar was in his pocket. He'd glanced at it when they'd stopped for gas. A set of numbers in sloppy handwriting. Not a phone number or other easily identifiable combination. He didn't know what they meant—Bianca might, but he hadn't shared the paper with her yet.

Secure. First, he needed to land somewhere they'd be safe for a few hours. He needed as many answers from her as he did from Rory.

They crested a hill and Cal slowed the car. He flicked on the brights and saw his turn twenty feet ahead.

The paved road turned into gravel as Cal left the highway far behind. Pot holes the size of Kansas made the car dip and shimmy. Maggie woke and sat up, watching out the windshield. The bumping also woke Bianca, one of her hands using Cal's leg to leverage her up, her fingers hanging on tight and shooting a renewed surge of lust straight to his groin.

"Sorry I keep falling asleep on you," she said. Her voice was low and husky. "The adrenaline crash is a bitch, isn't it? Where are we?"

"The cabin." He eased around a downed tree limb in the road. He hadn't been to the cabin since his father had died. His stepmom hadn't sold it yet, and from the looks of it, no one else had visited. "We'll be safe here until morning. Then we'll go see Halston."

Bianca righted herself, snagged her glasses from the dash and put them on. "Your dad's fishing cabin? In the woods?"

He saw her visibly shudder. He couldn't help the eye roll. She had a thing about snakes, bugs, poison ivy—pretty much nature in general, except the tornadoes and storms she seemed to gravitate to as a kid. He lived and breathed the outdoors, loved everything about it. How he'd ended up with such a nerdy prima donna, he didn't know.

The front of the cabin was overgrown with weeds. Vines covered the roof and snaked down the north side. Cal parked and got out. The nearby trees blotted out the partial moon and stars, keeping the cabin in dense shadows. He left the driver's side door open and went to the trunk, Maggie bounding out after him. From the trunk he withdrew a flashlight.

"Come on," he said to Bianca who was still stationary in the car. "Let's get you inside."

Her voice took on a higher pitch. "Aren't there bears and mountain lions in this part of the state?"

Getting her inside was going to be a challenge. "You went face-to-face with a hired assassin a few hours ago. If you can handle him, you can handle anything inside this cabin."

"I'd rather stay in the car."

Cal climbed the steps and inspected the door. A hard shove popped it open. Maggie started to rush through, but Cal stopped her. "Fine," he called over his shoulder to Bianca. "Just keep an eye out for the serial killer known to haunt this area."

He stepped in, shining his flashlight around. What the outside lacked in upkeep, the inside made up for.

Everything was tidy and neat, the couch and chairs covered with white sheets to keep the dust off. Inside the door, a coat hung on a wooden peg rack, a shotgun above it.

Cal's heart thudded a heavy beat. Except for the dust covers, which he assumed his stepmother had added at some point since the funeral, the place looked exactly as his dad had left it on his last fishing trip.

Maggie nosed around, her coat so black, she disappeared in the shadows. The flashlight beam bounced off the window panes as Cal carefully made his way to the kitchen. A fine layer of dust covered the countertops. An empty coffee mug sat in the sink and a set of fillet knives lay to one side on a dish towel. Just like the coat his stepmom had left hanging on the peg by the door, she hadn't been able to put the coffee mug away or sell his dad's prized knife set.

Out back was the cabin's solar-powered generator. It probably needed maintenance, but that would have to wait until morning. Crossing his fingers, Cal stood at the back door and flipped the nearest light switch. Several seconds later, he heard the engine kick on. A few seconds longer and the kitchen was bathed in warm light.

The front door slammed shut and Cal whirled around. The living room was still in darkness, but he saw Bianca leaning against the door, panting heavily and looking like she'd just seen a ghost. The bandage on her cheek had come loose on one end and dangled beleagueredly down the side.

Maggie barked once and rushed to Bianca.

"What is it?" he asked, his hand tightening on the flashlight.

She heaved a breath and made funny motions with her hands. "Big...long wings...yellow eyes..." She did that shuddery thing again. "Lots of flapping."

The tension in his shoulders eased. He set the flashlight on the nearest counter. "It's called an owl."

She shook her head. "Owls are cute and cuddly. This...this was an owl on steroids."

"You've been in your cozy, sterile cubicle in D.C. for far too long." Making his way back to the living room, he turned on a lamp. "I'm going to get a few things from the trunk and move the car so it's not visible. I'll grab wood from the woodpile and we can build a fire."

"Is this place safe? Won't Tephra know this cabin is owned by your family and look for us here?"

Possibly, but it wasn't an easy place to find if you'd never been there and Tephra had no idea which way they'd headed. Of course, he'd already found them once...probably because Emit, the asshole, had given them up. "If he's good enough to track us to Emit's, he's good enough to track us here or anywhere else we go, but it will take him time. We won't stay long. Just a few hours."

"He found us at Emit's because of the tracker in the bullet."

Cal paused. "The what?"

She fixed her glasses, askew on her face. "There are special bullets in use by some government covert operatives. They have a miniscule GPS tracker inside them. He shot the boat with the bullet and the tracker led him right to us."

Well, wasn't that convenient? Bullets with trackers. He'd heard of them but his team had never used them. At least that cleared Emit from Cal's capture-and-kill list.

If I'd wanted her dead, I wouldn't have missed that shot and you know it.

Another possible truth from Tephra. Cal walked over to Bianca. She continued to lean on the door as if barring nature, and that owl, from coming in. Her eyes were wide as he stopped in front of her and fixed the bandage on her cheek. She still wore his T-shirt, her hair a mess, and her expression completely trusting.

After he secured the bandage, he brushed his hand over her jaw. Her breath hitched, but not from running from mutant owls.

When was the last time he'd taken her breath away?

Thank God Tephra's bullet had missed. No matter how much she drove him crazy, Cal couldn't imagine a world without Bianca in it.

He'd never been an affectionate guy. Expressing his emotions didn't come naturally. After his mom died when he was five, he'd rarely hugged anyone. Not even Bianca, who'd given up so much for him. Sometimes it wasn't hard to understand why she'd pushed him away. Why she'd filed for divorce. He wasn't an easy person to live with. He hadn't been there for her when she really needed him.

Reaching out, he drew her into his arms. Her body was warm and soft in all the right places, and even after their day from hell, she still smelled like vanilla. Familiar. He stroked the back of her hair, nuzzled her neck. He closed his eyes.

She melted into him, the same way she always had, an amazing blend of softness and strength. For several long seconds, they stood that way, nothing between them. Not anger, not disappointment, not their tumultuous past. Just a man and a woman seeking comfort in each other.

Deep in the woods, the owl she'd been scared by *whoo-hoo'd* and crickets chirped. A tree frog joined the chorus.

Bianca's hands treaded lightly up his back muscles and her breasts rose and fell against his chest, her chin on his shoulder. "I don't know how I ended up here."

He stroked her hair with one hand, the other on her lower back. He should call Emit, get his extraction crew to meet them here as soon as possible, but he needed another minute to savor this. Another minute to hold Bianca close.

The stubble on his cheek rasped lightly against her skin as he shifted to speak near her ear. "I drove you, remember?"

She playfully whacked his shoulder and leaned back to look at him. "I mean, in this situation. I love my job. Love working for the NSA and being part of Command and..." She stiffened slightly, looked away. Her tone grew angry. "I don't know how I ended up being the enemy."

"I know the feeling."

Her gaze returned to his, her eyes scrutinizing. "What happened out there? With Warfighter?"

The spell was broken. Cal loosened his hold, drawing away even though he didn't want to. What he wanted to do was kiss her so she stopped talking. Drag her into the bedroom, strip her clothes off, and watch her willingly open her legs to him. Anything to keep her in the moment and not asking questions he couldn't answer. Didn't want to answer.

So long. It had been so damn long since he'd lost himself in her heat. "You know what happened."

Bianca squared her shoulders. "Actually, I don't. I was given a summary report—a whopping paragraph—about the outcome, but no details concerning the infiltration or ambush. When I asked Justin, he refused to share any details, claiming it was a national security risk for him to even talk to me."

Every night since the mission failed, he'd lost sleep trying to force his brain to remember the details. A never-ending loop played in his head—was there anything he could have done differently? Why wasn't he dead instead of three of his men? The hell of it never stopped. If only he could remember...

He knew in his soul the only way to come back from the brink of this insanity was to talk to someone. Bianca was the ideal person. She knew him, knew the way his mind worked.

He'd been her shield all these years, but she'd been his life source. Like the blood that pumped in his veins, he needed her. Needed her more than she'd ever known.

Tell her. Right now. Before another day passes. Tell her you love her, and no matter what happens, you're not walking away from her again.

He stared down at her tangled hair and the shadows under her eyes. His hands dropped to her arms, her skin cool under the sleeves of his T-shirt. She shivered at his touch, her eyes meeting his. They were clear, truly concerned, but he saw a hint of other emotions. Anger mixed with disheartenment. The fear of the future, not just for her, but for him too.

He touched the edge of her jaw. "Everything will be okay, B."

"How do you know?"

"Because that's what we do, you and I. We figure things out, make things work, no matter the circumstances. We survive and every challenge makes us stronger. We'll get to the bottom of this. We'll figure it out and expose whoever's behind it. Trust me, you'll be back to work before you know it."

Her hand rose almost hesitantly, her fingers stroking through his hair. Heat shot straight to his groin. "I wish I could believe that, Cal. I really wish I could."

CHAPTER SIXTEEN

Bianca bit her tongue. Cal was living in an alternate dimension if he believed everything would be okay.

Trust me. She'd learned at an early age not to rely on people who said that. People who told you they loved you, that everything would be okay. *Sit down, shut up, and be a good girl, Bianca.*

Too many times in her life, those who were supposed to take care of her and have her best interests at heart did the opposite. Her mother beat her when she said or did the wrong thing— and she always seemed to say or do the wrong thing. Cal had withdrawn his love and neglected her after the loss of both babies. And now her employer, the government of the United States, had betrayed her loyalty and wanted her dead.

By the time she was four years old, she'd learned to withdraw, to go inside her mind and live in an imaginary world in order to protect herself. Her mother wouldn't put her in preschool, so kindergarten was her first taste of life outside their shabby apartment. Kindergarten...a kind teacher, other kids, books and music and fresh air at recess. Bianca asked her teacher if she could live at school. When Ms. Olin said no, she asked the woman if she could live at her house. Another no, and the next day when Bianca's backside was too sore to sit in the tiny chairs because of the spanking her mother had given her when Bianca told her she wished Ms. Olin was her mother, Bianca was sent to the guidance counselor's office.

The man smelled funny and wouldn't look her in the eye. Bianca refused to tell him what had happened, and in return, he'd said something about the school didn't like to make waves but would contact social services. On her way back to Ms. Olin's room, Bianca wondered how a school with no water in sight could make a wave.

By second grade, her mother had been investigated by the state, but Bianca was still living with her, taking her abuse. Teachers, the principal, the social workers—people who were supposed to care about her and protect her—left her with her monster of a mother. Bianca ended up in the hospital twice, once with a broken arm and once with a mild head concussion.

She found refuge in books and gobbled up the school's library in no time. She earned perfect scores in all her classes, thanks to her memory, and at the end of the year, her teacher recommended she be tested for the gifted program. Bianca's mother refused to sign the permission slip, so Bianca forged her signature. She'd already learned how to perfectly replicate her mother's sloppy handwriting.

There was one other student in the principal's office that day. Callan Reese. A boy whose father wore suits to school events and coached little league in the summers. Cal seemed to be lacking a mother, but he didn't seem to care. Bianca wished she could give him hers.

He said nothing to her before or after the test, but something passed between them. A grudging respect that they were both unique on some level. In the hallway, when Marcia Linkletter shoved Bianca away from the water fountain, Cal told Marcia to knock it off.

That day, Cal invited Bianca to play dodge ball on his team. She hated dodge ball, but she was good at it. She could analyze the players and she knew how to move quickly to avoid getting hit. Cal's invitation was the first she'd ever had, so she threw her shoulders back, walked over, and played her heart out.

She won the game for them by sheer determination, earning

another solid stare from Cal that told her she'd upped her status with him once more. Later, when they met in the principal's office to receive their testing results, Cal punched her in the arm, a type of congratulatory high-five. But Bianca froze and then ran off, embarrassed. Cal caught up with her after school and apologized. His father had told him never to strike a girl, and he hadn't meant to hurt her.

His sincerity killed her, but she tried to laugh it off, refusing to tell him the real reason she'd ran away from the physical contact. Her laughter turned to tears, and then anger at herself for crying. Cal didn't seem to care. He started walking her home every day—they only lived a block away from each other, yet it felt to Bianca as if they lived on completely different planets. Her with her crazy mother, and Cal with his handsome, caring father.

And then he saved her from the school ground bully, and the deal was sealed. That day on their way home, she told him everything.

The next day at recess, he taught her how to block her mother's punches. How to bend her arm back and let her know Bianca was done cowering. How to dodge her kicks. His father had a black belt in karate and had taught Cal a few moves.

Seeing Cal now, knowing he was suffering but refusing to talk about it, reminded her of herself back then. If only she had a black belt in fighting his mental demons so she could fend them off for him. Protect him like he'd always done for her.

Reaching Cal on an emotional level was equivalent to running into a brick wall. Logic, her best friend, might work, though. "Talking about Warfighter might serve two purposes." He was still standing in front of her, seemingly reluctant to let her go. She ran her fingers down his arm. "One, I might be able to tie Senator Halston to the disastrous outcome which has put us both in this situation, and two, you might feel better."

He shifted his focus to the night outside the window. "I need to move the car. Can you get Maggie some water and check the pantry? See if there's anything she can eat."

Brick wall, we meet again.

Fine. She could be bullheaded too. "We *are* going to talk about it at some point, Callan Reese. I saw the gun on the boat."

"The gun?"

"The one with a single bullet." She paused, gathering her mental shields. "Were you really contemplating suicide?"

He made an exasperated noise in the back of his throat, looked away. "It crossed my mind, but I would never do that. Not to you."

An image of her mother's face flashed through her mind. The gun she'd held in her hand. Bianca shut down the images. "Tell me what happened in Afghanistan."

He shook his head and patted her cheek. "We *are* going to have a detailed conversation about a few things. You're going to tell me what was on your phone, and I'm going to tell you a few things Tephra said at the house that don't make sense."

"You *talked* to him?"

Cal headed for the door. "I'll be back in a minute."

The door shut. Maggie, lying in front of the fireplace hearth, raised her head, giving the door a curious look. Bianca patted her leg to call the dog as she walked to the kitchen. "Let's find you something to eat."

The dog bounded up, wagging her tail.

A few minutes later, Maggie had dined on a can of beef stew and a bowl of water. Cal returned from moving the car with an armful of wood for the fireplace. Dirt was smudged on his cheek and he had a leaf stuck in his hair.

He unloaded the wood, opened the flue, and knelt to build a fire. Maggie stretched out next to him and closed her eyes. Bianca watched his sure movements as he placed the wood just so and balled up a newspaper from the stack nearby to use as tinder. Her heart pinched at the normalcy, the hominess of the scene.

She picked the leaf from his hair and he glanced up. His dark eyes were serious like always, but behind them, she saw the intelligence and magnetism that had drawn her in since the first day they'd met in the principal's office.

And behind that, she saw the truth—they weren't making it out of this alive.

That wasn't going to stop him from trying. She could see that in his gaze as well. The same confidence she saw in his movements as he built a fire reflected back to her. That and the fact he was still attracted to her after all these years.

That they'd been through a hell of a day—that she'd brought this all on him—didn't seem to dampen his libido.

It hadn't dampened hers either. Especially when he looked at her like that.

"I thought I was going to die in that house," she said, twirling the stem of the leaf between her fingers. "And then, after I made it out and I was sitting in the car waiting for you, I was terrified *you* were going to die."

He struck a match and set the kindling on fire. Once the wood caught, he took the leaf from her hand and tossed it into the flames. He reached up, grabbed her hand, and pulled her into his lap.

"I never should have left you."

"At the house?"

"After the babies."

Her heart constricted. "Cal, I pushed you away. Both times. You know me. I suck at handling emotions. I hate showing them, can't share them like normal people. It wasn't your fault."

"I should have stayed anyway. No one should have to go through what you did alone. That first baby, and then your mother...died..."

"Sshh." She placed a finger against his lips. Even now, she couldn't go there. Couldn't talk about it. "I survived, and you found your true calling by entering the Navy."

For long seconds he stared at her. His lips kissed her finger. "I can't make up for the past, but I'm here now."

A small fissure opened in her heart. God, she loved this man. "That's all I've ever wanted."

His hands covered her face, smoothing her hair back. He showered her with kisses. They were soft but urgent, as if he were turned on and relieved at the same time. Happy she was there.

Her arms went around his neck and she ran her hands through his hair. Heat from the fire warmed her side; Cal's ardent ministrations heating the rest of her.

He massaged her neck and back, bringing his hands around to cup her breasts through the cotton fabric. A moan escaped her lips and she arched into him. This could not be happening— *should* not be happening—but her body responded the way it always did. Everything inside her wanted him and wanted him bad.

She kissed him back hungrily, moving her hands under his shirt and filling them with the solidness of his pecs and abs. In seconds, both of them were shirtless and Bianca knew there was no turning back now. No stopping.

This was wrong. Totally wrong. She'd filed for divorce. She was a walking time bomb. Sleeping with Cal after all these months—three months and sixteen days, to be exact—would not solve their problems. It would not resurrect their marriage, only make the final outcome more emotional.

Stop this insanity before he breaks your heart all over again.

But then Cal murmured against the skin of her neck, "You're not going to die, B. Whatever happens, you have to live." He licked her bottom lip, his gaze locking on hers. "For me."

Game over.

She wrapped her legs around him, ground her pelvis against the hard length of him. He tweaked one of her nipples—where had her bra gone?—and she nearly orgasmed right there.

"I need you inside me. Now," she heard herself say, and Cal, bless his Cro-Magnon heart, wasn't about to turn her down.

In one slick move, his strong arms lifted her from the floor and tumbled her onto the nearby couch. She helped him remove her pants, but he didn't remove his. Instead he put his hands on the insides of her knees and spread her legs. Wide.

Goose bumps raced over her skin and her stomach clenched, knowing what he was about to do even before he lowered his head. Skilled fingers massaged her thighs, one finger slipping under the silk of her underwear.

She sucked in her breath at the contact. Wetting the tip of his finger, he slid it against her tingling skin. "God, you're so wet."

He murmured against the silk of her panties, his warm breath heating her skin right through the fabric. "So goddamn ready."

Sliding the panties aside, his fingers began a slow perusal, finding the exact spot to make her gasp again. He raised his head and looked at her, heat and lust clearly in his eyes, a satisfied smile on his face. One finger parted her folds, and then it, and a second, slipped inside.

She bucked her hips, clawing at the dust cover. He worked her for a moment with his fingers, going deep, drawing them out, then going deep again.

When she could barely stand it, he went to work with his thumb on her nub, starting a rhythm she met with gusto. The combination of his thumb outside and his fingers inside had her moving fast and hard against his hand.

It wasn't enough. She needed more. "Please, Cal," she whispered. "Please..."

His smile broadened. He moved aside her underwear with his free hand and lowered his lips to the spot where his thumb had been, his fingers working their magic from the inside.

He licked her with his tongue, then sucked gently, pressing up with those wicked fingers. At her whimper, he sucked harder and Bianca's vision went white.

She exploded, back arching off the couch and in the process, shoving Cal's fingers even deeper. How that was possible, she didn't know or care. Her hands clenched the dust cover and she cried out as he sucked her through the orgasm, extending it until she nearly passed out from the pleasure.

Once it was over, he climbed up next to her on the couch and pulled her into his arms. She was shaking from head to toe, all her limbs doing a trembling, joyful dance.

Bliss. Lying in Cal's arms like this was pure bliss. She'd been fooling herself filing for divorce. Cal was an addiction she would never be free of, no matter what some paper said. Never wanted to be free, no matter what her logical brain told her.

The entire day had been surreal. *If only…*

Bianca shut down the thought. She'd lived her life with *if onlys* and look where that had gotten her.

Instead, she blanked her mind and soaked up the feel of Cal's arms, floating for as long as she could. Her head lay on his chest, his heartbeat, stable and resilient beating under her ear.

After a moment, she realized there was a firm bulge in his pants. She reached for it, cupping him.

"It's after midnight, and I've been driving for hours." His voice was low and quiet, almost ragged. "I could use some sleep."

His rejection twinged in her stomach, but he didn't pull her hand away. He was trying to give her an out, let her know it was okay if she didn't want to follow through.

She rubbed him through his jeans. "You'll sleep better once I'm done with you."

She undid his belt, lowered his zipper. He laid his head back, closed his eyes. "You don't want to do that, B"

"Why not?"

"You'll hate yourself enough as it is come morning."

Probably. "My days are numbered. I might as well have fun."

She started to slip her hand inside his pants, but he stayed it with his own. "Tephra told me he doesn't want to kill you. He only wants to talk."

I just want to talk, sweetheart. I have something important to tell you…

She'd replayed Tephra's words over and over in her mind as they'd flown up the interstate.

Cal opened his eyes and raised his head. His fingers touched her bandaged cheek. "He said if he'd wanted you dead, he wouldn't have missed the shot on the boat."

Her throat grew tight. The bliss evaporated, the roller coaster of emotions taking a dive like the crash after too many energy drinks. "He almost *didn't* miss. If it wasn't for Maggie—"

"I know. He also said you weren't the only target on this mission. That my neighbor at the marina? Gus? He was an assassin after *me*."

She sat up, pushing off his chest. Her heart hammered as she stared down into his eyes. "What?"

"Bianca, what did you steal from the NSA?"

"I didn't steal anything."

"Your phone had top secret information on it."

Turning away, she sat on the edge of the couch, putting her head in her hands. Time to admit the truth. God, he would hate her. "My phone had nothing on it but a few of my personally designed apps and some pictures of us. That's why I wanted it back, not because I stole top secret info from the government. I wanted to see if I could salvage those pictures."

Silence fell like a heavy blanket. She couldn't look at him, didn't want to see the anger she knew she'd find on his face.

The couch's cushion depressed as Cal sat up, an unexpected sound rising from behind her. He was chuckling. More than chuckling…he was laughing. "I don't believe it."

Facing him, she saw he was shaking his head in exasperation.

"It's true. I had photos of us from the whale sighting expedition—the last pictures of us together—and I didn't want to lose them. Even though Tephra smashed the phone, I could probably get them off the SIM card. I never back up my phone or download the pictures—it's stupid, but that's me. My backup for important things is up here." She tapped her head. "But I didn't want to lose those pictures, Cal."

"You lied." He didn't sound shocked or surprised. Just...disappointed.

What's new? "Would you have made an effort to retrieve the phone if I hadn't told you it was crucial to national security?"

"If the only things on it were pictures and apps, why did Tephra take it?"

"If he's any good at tracking people, which he apparently is, he already knows all of my contacts." She froze as a new thought hit. "Except..."

"Except what?"

Her boss. Not Cooper Harris, but Jonathan Brockmann, her boss at Command and Control.

He wasn't in her contacts book and his private number was stored only in her memory, but he'd called four days ago. To check on her, he'd said. More likely, he was checking to see if she was still alive.

What had he asked her that day? *How's California treating you? How are things with your...family?*

She'd thought it weird he'd asked about Cal. No one in C&C talked about their personal lives. No one said it out loud—it was sort of an unspoken rule—if you worked for Command and Control, you had no personal life. No ties that could compromise your job. Bianca had been the exception.

Cal. Her only tie. "Do you believe Tephra was telling the truth about Gus? That he was an assassin after you?"

"I think Rory Tephra has lost touch with reality."

Cal's face, though, said he was worried. That he didn't believe Tephra wasn't a mental case at all.

Rare was the time Jonathan Brockmann called her or any of his agents. It just wasn't done. And although they used encrypted technology, per protocol, any communication with C&C was to be erased from the phone's call log.

Bianca hadn't erased it. Being paranoid, she had, in fact, taped the conversation.

Once more, Tephra's words surfaced in her memory. *There are people watching both of us, monitoring our every phone call, our every move.*

"Bianca." Cal's voice was low with warning. "What aren't you telling me?"

Tracing that call back to Jonathan and Command and Control would be difficult but not impossible. What would it gain Tephra? Jonathan might be the man who'd hired him in the first place.

"Who hired an assassin to come after *you?*" Bianca searched Cal's face, his eyes. "What aren't you telling *me?*"

CHAPTER SEVENTEEN

"You think this is about me?" Cal shook his head in disgust, hauled himself off of the couch, and poked at the fire. "If anyone wanted me dead, I would have gone down with my men."

"Maybe you were supposed to. Maybe you were all supposed to die. You didn't. You got out alive." She drummed her fingers against her chin. "But *why* were you all supposed to die? Did Otto Grimes put out a hit on you?" She stopped, took a deep breath, her naked breasts rising and falling. "Who could take out an entire SEAL platoon?"

Conspiracy theories. She loved them, the puzzle they presented. "Gus was not an assassin, B, and even if he was, he wasn't there for me."

"How do you know?"

"He lived in the marina long before I showed up, and he could have taken me out at any point over the past two weeks since I moved in."

"Did he tell you he'd lived there all this time or did someone else tell you that?"

Come to think of it…Cal stopped poking at the logs in the fireplace. Gus had been a loner. No one at the marina, not even Chewy, the marina owner, had said much about the guy.

He set down the poker. "If Gus was an assassin, he didn't take me out because he wasn't after me. He was waiting for you."

She visibly swallowed and gathered up her shirt. She

couldn't find her bra and gave up, slipping his T-shirt over her head. Pacing, she snatched up her pants but didn't put them on. "Two assassins? There are *two* assassins after me?"

Her nipples were still hard, jutting out the soft cotton. The hem brushed her thighs as she paced, her slim legs beckoning to him. "Gus, or whoever he was, is dead, so technically, only one. That we know of anyway," he added.

"Great. Just...peachy."

He tried to concentrate on more than her luscious body. The past few hours weighed heavily on him but the coming ones offered hope. "There's an extraction team on their way to help us out. Should be here by 0230 hours."

"Extraction team?"

He moved away from the fire and kept his eyes diverted from her creamy skin. "Emit is more than a risk management expert. He runs a high-risk security group. That's the real reason I took you to his beach house. I needed a secure line to contact him and see what he could do for us, and the part about him telling me to use the house whenever I wanted was true. He couldn't get his sister out of the jungle when she was kidnapped and my team did. He owed me."

"Why didn't you tell me this sooner?"

"The extraction team was on their way to the house when Tephra showed up. At first I thought Emit was in on whatever this is and sold us out. Now I know Tephra found us with that tracking bullet, so I called Emit and told him where we are. His team will take you to a secure hiding place until this over."

"What about you?"

"I'm going to Sacramento to find Senator Halston."

Her hands went to her hips. "Not without me."

"It's too dangerous for you, and now I have the option of keeping you safe while I go after Halston and whoever else is behind this." He hated to admit it, but the next sentence was entirely true. "You're a distraction I can't afford, B. Emit will keep you safe, and your safety will give me peace of mind while I get to the bottom of this."

"Not again!" She threw the pants on the couch, fisted her hands. "Don't do this to me!"

"Do what? I'm trying to take care of you."

"You're leaving me. It's your MO. You're always leaving me behind. We can't fix our relationship or our marriage if we don't do it together. You don't have a team of SEALs anymore, but you still have me." She waggled a finger back and forth between them. "You and me. We're a team."

It was an old argument. One he was tired of fighting.

He knew what it was to be part of a team. Bianca didn't. She'd always been more lone wolf than a pack member.

As if she sensed he was about to shut down her logic, she came around the end of the couch and got in his face. "You need me to talk to Senator Halston. He knows who I am and what I do, and I carry a lot more weight than you do in this situation."

Irritation roared through his veins. What the fuck did she want from him? "This is not about our relationship or your connections in Washington. This is about saving your goddamn life!"

Her face fell, all the life draining out of her. She walked a few feet away and quietly slipped on her pants. "If I can get the senator to admit he leaked the information, I can save your career."

Damn. He didn't want to fight with her. If anything, he wanted to spend a few more minutes keeping the world at bay. "My career is over. I'm due at a hearing at 0800 hours. I won't be there, and even if I was, I know it would end badly for me."

She came forward, determination hardening her eyes once more. "You have to let me try. I'm the one who overheard the conversation about him leaking information, and I happen to know the woman he was with the night he got the call is a foreign operative. I started digging around on her right after I intercepted that message, but my clearance access to the Scout database had been revoked. If I could hack back into that, I'm sure I could find a link between her and Grimes."

"The Scout database?"

"A cross-referencing tool I developed for Command, uhm, I mean...oh hell." She rubbed her forehead with a hand. "I might as well tell you everything, but you may want to get a drink before I do."

Cal stiffened. "Spit it out, Bianca."

She stood behind the couch purposely keeping it between them. "I work for Command and Control, a top secret branch of the NSA. I designed the latest threat matrix software that gives the president a daily...um, well, there's no other way to put it...a hit list. In C&C, we call it a disposition matrix. It's a grid that contains biographies of people who pose a threat to US interests and their known or suspected locations. I use it to develop a range of options for their disposal."

"Everyone knows about the threat matrix."

"The disposition matrix goes a step beyond a terrorist most wanted list. We don't make it public and the missions and subsequent kills are kept secret as well. Some of them have to be because they involve public figures whose deaths must be made to look like accidents or inside jobs by their own people."

Cal processed the meaning behind her words, didn't like what she was saying. "Like who?"

Her fingers fidgeted with the nonexistent lint ball. "I really shouldn't be telling you this."

Cal stayed silent. She glanced up, looked away, rubbed her hand over the couch fabric.

Finally, she cleared her throat, his use of silence seeming to wear her down. "Last month, China's assistant foreign minister turned up dead in his hotel room from an apparent suicide on a trip to Quebec where he was secretly meeting with a few top officials about a possible oil deal." She met his gaze. "It wasn't suicide."

"You had him killed over oil?"

"The oil deal was a cover for him purchasing a shoulder-fired grenade launcher and giving it to a Chinese-American family, sleeper agents, who planned to assassinate President Norman while he was in New York City at a campaign stop. I had the evidence and believed the official should be arrested and charged, not killed, but it wasn't my decision to make."

"What about the family?"

She shook her head, letting him know they were dead too.

"Ah, shit."

Keeping the president safe, and in turn, the entire country, was a monumental task. While he didn't like what she was saying, he saw the need for it, and by the slump of Bianca's shoulders, the sadness in her eyes, he could tell it was also an overwhelming task. Regardless of the accomplishments she'd made in her job, she'd always been a human rights supporter and this type of situation had to go against all of her natural instincts.

He couldn't stop his feet moving across the floor to get to her, or his arms going around her shoulders as he pulled her into a hug. He'd been forced to make decisions in the line of duty that wrecked him afterward, but rarely did he have any reason to question his orders or his superiors.

She sighed against his chest. "For months now I've been wondering how far the power of a single man should be allowed to reach."

He set his chin against her head. He hadn't been there for her, to support her and allow her to hash this type of situation over with someone. Unlike other women, she wasn't a talker, didn't vent about her problems. Which had always made him slightly uncomfortable since he always wanted to fix whatever problem she had, but most of the time he had no idea what was going on in her head.

It was folly to think she might have shared this level of classified information with him—after all, pillow talk about her job was not allowed any more than it was about his—but maybe if he'd at least been around, he would have picked up on her internal struggle and could have given her encouragement. A hug, a knowing caress, the offer to talk even if she didn't want to or couldn't. Yeah, he sucked at communicating verbally, but he *was* a good listener.

He stroked her back and felt her relax into him. "If you didn't like the job, why didn't you ask for a transfer?"

"You don't leave Command and Control. Not willingly. Which was another reason I was shocked when they offloaded me to the taskforce."

Blue elephant. She knew too much, never forgot a detail. Those in charge couldn't let her simply transfer or walk away. If she were captured by a foreign entity and made to talk, or she became disgruntled, she could expose dozens of high-level secrets, endanger operatives in the field, ruin military campaigns, and throw the US government into chaos.

My wife is a ticking bomb with a giant target painted on her back.

Clarity was a gift on any mission. This time, it was also a curse. He wasn't only protecting her from an assassin, he was protecting her from all enemies foreign and domestic...and that was one long fucking list.

She drew away, turning so she could prop her butt on the couch. "There's more."

On one hand, Cal was glad she was finally telling him everything. On the other...

He leaned next to her and crossed his arms over his chest, preparing for the next round of things he was pretty sure he didn't want to know. "Let's hear it."

She looked down at her feet, tapped one on the floor. "I also analyze every credible threat made on the president's life, and believe me, lately, there have been a lot. Since Norman and Grimes have been one-upping each other in the media, threats to the president have tripled. Norman wants Grimes bad, and in his latest YouTube video, he threw down the gauntlet, challenging Grimes to come after him in Chicago at his final campaign stop.

Norman isn't stupid. He wanted Grimes dead before Chicago. That's why he tasked me with the job. I failed, as you know."

"Because Senator Halston leaked the info."

"Three of your men died, but you lived, and even with the lockdown on the details about the mission, too many people know about this failure. They're asking questions, and it won't be long before the media snaps it up and causes a fuss. Not about your role in the mission, but about Norman's decision to send a team in. And now Grimes knows Norman is trying to take him out before he can do anything in Chicago. He's already made a new video to tell the world about Norman's duplicity and that Norman's secretly scared shitless about Grimes accepting his challenge."

She shook her head. "I'm beginning to think Norman is as nuts as Grimes. Who would challenge a well-known terrorist to a Wild West-type showdown? Grimes isn't stupid enough to try to enter America and show up at the campaign stop in Chicago, but he's devious enough to activate one of his sleeper agents to do something."

"Egos," Cal said. "President Norman's videos, Facebook posts, and tweets have raised his standing in the pre-election polls monumentally, according to CNN the other day. He needed that after the university bombings."

Her fierce eyes pinned him. "He's putting hundreds, if not thousands of innocent people at risk. Even with the highest security in place, someone could slip through."

Grabbing her hand, he squeezed.

"If only I was back in D.C.," she said. "I could analyze the situation and advise the president's security team on possible scenarios."

"Hopefully, someone already has."

"No one knows the ins and outs of that disposition matrix the way I do. No one knows Grimes like I do."

"Forget Grimes for now. You need to worry about staying alive."

She withdrew her hand from his, spotted her bra, and made a production of putting it on. Then she raised her head and looked him square in the eye. "What happens when you're not at the hearing tomorrow?"

It was already after midnight and tomorrow was officially today. "I'll be considered AWOL and probably be court-martialed."

Her heavy sigh matched the sadness and disappointment on her face. "You have to go back."

In the soft glow of the firelight, she looked beautiful. Sad, but beautiful. All he really wanted right now was her. Not the SEALs, not the Navy, not anything but the woman who'd stuck by him through thick and thin.

Until she hadn't anymore because of his career.

The Navy or Bianca? He took her hand again. "I'm not leaving you."

She was in his arms, kissing him, before his next heartbeat. Her arms went around his neck, drawing his face to hers. He held her to him, parting her lips with his tongue, his cock jumping at her deep, sexy moan.

Easing her to her feet, he lifted her off the floor. Her legs went around his waist and he walked slowly and purposefully to the bedroom, ravishing her lips as he went. One hand cupped the back of her head to hold her steady and the other hugged her ass.

She pressed her pelvis into him, kissing him back with so much ardor, he nearly went down on his knees and took her right there on the floor. But he made it down the short hallway, kicked open the bedroom door, and laid her on the homemade quilt draped over the end of the bed.

Maggie tried to follow, but Cal used a foot to close the bedroom door.

Bianca's eyes were shadows in her face as she looked up at him, soft moonlight coming through the window on the south side to touch her cheekbones. "God, I've missed you," she whispered.

He was in the process of taking off her shirt—his T-shirt—and he couldn't help but tease her. "You wanted to divorce me only a few minutes ago."

The shirt's fabric was over her face when she mumbled something that sounded like, "I never wanted to divorce you. I had to."

The shirt came free a second later, and Cal threw it on the floor. She lay semi-naked, her full breasts overflowing her bra and making Cal's mouth water. He almost lost his train of concentration. "What?"

"We have our problems, and ours are somewhat different than your average couple, but the reason I finally filed for divorce was because I knew you were married to the SEALs in a way you'd never be married to me. Plus, you weren't safe being with me. Working for Command and Control is a dangerous job, one that doesn't foster relationships of any kind. I didn't realize how dangerous until it was too late."

Talking was not what he wanted to do right now, but he couldn't ignore her ridiculous ideas about him, his job, or their current situation. "I'm not married to the SEALs, but a unit like that is as close to a brotherhood as it can get. I *am* married to you, and let me be clear here, I *do not want to lose you.* And finally, your job should in no way endanger me anymore than mine endangers you. The responsibility the NSA and the president have put on your shoulders, B, is astronomical, but it shouldn't be deadly. They wanted you for your brain and your intelligence. They can't turn around now and decide you're a liability for the same things."

She sat up and grabbed him by the waistband, her deft fingers undoing his zipper again. Moonlight glinted in her eyes as she smiled up at him. "As long as we've both fried our careers and nearly destroyed our marriage, what do you say we live like the next few hours are our last?"

Behind the smile and eager fingers was a hint of disheartenment. Cal knew that feeling. All seemed lost.

He stopped her fingers, bent, and kissed her before he brought her forehead to his and locked his gaze on hers. "We're not going to die, Bianca. Trust me."

Her response was to smile. For real this time. "You're the only person I ever have trusted, Cal. Now make love to me like you're never going to leave me again."

CHAPTER EIGHTEEN

She loved it when Cal touched her. His big hands deftly removed the rest of her clothes, taking his time with every button, every zipper, his fingers gliding across her sensitive skin. Teasing. Torturing.

When they were both naked, kneeling on the bed facing each other, she leaned forward and kissed him full on the mouth, letting her nipples brush across his chest. He moaned and pressed a warm palm against her lower back, encouraging her forward. She complied, bringing herself against his rock-hard penis.

His recent scar was still pink. Her finger traced its outline, even as their kiss turned hot. He caught her wrist and drew her hand away so she took it and wrapped it around the hard, thick length of him. She spread her knees on the bed, giving him fuller access as she guided him to her folds, still wet and ready from their previous sexual encounter on the couch.

He gripped her butt cheeks, spreading her wider and rubbing himself against her swollen folds. Lust, dark and smooth, flowed through her, and she welcomed the emotions it brought.

His mouth sucked at the side of her neck, his hands holding her in place as he teased her now with his penis. She arched backward, lost in his heat.

"You're so beautiful," he murmured against the skin under ear. "So perfect. You make me forget."

Her breath came in short bursts. "Forget what?"

"The ugliness."

The ugliness he wouldn't talk about. This was a good time to make him spit it out. Right when she had him in the grips of lust.

Yes, that was it. *Make him talk.*

But then his lips moved to the base of her throat, kissing and licking at the pulse beating there, and she lost her train of thought. Later. She'd make him talk about the ugliness later.

Her hands massaged the strong muscles of his back, her mind blissfully blank. "Take me, Cal. I need you."

He grabbed her thighs and pushed her back onto the bed. His penis, now slick from her juices, zeroed in on its target, plunging inside her to the hilt.

She cried out, digging her nails into his shoulders, her heels into his butt cheeks. *So good.* He fit her like he was made for her.

"God, I want to fuck you so hard you won't be able to walk tomorrow."

Tilting her hips up so she could take more of him in, she gave him an evil grin. "Go for it."

He pulled out, thrust deep. His mouth lowered to suck on her breasts. She moved in rhythm with him, reminding him he had a lot of work to do. "Three months," she managed between thrusts. "You have three months of separation to make up for."

Bracing himself on one arm, he raised his head and looked her in the eye. "Then we better slow this down and make it count, love."

She didn't want to slow down...until he pulled out and stroked between her folds with the plump end of his erection. "Oh, God."

The side of his mouth quirked. He tweaked a nipple, catching it between his finger and thumb and gently tugging. He massaged her breasts, lowered his mouth and began to suckle, building her pleasure as his penis continued dipping into her and pulling out to rub her spot, only to dip inside again. Over and over and over, he took her to the brink of orgasm, then withdrew.

Bianca let the sweet torture take her higher, opening herself to the feelings she always kept buried. With Cal she was safe. Safe and loved and treasured.

"Now," she finally whispered when she couldn't stand it anymore. "I need you *now*."

He placed his hands on the side of her face, dropping light kisses on her cheekbones, her closed eyelids, her jawline. "Look at me," he demanded and she opened her eyes and did.

He moved inside her, picking up the pace, driving himself into her again and again as he stared into her eyes. The intensity of the love she saw shining there undid her.

It's only lust, logic said.

She slapped logic in the face.

"I love you, Cal," she whispered, matching each trust of his hips. "I've always loved you."

He parted her lips with his tongue, melding them together, and continued to move her hard and fast, making the bed springs protest. Her insides spasmed, the first wave of the orgasm breaking over her as he, too, gave into the overwhelming lust they'd built. His erection drove deep, once, twice, three times, teasing out her orgasm, until he thrust one last time and collapsed on top of her.

His chest heaved, his breath came in bursts as if he'd just sprinted uphill for a mile. "I love you, too, B. I love you, too."

In the aftermath, he dozed, his head on her chest. Bianca smiled into the darkness and held onto him for all she was worth.

CHAPTER NINETEEN

"Cal!" Bianca shook his shoulder, but he batted her hand away.

His eyes were closed, his body twitching. Back and forth, back and forth, his head rolled on the pillow. Sweat beads dotted his forehead and his skin was ashen. He cried out, the words a jumble that didn't make sense but that made the hair on her neck rise.

Maggie whined and Bianca chased her out of the room. Kneeling on the side of the bed, she patted Cal's face and shook him again. "Cal, you're having a nightmare. Wake up."

He mumbled something and she finally resorted to an old trick. She pinched him in the side.

He bolted upright, knocking her off the bed. She smacked into the dresser, ricocheted off the corner, bumped her big toe on the bed frame, and fell unceremoniously on her ass.

"Ouch. Dammit!" She rubbed her toe and tried to fix her glasses, which had gone kittywampus on her face.

In a split second, he was out of bed, on his feet, weapon in hand and pointed.

At her.

Bianca froze, staring at the dark hole at the end of the looming gun. Her mouth went dry.

Dangerous. He'd always been dangerous but not to her.

PTSD was a bitch. She'd seen no sign of it until now. Heart hammering, she lifted her gaze and met his over the barrel. The dark orbs were distant, as if he weren't seeing her but something—some*one*—else.

"Cal, it's me. Bianca."

Nothing changed in his demeanor. He kept the gun pointed at her, his body rigid and ready for action.

Years ago, her mother had held a gun in her hand and looked at Bianca the same way—blank eyes, emotionless facial affect—right before she'd turned the gun on herself and put a bullet in her brain. Talk about PTSD. Bianca still had nightmares.

She'd failed with Annabelle, talking her off the ledge had been futile, but this was Cal, not her mentally unstable, alcoholic and drug-dependent mother.

Bianca was an adult now with a lot of skills and experiences under her belt, not some scared seventeen-year-old who'd recently lost a baby and was about to lose her mother.

I will not let the demons get you, Cal.

"We're in your father's fishing cabin in upstate California," she said in a calm, soothing manner, even though she was anything but calm. "I was attacked by an owl, remember? We made love and you fell asleep and had a nightmare. That's all it was, a nightmare. I've kept watch on the house and grounds while you slept, and Emit texted your phone an hour ago. His extraction team will be here any minute. I, of course, informed him I wasn't going to any safe house to hide out while you went to see Senator Halston."

Cal's head jerked slightly, as if he were trying to clear the fog. The distant look in his eyes faded. Not completely, but she could see he was truly waking up.

The gun, however, didn't lower. The barrel was still aimed at the spot between her eyebrows.

Give him a little more time. Keep talking.

"You're not in Afghanistan. You're here with me in America. You're safe."

Another blink. The gun lowered an inch.

"That's right. You can do it. Fight the demons. You had a nightmare, that's all it was. What happened was not real. I'm real and I need you."

Maggie rushed to his side, wagging her tail and leaning against his leg. Confusion entered his eyes, and a second later, he frowned. "Bianca?"

Relief swamped her. She swallowed hard, wanting to jump up and hug him, yet knowing any sudden movement could trigger another episode. "Yep, it's me. Your pain-in-the-ass wife."

He looked down at the gun, back up to her face. "What happened? Why are you on the floor? Oh, God. Did I...?"

The weapon fell to the bed and he backed away, a look of abject horror on his face.

"It's okay," she said, rising slowly. "You had a nightmare and were having trouble coming out of it, that's all. No harm done."

The look on his face said differently. He rubbed his eyes with the heels of his hands, flattened himself against the wall. "I'm sorry." He turned a tortured face to her. Maggie whined up at him. "I would never hurt you. *Never.* I would never lay a hand on you like your mother did."

She couldn't help herself. She launched herself across the space between them and threw her arms around him. "I know that. Stop beating yourself up." She pushed her hands through his hair, holding his head so he had to look her in the eyes. "You didn't hurt me. I'm fine."

Maggie jumped up on both them, barking and acting like it was a game. Bianca laughed and bent to hug the dog. Her presence had seemed to snap him the rest of the way out of it.

Cal scratched the dog's ears and took a deep breath, his body sagging slightly with what appeared to be relief.

Bianca almost mentioned the PTSD, then decided against it. After her mother had committed suicide right in front of her, the one thing that pissed her off was the clinical jargon the medical and psychiatric experts threw around. As if grief and anger and the awfulness of such a thing could be summed up by a sterile, unfeeling label. As if she, the victim of her mother's neuroses and final act of desperation to escape them, could ever get over it without industrial-sized therapy. Maybe not even then.

It would be best to let Cal talk if he wanted to and to leave him alone if he didn't.

On the other hand, Cal excelled at Houdini-ing his real thoughts and emotions. *Now you see them, now you don't.* She'd never known him to admit anything was wrong, ever. Never in a million years would he voluntarily mention his feelings and emotions.

He needed to talk about what had happened. Needed to express the anger and terror and shock of what he'd lived through, and she was probably the only person he would ever confide in. Yet, she couldn't force him to do it. The best way to get him where he needed to be was to simply open the door and let him walk through when the time came.

If it ever did.

"I shouldn't have fallen asleep." He ran a hand over his face. "What was I thinking?"

"You were exhausted, and I was wide awake. Energized. I didn't mind staying up." It was true. After their love-making, she'd felt animated. Ready to take on Tephra and the whole goddamn US government. "I kept an eye on things, and Maggie was with me." She patted the dog's head. "We make a good team."

He was still in his underwear, his broad shoulders and naked chest rippling as he moved to the bed to grab his clothes. As he pulled up his pants and worked his shirt over his arms, something dark and delicious quivered between her legs. Of course, he had to get dressed, but what a shame.

She touched her lips, remembering the feel of his against them. The control he always took of her in bed. As he finished dressing and headed to the bathroom, she sat on the edge of the bed and closed her eyes. The smell of sex emanated from the sheets and she rubbed a hand over the spot where Cal had lain, the sheets still warm from his body heat. If only they had a little more time to keep this rekindled flame alive.

No more *if onlys*. By God, if it killed her, she *would* keep this flame alive. No more giving up; she was going to fight for her marriage, whether she had a day left or another fifty years.

"Hey, I almost forgot." Cal came back from the bathroom, holding out a piece of paper. He appeared back to normal, his interior armor back in place with his usual confidence. "This was on the kitchen island at Emit's place after Tephra ran. Is it yours? Didn't look like your handwriting, but I grabbed it anyway."

She took the paper. Two strings of numbers were written on it, the impressions made from a black ink pen deep.

418531

876121

A heavy hand had written them.

Tephra.

She glanced up and saw the same conclusion in Cal's eyes.

"What do they mean?" she asked.

"I was hoping you could tell me. Is it a code or something?"

She read the two lines of numbers again, her brain breaking and regrouping them into plausible combinations. Not a phone number, social security number, or bank account number. Not any type of cipher or computer code she'd ever seen.

And yet, there was something familiar about them. Two lines, six numbers each.

Damn. She looked up. "I need my phone, but since we don't have that, how about a map?"

Cal frowned. "Of California?"

She shook her head. "The world."

CHAPTER TWENTY

There were no maps at the cabin, world or otherwise. Who needed a map to fish?

No computer either, and the cheap burn phones Cal had bought didn't have internet service.

Bianca was sure the numbers were a longitude and latitude location. Missing from the two sets of numbers were the degrees, minutes, seconds, and directions, but if they had a map, they could pinpoint the possible locations and theorize which was most likely to be the right one.

What did it mean, though?

Cal didn't have the answer, but he did have Emit's team. He replied to the text he'd slept through earlier. *Bring a world map.*

Exfil teams like Emit's were run on the same premise the SEAL teams used. How they performed the job depended on whether or not their target was hostile or friendly, the type of terrain—sea, air, land—and whether they were under fire or sneaking in.

The team meeting them at the cabin was labeled Tier Three. Since Cal and Bianca weren't under fire, the team probably expected an easy mission.

However, Bianca still hadn't warmed to the idea of going off with them to a safe location, so when the black SUVs pulled up outside, she gave Cal a look that brokered no argument. "I'm not going to a safe house."

He had to make her see reason. Not only would she be safer

with Emit's team, she'd be safer away from him. *My God, I almost shot her.*

His skin crawled. The nightmare had sucked him in again. The same one he'd had every single night since the mission. At least on his boat he'd been able to drown the sharp edges with alcohol. Here, his stepmom had removed the bottles of alcohol long before his father died from liver failure.

The only way to make sure he didn't inadvertently hurt her was for Tier Three to take her away. His phone buzzed with a text. *All clear?*

From behind the curtain, he watched one man from each of the two SUVs exit their vehicles. Dressed in black, they moved with the precision of trained operatives. Hyper-alert, the one in front held up a hand to stay the other who had an M4 sweeping back and forth over the drive and woods.

Cal typed back. *Clear. Front door is open.* "You can't stay with me, B. Not after tonight."

She stood near the kitchen table, hands on hips. "What are you talking about? We had an amazing night."

"I knocked you down and pulled a gun on you."

"You would never harm me."

I almost killed you. "You don't know that."

The leader of TT moved to the door, the other man covering his back. Standard protocol. Cal had his gun in his hand hanging by his leg. He turned the knob and opened the door as Bianca huffed. "I do, too, know that."

TT's leader moved into the room slowly, nodding at Cal and sizing up Bianca and the dog. His hair was Marine short, his body built like a semi-truck. His left earlobe was pierced with a tiny gold hoop.

Maggie started to lunge forward but Bianca caught her by the collar and told her to stay. "I'm not going with you," she promptly informed the guy.

His gaze cut to Cal as he held out his hand. "Hubble Warwick, Tier Three team leader. What's our status?"

Cal shifted his gun to his left hand and shook Warwick's. He'd hand off Bianca in a minute. "Did you bring the map I requested?"

The man closed the cabin door and withdrew a paper map from inside his black jacket. "My men will watch the place, but I'd advise we move out quickly."

Cal took the map and smoothed it on the coffee table. Bianca allowed Maggie to greet Warwick as she knelt on the floor next to Cal.

Her finger found the latitude line she was looking for, running horizontally across the map. "Let's initially assume the coordinates are in North America..."

Warwick approached watching. "What are you looking for?"

She stopped her finger and handed him the piece of paper with the numbers. "I believe these correspond to a location."

"Longitude and latitude?" he asked.

She nodded.

He pulled out his phone. "I have an app for that. Let's type it in and see what we get."

"We don't know the directions," Cal said. "North, South, East, or West."

"Doesn't matter. It will give us a list of possible places."

Bianca sat back on her heels, smiling like Warwick had just given her a box of her favorite chocolates. "That's all we need."

A second later, Warwick turned the display so they could see it.

Bianca scanned the results and her smile faded. "Oh crap."

"What?" Cal said.

She pointed to a Chicago address.

"McConnell Place?" He shrugged. "What's significant about that?"

"The president will be there tomorrow for his last election speech before he returns to DC," she said.

"And?" Warwick asked, seeming to be as lost as Cal was.

Bianca put her face in her hands and released a heavy sigh.

"That's where he challenged Otto Grimes to a showdown."

Warwick gave Cal a look that said he still didn't understand. He wasn't the only one. "Grimes can't get in the country, B. The president isn't at risk."

She lifted her eyes and met his. "Oh, but I think he is."

CHAPTER TWENTY-ONE

0900 hours
San Diego

He couldn't believe they'd lost the Chevelle.

A yellow '69 Chevelle that should have stood out like a sore thumb.

Cooper stood at the window of the office in the low-rent district part of town his team met at each morning for their situation report and stared out at the parking lot. The building housed the social security office and a chiropractor; the majority of people coming and going were well into middle, if not old, age.

Ronni stepped up beside him and handed him a fresh cup of coffee. "Bobby will be in shortly. He just got a call from the team hunting for that fishing cabin."

Her voice conveyed that she thought it was good news. Cooper wasn't holding out hope. So far, they had nothing. Most of the crime scene reports weren't back yet. The car had last been spotted off Interstate 680 near Freemont, then disappeared. Cal Reese and Bianca Marx seemed to have dropped off the face of the earth.

Bobby, Ronni, and ICE agent Nelson Cruz had worked all night digging up information on Cal and Bianca's families, past history, and possible locations they might go. The fishing cabin was in Bumblefuck, USA, way out in the rolling hills of

Northern California, but Cooper prayed that's where the two had holed up for the night.

When Bobby rolled in a minute later, Nelson was with him and Cooper could see from the look on both men's faces that there was no happy ending in sight.

He just hoped Bianca was still alive. "What'd you find out?"

"Cabin was deserted," Bobby said, "but someone had recently been there. Embers in the fireplace were still warm. My guys found a long, blond hair on the couch and several in the bed."

Ronni's face lit up. "Bianca's? The CSI techs found several of her hairs in the shower drain at Emit Petit's."

Nelson drew out a chair and rubbed his eyes as he sank into it. "Won't know for sure unless we run a DNA test. There were also other short, dark hairs found on the floor at the cabin. Similar to those found at the beach house. Guessing a dog."

Cooper set his undrunk coffee on the conference table. Cal Reese was a dog alright. "Any blood? Any signs of a struggle?"

Bobby answered. "None."

Cooper could see his friend was holding something back. "But…?"

"The team I sent is thorough. Very thorough. They found some, uh…something that appears to be bodily fluids. On the bed sheets."

Ronni took a seat across from Bobby. "Semen?"

Thomas, who'd been dozing in the corner after their all-nighter chasing the Chevelle, opened his eyes and cracked a grin. "Bianca, you naughty girl."

If he could have reached Thomas, Cooper would have smacked him upside the head. "We don't know it's them, and even if it is, as long as it was consensual and Bianca's not a kidnapping victim, that's none of our business."

"It's them," Bobby said, setting his tablet on the table and scooting it over to Cooper. On the screen was a picture. "They found the Chevelle."

Thomas meandered over to peer at the photo of the yellow

car, half covered with vines and tree limbs. Reese had hidden it. "They left on foot?"

Bobby touched the screen, flipping to the next photo of tire tracks. "Two vehicles stopped in front of the cabin. Those tracks were made from some heavy-duty, off-road terrain tires. One of my guys is a car nut. Says the treads belong to something that works off-road as well as on. GMC Yukon, Range Rover, that sort of thing."

Cooper leaned on the table, staring at the photo. Two vehicles, no signs of a struggle, semen on the bed. "Any idea which direction they went?"

"Yep." Bobby tapped the screen again and a grainy satellite shot of a highway with two burgundy-colored Land Rovers, one behind the other, appeared. "This might not be them, but if it is, they're headed north on I-5."

Ronni frowned. "You snagged satellite images? I thought that's what we had Bianca on the taskforce for. Spying on people."

Bobby smiled. "She does it legally. I do it...well, less legally. Besides, you didn't really think the NSA sent her to help us, did you? She was sent to spy on Dupé."

"Holy shit," Thomas said. "I didn't know that."

Neither did Cooper, and it gave him pause. "Spy on him for what?"

"Maybe someone doesn't like the way he's running our taskforce?" Bobby offered.

"How do you know that's why NSA sent her?" Cooper asked.

"I'm a hacker, remember?" Bobby tapped the side of his head. "And I'm smarter than all of you put together. I know things."

"Did she find anything on Dupé?" Ronni asked.

"Not yet."

Nelson, seemingly unconcerned, passed Cooper a piece of paper. "I ran the plates on the vehicles in the photo. They belong to Roman Enterprises."

"What's that?" Thomas asked.

"A shell company for several businesses owned by someone you might be interested in."

For the first time in the past twenty-four hours, Cooper felt a ray of hope. "Who?"

Bobby rubbed his hands together with glee. "Emit Petit. Along with a couple of other businesses, this guy runs a security service. High-end. He only takes rich and/or famous clientele, and his employees all happen to be former Special Forces men. A few of them were referred to him by Reese."

"So Emit and Reese have something going and they've taken Bianca along. Why?"

"She's NSA," Ronni said. "She knows everything and can hack into anything they want."

Cooper ignored the scenarios that particular comment sent running through his head. "What's north?"

"Sacramento."

"What's in Sacramento?" Ronni asked.

Bobby shrugged. "No idea. Neither of them has any ties to the area that I can find."

"Any government installations?" Cooper said. "Anything they would need Bianca's expertise for?"

"Nothing I've found so far." He took back his tablet and rubbed his eyes, mimicking Nelson. "I'll keep digging."

Cooper paced to the window and back. "What about the guy who was in Petit's beach house? The one who got injured? Any ID yet?"

"Let me check." Bobby tapped a few keys, entered his password for his email. His eyes scanned the incoming mail and he shook his head. "Nothing yet."

Thomas held out his hand to Cooper. "Looks like a road trip to northern Cali. I'll drive."

Driving would take too long. "We need to get ahead of them. Get to Sacramento ASAP."

Ronni pulled out her cell phone. "I'll call the airlines about flights."

"No," Cooper said. "Call Dupé. We need a helicopter."

Bobby looked up from his email. "Sacramento's a big place, Coop. You need a starting point."

Bobby *was* smarter than all of them put together. Didn't mean Cooper liked it. "Do your best to track those vehicles and alert Sac PD. If they spot the cars, they should contact us and not engage. I don't know what's going on, but I don't want Bianca in the line of fire. I want to know what Reese and Petit are up to first and have a solid plan in place before we go after them. Clear?"

A knock sounded on the door behind him. Through the plate glass, Cooper saw a figure. No one visited this office except for Dupé, unless it was an aging senior citizen who got lost looking for the social security admin office.

Nelson and Thomas both went on alert. Cooper made a hand signal to stand down and both men returned to their relaxed positions. Cooper didn't buy it. He knew they had their hands on their weapons. But at least they wouldn't give some poor old woman a coronary.

To his surprise, it wasn't a senior citizen on the other side of the door. Instead, he found a man in navy whites. From the insignias decorating his jacket, he looked to be an officer. "Is this the SCVC Taskforce?"

"It is," Cooper answered.

The man removed his hat and ran a hand over his short hair. "I'm looking for Bianca Marx."

Inside the room, Thomas snickered. "Join the crowd."

"And you are?"

"I'm her husband's Senior Chief, Justin Lugmeyer."

"Cooper Harris. I'm her boss."

They shook and Cooper motioned the man inside. "What's your business with Agent Marx?"

"I believe she's kidnapped my platoon leader, Cal Reese."

This time, Thomas laughed out loud. "Bianca kidnapped *Reese?* What alternate reality do you live in?"

The senior chief didn't look amused and Cooper once again wanted to smack Thomas upside the head.

Lugmeyer did a quick inventory of all of them, returning his cool gaze to Cooper. "Do you know where Agent Marx is? Reese missed a very important military hearing this morning, and I believe she's the only person who would keep him from showing up. It's imperative I find him."

The guy was a no-nonsense SEAL unit chief. Cooper respected that, but this guy sent alarms ringing in his head. Every time he mentioned Bianca, he acted like he'd swallowed a lemon.

"Bianca didn't kidnap your man. We believe, if anything, the situation is reverse, that Cal Reese may have taken her against her will."

The chief studied Cooper for a minute, seeming to consider the scenario. "I'm aware of what happened at the marina yesterday. I'm not at liberty to discuss Reese's current state of service with the Navy, but I will share with you that he's been diagnosed with post-traumatic stress disorder after his last field mission went south. He's..." The guy paused, rubbed a thumb over the brim of his hat. "He's unstable."

The hope Cooper felt a minute ago evaporated. "Unstable enough to kidnap his own wife and disappear?"

The man said nothing, didn't even nod. His lack of an answer was enough.

"I don't involve myself with my men's personal problems, but Reese and I go back a ways. Agent Marx recently filed for divorce and I believe that's what messed him up on his last mission." Lugmeyer glanced out the window and stated without emotion. "He refused psychiatric help, and regardless of what's going on, he's a SEAL under great emotional stress who's suffering from PTSD. That's a dangerous cocktail."

Exactly what Cooper feared. He started to grab Bobby's tablet and show Lugmeyer the photos and tell him what they knew about Reese and Bianca's whereabouts, but something held him back.

As far as he could tell, Bianca hadn't been harmed. She'd said there was a man after her, but never mentioned it was her soon-to-be-ex. Seemed kinda key to the whole thing.

"How'd you know where to find us?" Nelson asked, still slouched casually in his chair. Only, his eyes were sharp on Lugmeyer's back. Watching, assessing.

So Nelson felt it too.

Ronni's phone pinged.

The chief turned from the window. "Bianca talked about the taskforce the last time we spoke. She mentioned how much she loves it here. She told me this was your HQ."

Cooper stiffened. Bianca hated it here. She'd never said as much, but he knew from her body language and from what she *didn't* say that she knew working with the taskforce was a step down for her. A demotion. And while their meeting location wasn't top secret, none of the taskforce members talked about their jobs or this place with anyone outside of the team. Their undercover ops *were* top secret and no one but them and Dupé needed to know where they met to discuss missions.

Ronni had received a text, but at the mention of Reese being dangerous and Bianca supposedly telling Lugmeyer about their meeting place, she'd glanced up from reading it. Her eyes sent Cooper a clear message. She didn't buy Lugmeyer's story either. "Why would Bianca go with Cal if she knew he was dangerous?"

The chief gave a stiff shrug. "Maybe she doesn't realize he is. Or maybe she does and thinks she's saving him from a court-martial. Doesn't matter. If she's assisting him in going AWOL, she's in effect conspiring against the United States Navy. I will bring charges against her."

Cooper didn't know Cal Reese, and he certainly didn't trust him, but he didn't trust Cal's senior chief either. There was something more going on here. Something Lugmeyer wasn't telling him.

Or maybe the guy really didn't know any more than Cooper

did. Either way, the one person Cooper *did* know was Bianca. They weren't close friends, but she'd been with his team long enough for him to get a read on her. Outside of discovering she was investigating Dupé on the side—which meant she was doing her assigned job—he believed she was trustworthy.

Ronni gave Cooper another look. She was tapping one long finger against her phone as she handed it to Bobby, showing him the message.

Cooper stepped in front of the SEAL and made no bones about hustling him back to the door. "If we learn anything of value, we'll be in touch."

Lugmeyer resisted for half a second, then relented, stepping across the threshold. "Cal Reese was once a hero. Now he needs to set the record straight. He can't run from the United States Navy."

The chief stopped and faced Cooper as he set his hat on his head. "If your agent is involved in Reese going AWOL, you can be sure I'll find her and bring her to justice as well."

Cooper put his hands on either side of the doorframe and leaned forward, getting in Lugmeyer's face. "You let me handle my agent."

The senior chief held his stare for a moment and Cooper let all kinds of threats run through his head. Threats he couldn't say out loud to a military man without breaking a few written laws, along with his own personal code of conduct. But Lugmeyer understood the body language and the glare. He turned on his heel and marched away.

Cooper drew a satisfying breath, and with renewed determination, he closed the door and faced his team. Ronni and Bobby were staring at him with grins on their faces. Grins? Not what he was expecting. "What?"

Ronni pointed at her phone. "Bianca's okay. She texted me. No details, but she said she'll explain everything once she has the proof she needs."

"About what?"

Bobby snapped his fingers as if the idea light bulb had gone off over his head. "Reese's last mission. I went through her laptop. Not much there, but I was able to find some of the searches she was doing. She had notes and a timeline on the mission. That must be why she went to see him."

Thomas rubbed his bottom lip with his thumb. "So Lugmeyer may be right. If Reese is being court-martialed, something definitely went wrong with that mission, and Bianca may well have helped him go AWOL until they find proof it wasn't his fault."

Nelson sat up, all traces of casual gone. "I don't trust Lughead. He's up to something."

It was normal for Cooper's team to be suspicious. In this case, he was one hundred percent right there with them. "Follow him. See where he goes."

"You got it." Nelson rose.

"Want me to go with him?" Thomas asked.

Cooper shook his head. "This is not official, Cruz. Just keep an eye on him. See if he shows his cards. Anything suspicious, text me. Meanwhile, Bobby can do some digging on his background."

Nelson left and Bobby spoke after the door shut. "Reese and his team were going after Otto Grimes. Three of the SEALs were killed. The Navy claims Reese was negligent."

"Grimes?" Cooper said. "The terrorist President Norman is having YouTube wars with?"

"The one and only."

Ronni's phone buzzed and she and Bobby both reached for it. "Another text," she said slapping Bobby's hand away. "'Tell Cooper something big is going down at McConnell Place, Chicago, tomorrow night. Campaign stop. Don't know what.'"

"Give me that." Cooper reached out and took the phone. Typed back. "Tell him yourself. I'm right here. Call me."

He tapped his thumb against the side of the phone, waiting, waiting, waiting…

Nothing came back. No text. No call.

Dammit.

He glanced at Bobby. "Any way you can track where these messages came from?"

"Already tried. The number is blocked."

Big surprise. Cooper handed Ronni the phone and pulled out his. As he stewed, he dialed Victor Dupé's direct line.

"I've got a lead on her," he said without preamble when his boss answered. "I need your helicopter on the pad and ready to go in thirty minutes."

"Done," Dupé said. His voice was quiet. "Go get her and bring our agent home."

Done, Cooper's mind echoed. Whether Bianca liked being a member of the taskforce or not, she *was* part of his taskforce, and there was no way the Beast was letting anything happen to her.

CHAPTER TWENTY-TWO

They'd left I-5 several miles back, drove northwest on county roads, crossed a river, and were now at the Life Is But A Dream winery and retreat in a large, sweeping valley carved out in the Ice Age by giant glaciers.

The sign at the gate stated the winery had once been a Spanish monastery, and looking at the gothic arches, stained-glass windows, and ancient stone walls of all the buildings, they weren't kidding.

The SUVs drove through the wrought iron gates and followed a road that wound its way past a wooded area. They passed a lake where cattails and some kind of wild flower grew in luscious abandon. Maggie pressed her nose against the window and panted, the dog seeming to wish she could get out and run free.

Bianca knew the feeling. She was tired of riding. A wooden sign by a fork in the road claimed that to the left was forty acres of grapes and to the right was Prosperity, the wine production and tasting building. The driver turned right.

Prosperity was another Spanish gothic building, this one more open and attractive, reminding Bianca of architecture of Spain and Italy. Flowers and bushes adorned the portico where matching arches of sun made a pattern on the stone walkway. The entrance was back ten feet and nestled on each side of the double wooden doors were what appeared to be stone fairies with grape vines wound in their hair.

Sergeant Warwick drove the SUV around back and when it came to a stop, Bianca was hustled out by Buckcherry and Death Punch, the code names of her bodyguards. They guided her into a smaller and less grand private entrance in the shade of the building.

Bianca wasn't allowed to know her bodyguards real names. *For security purposes,* they'd told her. Each man, outside of Warwick, went only by the name of a hard rock band.

Maggie ran around, sniffing and wagging, and did a quick pee under a nearby pinyon tree. As Bianca passed through the thick door, she cast a glance over her shoulder and saw Cal and his guards, Soundgarden and Alice in Chains, bringing up the rear. Maggie rushed to greet Cal and he bent down and gave her ears a scratch.

All through the drive Bianca had anticipated Cal's SUV peeling off and heading somewhere else, leaving her with Buck and Death and a seedy hotel room. When they all arrived here together, she wondered if maybe her speech at the cabin had done some good. Cal had seen the logic of keeping her with him, rather than sending her off to who-knew-where in an attempt to keep her safe, while he took on Halston and whoever else was behind this disaster.

Right. And she was Beyoncé. *Dream on, Bianca.*

Buck and Death led her down a hallway, through an office, and to a hidden door behind a bookshelf. The moment it opened, Bianca smelled food—bacon, pancakes, and coffee—and her stomach growled. Steps led down to a circular room partially underground with stone walls, a dining table that could seat at least twenty, and tall, slender windows adorned with wrought iron scrolls. Two men dressed in the same black attire and armed with semiautomatic weapons stood in the corners. A silent greeting passed between them, Buck, and Death.

Along one wall was a fireplace. The opposite wall had several rolling carts lined up under the windows and topped with stainless steel warming pans, a bowl of cut fresh fruit, and carafes of coffee, water, milk, and orange juice. Maggie's nose went nuts as she sniffed first the air and then started looking for crumbs on the floor near the carts.

As Bianca allowed her eyes to adjust to the dimmer surroundings, Cal sidled up to her. She glanced up at him and hoped this wasn't the part where he said goodbye and tried to ditch her. *So not going to happen.*

"I'm starving," he murmured.

"Me, too."

From the moment they'd arrived, Bianca had seen no one on the grounds or coming and going from any of the buildings. "Where is everyone?"

Cal placed a hand on her lower back. "I wondered that too. Apparently, they're all at the church, praying."

"This place is still run by monks?"

"Worse." He teased. "Nuns."

Buck and Death, along with Cal's bodyguards, exchanged a few muttered words with their counterparts. Death and one of the other men left, and a moment later, Emit Petit came jogging down the stairs.

A wide grin broke over his face when he saw her and Cal, and he stretched out his arms as he walked over to them. He was Cal's opposite—green eyes, fair skin, lanky body—and as he clapped Cal on the back in a man hug, Bianca thought of the Chinese elements yin and yang. "Good to see you, bra."

Cal returned the hug and the back slap. "Damn good to see you too."

Emit turned his green eyes on her, assessing. There were shadows under them and she remembered Cal telling her Emit had been in London and had flown back to help them. "Ten years, and you're still as beautiful as I remember."

Bianca's cheeks heated slightly. He looked like he wanted to hug her but hesitated. Instead, he gently took her hands in his and gave them a light squeeze. "Welcome to Life Is But A Dream. You're safe."

The winery was also a safe house. Go figure.

She removed her hands from Emit's grip. "I appreciate all your help so far, but just so we're clear, I'm not staying. I'm going to see Senator Halston."

Emit flicked his eyes to Cal and returned to Bianca. "How about we have some breakfast and you can tell me what's going on?"

She'd been forced to tell Cal about her job and the information she had, but Emit was all but a stranger. Maggie seemed to sense her anxiety and came to stand next to her, pressing her weight into Bianca's leg. "Breakfast sounds good, but I can't share classified information and I'm capable of handling the situation on my own. As long as you and Cal can keep me alive."

"Tough as nails, like always," Emit said. He eyed the dog as he withdrew a folded sheet of paper from his jacket pocket and held it up for Bianca to see. "I have Senator Halston's schedule for today, and I can access the place he's staying tonight. Sneak you in. Perhaps over breakfast, we can barter."

He waggled his eyebrows and Bianca didn't know whether to laugh or kick him in the shin. Same old Emit.

Cal trusted him, and maybe she should too. At least with a few of the bare facts. Nothing more. If he could get her into the senator's hotel room... "Coffee first, and then I'll think about it."

———

Cooper's phone buzzed. He almost didn't feel the vibration over the shuddering of the helicopter. He drew out the phone and found a text from Nelson. *Lughead got a call. Went to airport and boarded a private plane bound for Sacramento. Keep following?*

What the hell was in Sacramento?

Negative. In air now. Stay with Bobby, find out what's up in Sac. Find those vehicles. And check into McConnell Place.

What am I looking for?

Hell if he knew. This whole thing was like a giant puzzle. He took a best guess. *Something to do with prez.*

Roger that.

A minute later, the pilot came over Cooper's headphones. "We'll be setting down on the south side. Lots of commotion in our usual spot with the senator's visit and all."

"What visit?" he asked.

"Senator Halston. He's in town for the weekend stumping for the president. He's got a passel of security."

Halston. "The head of the Intelligence Committee?" Cooper asked.

"The one and only."

He and Thomas, sitting in the seat next to him, exchanged a look.

Coincidence? Cooper didn't believe in them.

It wasn't a *what* in Sacramento. It was a *who.*

Hacking at his phone's touchscreen, Cooper sent Bobby a note. *Sac = Senator Halston. Need today's itinerary.*

By the time the helo touched down, the itinerary was on his phone. So was another text from Bobby.

Emit Petit entered Dulles at 0300 hours this a.m. from London. Stopped in Chicago, then went straight to Sacramento.

"Get us a car," he told Thomas.

"Where we headed?"

"To see Senator Halston. We're attending every one of his stops today."

———

Cal, Bianca, and Emit snagged plates and helped themselves to the food. Cal filled Maggie a plate with scrambled eggs and a couple chunks of ham.

While they all ate, Cal and Emit rehashed old times spent in their neighborhood and at school. Some Bianca remembered, others she didn't. It was nice to listen to the two of them reminisce. Cal's relaxed voice and deep laugh was a balm to her heart.

So different than the zombie soldier ready to shoot her earlier that morning.

The bodyguards rotated through the food line as well, but situated themselves at the other end of the table. She hadn't eaten this well since Cal's mission had blown up, and after Bianca had had her fill and her pants needed loosening around the waist, she sat back and sipped coffee with a contentment only good food and a peaceful meal could bring.

When Cal and Emit finished a few minutes later, Emit rose and cleared away the plates. Cal leaned over and whispered in her ear. "You can trust him, B. You don't have to tell him everything, but the more he knows, the more effective he can be in helping us."

Bianca said nothing, weighing her choices carefully. All she really needed was to stay out of Tephra's crosshairs and speak to Senator Halston. "Are you going to tell him about your mission?"

Cal sat back, lips pressing tight.

"Didn't think so," she murmured.

Maggie was laying at Bianca's feet, asleep after her breakfast. The guards exited the room, but Bianca knew they were right outside. Emit returned and laid the paper with Senator Halston's schedule on the table in front of her. "Busy day for the senator. Lots of campaigning. Lots of public places. His security is tight. Sure you want to go after him?"

Bianca didn't look at the paper. "He'll make time for me once I tell him what I know."

"Figured you might say that." Emit pointed at the paper. "His last stop is here at the winery. He and his entourage are staying overnight."

"I saw his itinerary yesterday morning. This place wasn't on it."

Emit looked like the cat that had swallowed the canary. "You saw the public-issued itinerary that said he'd be staying at the Hilton in downtown Sacramento. I pulled some strings with his assistant and now he's staying here."

"Strings, huh?" Bianca took a second to process how much effort Emit had gone to for her and Cal. Letting them use his beach house, sending a team of bodyguards to bring them here, arranging for the senator to stay there that night. "You're good."

He made a silly, mocking bow at her. "Just doing my job."

She had the feeling Emit's job was a lot like Cal's...one big, fat secret. "I appreciate you doing this. Coming here and helping us. I'm sure you'd rather get home and see your son."

Emit gave her an odd look. "My son?"

"Austin? I saw his bedroom at the beach house." She bit her bottom lip. "I didn't mean to snoop, but your son's room is charming, and from his picture, he's adorable."

"He's awesome."

Cal fidgeted. "Yeah, about the house. We kind of left it in a mess."

"The authorities already contacted me and gave me the low down about it being a crime scene, yada, yada. It's being handled. No worries."

No worries, except that was the last time they'd seen Tephra. Where was he? What was he up to?

"How much did Cal tell you?" Bianca asked, getting up to refill her coffee. Maggie opened her eyes, following Bianca's every move, but didn't so much as lift her head.

Emit pulled out a chair and settled in. "Only the mission critical details. You're under the gun. You believe it's a former SEAL named Rory Tephra. You need a computer and a way into the NSA's databases."

She returned to her chair and sat down. "My passwords are all burned. Even with a computer, I can't log in."

"Can you hack in?" Cal asked.

She could if she needed to find a link between the operative nicknamed Killer Kathy, Halston, and Grimes, but doing so, no matter how careful she was and how well she covered her tracks, could jeopardize their safe location. "I want to start by talking to Senator Halston. If he won't cop to leaking intel, I'll go after him another way. If that's necessary, then and only then will I hack into NSA."

"What about the numbers Tephra gave you?" Emit asked. "Sergeant Warwick said you think they're coordinates for Chicago."

"McConnell Place to be exact. I can't be one hundred percent sure," she said, "because there wasn't designation of direction or degrees listed by hours and minutes, but it makes sense from the standpoint that Linc Norman will be there tomorrow and that's where he told Grimes to meet him for a showdown."

Emit scratched his sparse goatee. "Why would an assassin who's supposed to be MIA hand you coordinates for that? Does he want you to be there?"

"Like I mentioned to you earlier," Cal said. "Tephra told me he didn't want to kill Bianca, only talk to her. He said she wasn't the only target. But hell if I know why he didn't just say, 'Be at McConnell Place in Chicago tomorrow' if that's what he wanted."

Emit raised an eyebrow at her. "So if we believe Tephra, you're not the only target either on his hit list or overall. Any idea who else might be in danger?"

She'd thought about it a lot on the drive and had only one conclusion. Cal might not be on Tephra's agenda, but the numbers, if they truly did designate McConnell Place, were an invitation. An invitation she wished she could turn down. "It's the president. He's going after Linc Norman."

CHAPTER TWENTY-THREE

Cal couldn't find Bianca. After breakfast and a lot more discussion about Tephra, the president, and why Bianca was on someone's hit list, he'd stayed to talk to Emit and Bianca had disappeared into the bowels of the building with two of Emit's bodyguards to get "cleaned up."

He and Maggie were taking the abbreviated tour of the place searching for her. Even though she never wore much makeup and kept her long hair in a ponytail most of the time, he remembered how obsessive she was with bathing and staying clean. The small bathroom in their apartment had always been cluttered with beauty products. Lotions, creams, and specialty soaps. The shower had been filled with stuff too. Smelly oils, herbal shampoos…the memory made him shudder and smile at the same time.

Here, she had none of her stuff, but probably wanted to wash off the dustiness of the cabin and her brush with Mother Nature. Emit assured him her bodyguards would keep her safe while she used a special bathroom in the suite reserved for important overnight guests. The suite Senator Halston would be using later.

Finding the suite wasn't easy. Cal took another turn and a second set of stairs, Maggie by his side.

During his conversation with Emit, Emit had tried convincing Cal to come to work for him. The idea was tantalizing, but Cal knew the PTSD would be an issue. He begged off, saying he wanted to take a shot at saving his career.

The whole time Emit talked, Cal's mind kept wandering to Bianca. He couldn't concentrate on what Emit was saying, the offers he was making. He needed a good scrub himself, but mostly he wanted to see her naked in the shower, the water skimming over her high breasts and slender legs. He wanted to scrub her back and wash her hair and take her in about six different positions...

An image of one of those positions made him stop and catch his breath. Ahead was the door to the suite and his heart pinched at the idea of having her alone again.

She'd gotten under his skin like always. And now he couldn't wait to get back under hers.

The door was unmanned. Where were the bodyguards?

Cal covered the last few steps in quick strides, flung open the door, and found an empty room. For a suite, it wasn't that big—a king-size bed at the far end, a reading area in the center with a desk, a fireplace at the other end with a comfy looking couch.

The door to the bathroom was closed. He approached, listening, his heart jack-rabbing in his chest. Leaning one ear against the door, he waited. Heard nothing. "Bianca?"

No reply. His hand went to the gun in the waist of his pants, the other turning the knob. Slowly, he eased open the door.

The air was heavy and warm, the mirror still fogged. Rivulets of water ran down the glass shower enclosure. She'd been there...but now she was gone.

Where?

Maggie sniffed a washcloth hanging on the edge of the tub. Knowing Bianca, she could be anywhere. As long as she hadn't ditched the bodyguards, he had nothing to worry about.

Right. He tucked the gun away and rubbed his forehead. He wouldn't be happy until he knew where she was and that she was safe.

Drawing out his cell, he texted her burn phone's number. *Where are you?*

Service here was intermittent, but he currently had two bars and two seconds after he hit SEND, the phone told him the message had been delivered.

He stayed there, hoping to keep the service bars and get a reply. His patience was rewarded a minute later when she replied, *tasting room.*

Breathing a sigh of relief, he left the suite and went to find the tasting room.

One of Emit's bodyguards had been trailing him, staying out of the way, but keeping tabs on him all the same. Cal knew it was for his own safety but it made him antsy. As he and Maggie hit the first-floor landing, he noticed the guy had traded places with one of his cohorts. A tag team.

Lovely. He'd told Emit he didn't need protection, especially inside these walls. That they should focus on Bianca. Apparently, Emit had ignored his request.

Cal would take it up with him later, when they all met up again to discuss their plan for confronting Halston. For now, Cal was intent on finding Bianca. She wasn't going to like what he had to say, but she needed to look at the situation realistically.

The basement was cool and dry. Cal took a wrong turn and ended up in the area where three men were loading grapes into a cold press. He turned around and found Emit's goon slouched against a wall. The guy didn't look at Cal, apparently more interested in his cuticles; he simply pointed in the opposite direction.

"I don't need a bodyguard," Cal mumbled as he walked by.

"Just following orders, sir."

Sir. The title rang hollow in his ears. "Does Emit really think the assassin is going to find us here?"

The guy fell into step behind Cal. "An assassin could already be inside the walls. Emit doesn't trust anybody."

"Not even monks?"

"Especially not monks."

Cal had to laugh. "I never realized he was such a paranoid SOB"

"Try working for him."

It might come to that. He shook off the idea. There would be no working for Emit, no field work of any kind. Put him under stress and his mind would snap. Look at what had happened at the cabin.

He'd vowed to stay away from Bianca, and he would. As soon as he helped her clear his name, and stopped Tephra, or whoever, was after her.

Her bodyguards flanked each side of the wine tasting room door. "She in there?" he asked.

One of them nodded. "We were getting on her nerves so she asked us to stay out here."

"Asked?" the other guy snorted softly. "She told us to park it and leave her alone."

Sounded like B. Cal left his bodyguard and hers and went inside.

The room was dark, the smell of old wood and years of spilled wine hanging in the air. Dark hardwood floors, dark wooden tables, small alcoves here and there with porcelain figurines and fake grapes. Maggie didn't seem to like it and stayed close to the door.

Pot lights in the ceiling over the bar reflected off the high gloss of the thick bar top. Over time, the wood had been scarred and nicked, its dark stain worn lighter in some spots.

There were three glasses set up with varying amounts of wine. A fourth was being held up by its stem, Bianca's slim, pale fingers in stark contrast to the ruby redness of the liquid. Her hair was lose and flowing in sexy waves down her back, Cal's way-too-long T-shirt tucked under her butt and outlining her perfect ass cheeks on the bar stool.

As always, his gaze zoned in on her and he had trouble focusing on anything else.

Except the dickweed standing across from her.

Cooper's phone vibrated in his pocket. The screen ID read, "My Lover."

Celina had been playing with his phone again.

Quietly slipping away from the walking tour of the vineyards, Cooper stopped under a nearby oak. "Hello, beautiful."

"Where are you?"

He'd gotten in late the night before and left before Celina was out of bed. "Northern California."

Instantly, his Cuban girlfriend raised her voice. "Northern California? We're supposed to go to Owen's soccer game after school. Tell me you'll be back in time."

He couldn't promise her that. "Bianca Marx disappeared yesterday. That's why I got home late and why I'm now in Sacramento. I think she's in trouble."

"Oh, God." The fire went out of Celina as fast as it had come. She knew how protective he was of his agents. She'd been one. "What kind of trouble?"

"I don't know. Thomas and I are shadowing Senator Halston. We think it has something to do with him."

A long pause and a sigh. "Don't worry about Owen. I'll smooth things over with him and take him for ice cream afterward."

"Have I told you how much I love you?"

"You can make it up to me by bringing home a couple bottles of wine."

"Cab Sauv or Pinot?"

"Some of each. And while you're touring around, make reservations at one of the bed and breakfasts for next weekend. You and I need to get away for a few days."

Bobby had texted and told Cooper about a change to

180

Halston's itinerary. He was staying at a winery that also hosted overnight guests. When Cooper was there, he'd check into a weekend reservation. "You got it, boss."

She snorted at the reference. She used to call him that to get under his skin when she worked for him. He'd been an idiot to put her off for so long and not let her into his heart.

But that was over. She asked so little of him, yet gave so generously. It was time for something more permanent between them—if she would have him. He'd sworn after his divorce from Owen's mother that he would never marry again, but now...

Never say never. "It's beautiful up here. You would love it."

She was quiet for a moment, then said, "I already miss you. I want you home safe and sound. I hope you find Bianca soon and she's okay."

The tour group was nearly out of sight. The hostess was explaining the different types of grapes to Senator Halston, photographers and fans alike snapping pictures as they trailed behind.

"I miss you, too. I'll be home as soon as I can, and in the meantime, I'll keep you posted."

They said their goodbyes and Cooper caught up to Thomas, lingering on the fringes of the group. "We have a visitor," he said, his voice low.

They let the group move forward several feet as Cooper scanned the crowd. He didn't see anyone he recognized. "Who?"

Thomas discreetly pointed to a man's back hidden in a group of tourists. He wore a baseball cap, jeans, and a leather jacket. "I didn't recognize him out of uniform, but I'm sure that's him."

Cooper squinted. The noonday sun was too bright or his eyes were weak. He couldn't tell who it was. "Reese?"

"No," Thomas said. "Lughead."

As if on cue, Justin Lugmeyer discreetly broke away from the crowd, head down, a cell phone in his hands. He didn't stop until he was near the line of grapevines and out of hearing distance from the crowd. He took a call, his back to everyone.

"What's he doing here?" Cooper muttered.

"Good question," Thomas said. He started walking forward. "I'll go ask him."

Cooper grabbed the younger man's arm, stopping him as he watched Lugmeyer nod and disconnect. "Wait. Let's see what he's up to."

Thomas faded back and Cooper followed, the two of them keeping close to the same grapevines and trellises, only farther back.

The tour of the vineyard complete, the hostess was wrapping up her speech and inviting everyone inside for the wine tasting. That was to be followed by lunch and Senator Halston's address. People clapped, cameras snapped, and everyone followed the senator and hostess to the main house.

Lugmeyer hung back, typing something on his phone. As if he felt Cooper and Thomas watching him, he looked up and glanced around. They kept out of sight, and finally, Lugmeyer jogged off to catch up with the group.

Shadowing Halston was one thing. Shadowing Halston without being seen by Lugmeyer was another. Maybe Thomas's idea was better. Confront Lugmeyer and see why he was there. Did he have a lead on Reese and Bianca or was he simply a fan of the senator?

"We've scoped this entire place," Cooper said. "Reese and Bianca aren't here. I say we go down the list and check out the other sites. See if anything pops. If we come up empty-handed, we'll catch up with Halston and continue to shadow him."

"Damn, I was looking forward to a nice glass of wine and some lunch."

The kid was always thinking about his stomach. "You don't drink wine."

"Maybe I'll start."

"Focus. If you were Reese and wanted to talk to the Senator for some reason, say about your last mission, which winery would you set up camp at?"

Thomas brought up the itinerary on his phone's screen as they walked toward the parking lot. "The last one. It's the end of the day, most of the journalists have their story and pictures and have left to make their deadlines. The tourist crowd is thinner—those that are left are probably drunk and not paying much attention. The senator's feeling good and ready to call it a night. Bianca would know it's the perfect time to approach him, if that's Reese's plan."

"I say we start there and see if we can flush them out."

"Anything beats another tour."

The two bumped fists and headed for their rental car.

A male bartender with a goatee and wavy dark hair was making eyes at Bianca as Cal stood in the doorway.

She was swirling red wine in a glass. "And how does this differ from the first Zinfandel?" she asked.

Bianca had never been much of a drinker...a beer would make her loopy. Two and she'd fall asleep on him. Since he'd never been much of a drinker either, that suited him just fine.

At the moment, he wondered why the hell she was tasting wines. He figured she'd be making plans for the Halston encounter, and possibly going off on a tangent and calling the president to warn him about a terrorist threat or assassination attempt in Chicago.

"This Zin is lighter bodied," the bartender said, his voice smooth, and his gaze seeming to find a different body more interesting as he not-so-subtly undressed her with his eyes. "Great berry fruit with a touch of vanilla."

She sampled it, licked her lips, and held the glass out in front of her. "I like this one."

"Figured you would." He grinned. "Fits your personality."

Cal strode forward, a sudden urge driving him. An urge he

had to tame before the bartender ended up choking on his own wine. He stopped beside Bianca's bar stool and glared at the guy. "You don't know her personality." He jerked his head at the door. "Get lost."

"Cal," Bianca said, leaning toward him with a sly smile on her face. "Thought you'd never get here."

The bartender's gaze hardened. "Look, buddy—"

Laying his hands on the edge of the bar, Cal gripped it hard to keep from punching the guy. "Get out."

"It's okay," Bianca said to the man. "He's my husband."

The bartender scowled and Cal scowled back. The challenge in his face or the grip he still had on the bar seemed to change the guy's mind about staying. He threw down a bar towel he'd been wiping his hands on and headed for the door. On his way by Maggie, she growled low in her throat.

Before the door had even shut, Bianca was handing Cal one of the glasses. "Try this."

"I don't like wine."

Her eyes were mischievous, playful. Was she drunk? "You'll like this. It's a petite sirah. Heavy tannins, lots of blackberry. Dark and brooding like you."

"I'm not dark and brooding."

She leaned forward, tilting her face up to his and patting his cheek. He smelled the wine on her warm breath. "Yes, you are, Cal."

Taking the glass from her hand, he set it on the scarred bar top. Maggie was now making her way around the room, checking out the tables and chairs, nose to the floor. "What are you doing here, B?"

"Isn't it obvious?"

"You don't drink."

Her eyes sparked. "Maybe I do."

"Since when?"

She straightened her spine. "Since you left me."

God, not this again. He set his jaw so he didn't yell, and

placed his elbows on the bar so he could focus on something besides the accusation in her eyes. After the last miscarriage, he felt so helpless, the only thing he could do was lose himself in work. Bianca had been devastated, but from a life filled with disappointments, she'd taught herself how to become aloof and apathetic in order to hide the pain. When he reached for her, to comfort and offer some type of solace, she acted like a cat. Her hackles went up and she moved away from him. As if it were his fault. As if his touch were like sandpaper.

Finally, he'd given up. He was hurting too, but he couldn't express it. Couldn't stand to watch her deny her own feelings even though he knew it was the only way she knew to get through the blow of losing a second child.

His heart beat a heavy rhythm in his ribcage as he tried to give her what she needed. "I'm sorry, B. About leaving. About the baby. All of it. I tried to be there for you, but it seemed like you didn't want me. I never meant to drive you to drink."

Her anger vanished. She slumped against the bar, putting her elbows on it alongside his and sighed. "You didn't. I'm not a drinker. I don't know why I said that. It's this situation. The stress."

He knew the feeling. "You really think there will be an attack on the president?"

She shrugged. "I don't know."

"I'm surprised you aren't panicking and calling Linc Norman to warn him."

"I've notified the taskforce that something is going down. Cooper will alert the proper authorities."

Cal's pulse went into overdrive. "You did *what?* You weren't supposed to contact anyone."

"So sue me." She met his gaze head-on. "I have to report any credible threat to the president. I'm not sure there even *is* a threat, but I couldn't ignore the logic of this. I couldn't call my boss at C&C, but I could at least put Cooper on the trail. And don't worry, he won't be able to find us, and even if he does, he's not the one trying to kill me."

Famous last words. "You're unbelievable."

"Yeah, well, I'm not the only one in this room with a hero complex, thank you very much." She took another long sip and her voice was quieter when she spoke again. "My usual job at the NSA requires me to make tough calls to protect our borders and save lives, sometimes even the president's. I thrive at my job. But here I sit, my career burned while I twiddle my thumbs and a senator goes free to leak more information that could endanger hundreds, if not thousands of Americans. Otto Grimes is still free. My president, the man I've been protecting for three plus years, could be in danger. The men in your unit died because of me, and all I'm doing is trying to save my own ass at the moment."

"My men didn't die because of you. They died because of me. I knew something was off that night. I should have called off the mission."

She shook her head. "You were only following orders."

Maggie came over to nudge Cal's leg. He patted her head, and seemingly satisfied, she went back to the door and laid down. "Neither of us was playing with full knowledge of how the deck was stacked against us. We didn't know about the leak."

She closed her eyes, shook her head. After a minute, she said, "Do you know how many death threats the president gets a day?"

He had no idea. "How many?"

"The last president received on average twenty-four credible threats a day. Linc Norman receives on average *one hundred* and twenty-four."

"A day? That's a lot of damn death threats."

"Yes, just slightly over five an hour. I don't know how he does it. Ignore them, I mean. I have one death threat to contend with and I'm a basket case."

"The president has the Secret Service. You don't."

"I could have this whole thing wrong. Those numbers may not be coordinates. Tephra could be playing games with us."

Tephra didn't seem the type to play games. "But why?"

"That's what all of this comes back to. Why. I'm hoping Senator Halston can answer that for us tonight."

"About that. You really think the guy will cop to leaking information? You don't have any proof and he's not going to blow up his career and freely admit wrongdoing if you don't."

She dropped her head into her hands. "I have a plan."

He waited for her to expound on the plan, and when she didn't, he nudged her with his elbow. "What are you going to do?"

Her eyes cut to him, away. "Bluff."

She might not be good at handling her liquor, but she was an ace at holding her cards close to her chest. "With what?"

Capturing one of the glasses, she twirled the stem between her fingers. "Fake evidence isn't that hard to manufacture." She took another sip of the Zinfandel she liked and eyed him over the rim.

"You're going to falsify evidence?"

"Only in order to make him incriminate himself."

This wasn't the Bianca he'd grown up with. The one he'd married. This was the Bianca who lay in wait under the surface. The NSA agent and one person in the world willing to do anything in order to clear his name and give him his life back.

He loved her for that.

But it wasn't going to work. "And if Halston sees through your bluff and still refuses to admit he leaked the intel?"

"Then like I told you and Emit at breakfast, I'll hack into the NSA and finish my investigation on the senator and Killer Kathy. The problem is, that type of investigation could take days, weeks, even longer. I'm good, but I'm not that good. The NSA will figure out they've been hacked at some point and shut me down...even if I live that long."

He brushed a strand of hair back from her face. "I won't let anyone hurt you." *Not even myself.* "You're in good hands with Emit and his crew."

She set down the glass and turned her stool to face him. Leaned forward and put her lips to his cheek, laying a light kiss there. "I'm in better hands with you."

Her lips grazed his jawline, traced their way down the side of his neck.

"Bianca..."

She wrapped her arms around his waist and slid halfway off the stool, pressing her breasts into his chest as she kissed his collarbone. Her hair tickled his nose. "We have a lot of time to fill until tonight," she murmured against his chest.

True. And they were all alone, except for the bodyguards outside the door.

His cock twitched and his fingers wound around sections of her hair, gripping it and drawing her head back. She stared up at him with heat and lust in her eyes. He wanted her so bad it hurt.

But then an image of her terrified eyes from the previous night flashed through his mind. His stomach clenched.

She reached out and ran a finger over his lips. "Stop thinking."

If only he could. He closed his eyes and leaned away from her touch, mentally cursing. He didn't want to stop this, but he had to.

Her hand dropped to his belt, fingers working to undo the buckle. He grabbed it and held her by the wrist. Her pulse jumped under his thumb. Shifting them both, he pressed her gently against the bar. "We can't do this."

"The hell we can't."

"Bianca, I'm serious."

Her eyes were clear and steady. Determined. "So am I. You're my husband, and I love you, even if you love your career more. I'm not giving up on us."

His throat tightened at her admission. "I'm dangerous."

That sly grin slid across her face again. "Knew that when I married you."

Damn this woman. "I pulled a gun on you last night."

"You don't cure PTSD, but you do learn to live with it. Plenty of people have. I know some experts who can help."

He *would* get help. Anything to be with her again if she would take him back. "But right now, it's not safe. You can't be alone with me."

"You mean like, *right now* right now? Because I don't see you freaking out or being disoriented about where you are or what we're doing. Nothing's going to happen, Cal, except you and me enjoying each other for a little while."

He touched her cheek, slid his fingers into her hair, wishing he could believe that. "We can't take the chance. I don't know what could trigger an episode."

"Having sex with me could trigger PTSD?" She arched an eyebrow at him. "You really know the way to a girl's heart, don't you?"

"You know that's not what I meant." Jeez, he was digging himself in deeper. "I mean...oh, hell. You know what I mean. The stress of sex could trigger it."

She held out a hand. "Give me your gun."

"What?"

She waggled her fingers at him. "Come on. Give it up."

He withdrew the gun and handed it to her. Setting it on the bar top, she sent it sliding down to the other end. "There. Nothing to worry about."

He set his hands on her hips, pressed into her ever so slightly "I can kill you with my bare hands."

Her eyes were excited, eager. "Sexy."

Leaning in, he dropped his eyes to her lips. "You're sick. Or crazy."

"Don't use the crazy word with me."

"Sorry."

"You won't hurt me. I believe in you."

As she tried to kiss him, he drew back. "You shouldn't."

She grabbed his shirt, balling it in her fist and pulling him forward hard enough that he had to grab the bar to keep from falling completely into her. "Stop it. You're the only person in my poor, pathetic life that I've ever trusted one hundred percent. I still do."

"But I *have* hurt you."

"Not physically. Emotionally, yeah, we've both thrown our share of daggers at the other. Relationships are hard. Harder yet between people like me and you. We don't do well with emotions or sharing our thoughts and feelings."

"It doesn't come easy."

"Nothing worth fighting for does."

She was right. He searched her face. "This is different."

"How?"

God, how could he say all the thoughts crashing around in his brain? He started to say something, anything, but the words wouldn't come.

She waited, her gaze still steady and eager. He tried again. "You mean everything to me, B. Letting you down tears me up. And I've let you down time and time again."

"Because you're a hero. A hero I kept trying to keep all to myself."

She released his shirt, smoothed it. "It's me who needs to let you go. That's why I filed for the divorce. You're the real hero, here, Cal, and I've been holding you back. I wanted the white picket fence and all that. A real family. You, me, and a kid or two. But underneath, I was scared and stupid, so I kept sabotaging myself and our relationship."

Hero. He hated that word. "And now?"

She raised her eyes to his. "Like I said, nothing worth fighting for is easy. My whole life, nothing has ever been easy and I'm tired of fighting. For my career, for people's respect, fighting to make a difference in the world. But one thing has become clear to me over the past two days."

"What's that?"

"You're the one thing I *do* want to fight for."

Plunk, ping, smack... Tiny pieces of his resolve were crumbling to the ground in his mind. "You sure about that? I'm not exactly a prize right now."

She moved in close and clutched the front of his shirt again, drawing his face to hers. "I've never been more sure of anything in my life."

Her lips were on his before he could reply, her hold on his shirt keeping him close. The final pieces of his resolve collapsed under the realization his wife still loved him, no matter what.

He grasped her head between his hands, kissing her in return. He raked his fingers through her hair, as she released his shirt and she sighed into his mouth.

Relief.

Her fingertips slipped under his shirt, her nails raking his back, clutching him to her as he bent her back over the bar. He couldn't help it. He needed her, wanted her. He'd never been able to resist her and never would.

She laughed, low and wicked, laying back to give him access to her neck, her collarbone, her breasts. A smile crept across his face and he drew a breath...the first in weeks that felt right, normal.

Bianca was right; they were a team. Together, they could take on anything.

"You and me," he said to her.

"You and me," she echoed.

He dipped his head and kissed her jawline, then nuzzled her neck, making his way down to those glorious breasts she had put on display.

Everything was going to be all right.

CHAPTER TWENTY-FOUR

When the knock on the door came, Bianca was in such a lust-induced stupor, she didn't notice.

Cal had set her on the bar, pressing himself between her legs as he ran his hands over her body and murmuring how badly he needed her. How much he wanted her. She'd heard those words before, but this time they'd seemed more urgent, more...emotional.

Hot damn. She was really and truly making headway with him, and that alone was an aphrodisiac to beat all aphrodisiacs.

She'd lost her—*his*—T-shirt somewhere along the line and was getting ready to lose her bra when he froze, one hand cupping her left breast and his mouth gorging on her right. His lips vibrated against her skin...was that a growl coming from his throat?

"What...is it?" she murmured. Over Cal's shoulder, she could see Maggie facing the door, ears pricked and body on alert.

The knock sounded again, and oh, yeah, she'd heard the first one but had been too deep in Wonder-Cal-land to put two and two together.

Cool air replaced Cal's mouth on her breast and she groaned. He kept his back to the door, shielding her. "Go away," he called.

"Sorry to interrupt, bra." Emit's voice was muffled through

the wooden door, but his tone was serious. "We have a situation."

Cal let out a heavy sigh and hung his head for a second, his hair tickling Bianca's breasts. "Can't it wait?"

Bianca looked down at the top of his head, baffled for a moment. While she was completely annoyed at the interruption, it surprised her Cal hadn't switched gears in a heartbeat, ready to throw open the door and take on whatever Emit was worried about.

"Turn on the TV above the bar to the local news station. You're going to want to see the breaking story."

"Shit," Cal mumbled, his head coming up and his gaze locking on hers. He released her and scrambled around behind the bar, searching for the TV remote. Bianca found her lost shirt and pulled it back on.

A second later, the screen came to life, already on a local channel. The headline at the bottom of the screen read, *Senator falls seriously ill during wine tasting. Rushed to hospital.*

As Bianca listened to the reporter state the facts, Cal opened the door to Emit. The two men joined her at the bar as the reporter went on.

"*Senator Patrick Halston was on a wine tasting trip through the Sacramento Valley today, meeting with local farmers on a last swing through the state gathering votes for President Linc Norman. On his third stop of the day,*"—the reporter searched her notes—"*at Woodglen Winery off Interstate 80, the senator gave a rousing speech on President Norman's behalf, and then enjoyed a lunch and wine tasting ceremony. During the lunch, Senator Halston fell ill and was rushed here, to UC South Medical Center. Details on his condition are pending, but a source inside the hospital claims Senator Halston is seriously ill.*"

Emit used the remote to mute the TV. "I have a source inside the hospital who says Halston's initial symptoms resemble potassium cyanide poisoning. He's a very sick man. They don't know if he'll make it."

The air went out of Bianca's lungs and she staggered against the bar stool next to her. "A poison pill?"

Emit nodded. "Sounds like he thought it was his irritable bowel acting up when he got sick and didn't seek immediate medical attention. The cyanide was probably in his wine."

The room spun; the floor under her feet dipped. The wine in her stomach, while not much, threatened to come back up. Cal's warm hands landed on her arms, supporting her.

Thank God. Otherwise, her butt would be making quick friends with the floor.

Her voice sounded floaty and far away as she spoke. "Someone tried to kill Senator Halston?"

From the look Emit and Cal both shot at her, it was a dumb question. And yes, she knew it was before she even asked, but her brain couldn't seem to wrap around this latest turn of events. The man could die. The horror of it rushed over her and once more her legs went weak. "I need to sit down."

Cal started to help her onto the bar stool, but she shook her head. "Chair. I need a chair."

With his help, she staggered over to a table and plopped down. Maggie followed, wagging and head-butting Bianca's hand for attention. Bianca's fingers delved into the Lab's soft fur and held on. She needed something to ground her.

Not only had Halston been poisoned, he was the key to resolving the issues surrounding Cal's mission and the bounty on her head.

Not the only target on this mission...

Bile rose in her throat. She'd thought Tephra was insinuating Linc Norman was on someone's kill list. Instead, whoever it was had gone after Senator Halston.

Why? Because he'd leaked information? Or because he was her only hope of clearing up this mess?

Only Cal and Emit knew her plan to talk to him. No one else did, so whoever poisoned Halston hadn't done it because she'd been waiting to talk to him. At least she could take comfort in that.

Emit set a glass of water in front of her and pulled out a chair. He brought out a computer tablet and laid it on the table. "There's more."

More? She set her teeth, forcing herself to swallow the lump in her throat.

Under the table, Cal took her hand—the one not embedded in Maggie's fur—and squeezed. *Team.* They were a team. Bianca exchanged a look with him and nodded. He said to Emit, "Give it to us."

Emit touched the screen, bringing it to life. "I ran TrackMap, my people-mapping program that shows relationships between people and groups they belong to. Bianca would recognize it as a version of Net Map, used by her coworkers to track everything from human trafficking networks to targeted digital attacks on government and financial websites. Anyway, I put in all the variables I had. You two, Tephra, Halston, Linc Norman. An interesting correlation popped up."

On the screen were clusters of dots, some gray, some white, and some red. The clusters were labeled "Family," "SEAL Teams," "Congress," "White House." Emit pointed at a large gray dot on its own. The dot was labeled Rory Tephra.

From Rory's gray dot extended several lines. Emit traced one that led to the SEAL Team cluster. Inside that cluster were dots labeled with Patrick Halston's name and Cal's. "The three of you were all SEALs."

Cal shrugged. "We knew that."

Emit traced the finger back to Rory. "Rory Tephra entered the training program in 1996. Do you know who his BUDs trainer was?"

Cal shook his head. "Before my time."

Emit tapped the dot with Senator Halston's name. "Patrick. He left the Navy and became a senator in 1998. Two months after 9/11, he was appointed to the Senate Select Committee on Intelligence, and within ten days, Tephra was declared MIA."

Emit was looking at them as if he'd given them the answer to all their questions. Bianca's brain cells felt as frayed as her nerves. She blinked, hoping that clearing her vision would unscramble the message Emit was giving her. It didn't work. "I'm sorry, I don't see it. What's the connection?"

Cal released her hand and set his elbows on the table, staring at the tablet. "Tephra was commissioned by Halston to go MIA so he could do ghost work."

"Exactly." Emit sat back, seemingly proud that Cal had gotten it.

Bianca was still lost. "Ghost work for Halston?"

Cal nodded. "You said he was doing wet work for the CIA? Same thing, except in the Spec Ops world, we call it ghost work. Black operations in foreign countries that only a few top ranking officials ever know about. They perform missions similar to what you were telling me about at the cabin. Things the government doesn't want made public. The men and everything about the mission, right down to the budget is kept off-record."

"Lots of ops are run that way. Every division has a black budget and a specific team of experts to deal with sensitive targets."

Emit shook his head. "We're talking completely unofficial here. There's a specialized group called Command and Control. It's run by a ruthless SOB who has dirt on every politician and financial mogul in America. Thing is, he doesn't bother with blackmail. You cross him or whoever he's backing at the moment, and he simply wipes you off the face of the earth. His group does things that would make your hair stand on end."

Bianca's hair was already standing on end. A low tingling had started at the base of her neck the moment Emit had said Command and Control, and now a buzzing filled her ears. How did he know about C&C? About Jonathan?

Jonathan was made of steel, sure, and had one heck of a short list of enemies, but he did what he did to protect America and support the men and women of the military on the ground defending her. Jonathan looked at the big picture twenty-four-seven, and he wasn't afraid to pull the trigger to defend his country.

She kept her face neutral even though Cal was staring at her so hard, she felt the heat of his gaze down to her toes. "How do know about this group? This Command and Control?"

Emit met her eyes. "I know someone who works in it."

Did he mean her? "You have spies everywhere."

"You should see your face right now." The signature Emit-grin spread across his face. "You're shitting bricks, aren't you? It's okay, B. I know what you do when you go to work at the NSA, but you might want to fill Cal in on the details."

Cal ran a hand over the scruff on his face and chuckled without humor. "I already know, but it was like pulling teeth to get it out of her."

"I'm not your spy," Bianca said to Emit, "so how do you know about C&C? About Jonathan?"

"The other blue elephant was a friend of mine. Before she died, she was a client too."

"You knew Alisha?"

"She suspected someone was following her, bugging her phone, the usual. Of course Jonathan was keeping an eye on her. He kept a close eye on both of you. With Alisha, though, it was something different. She was worried. Unfortunately, she was on her way home from meeting with me about her suspicions when she had her accident. I never had a chance to set up security for her."

"Did you look into it? The accident?"

"I did, but everything was sealed. Jonathan didn't want anyone sniffing around her or what happened."

"Maybe I need to talk to Jonathan rather than Senator Halston."

"No," both men said at the same time.

"What we need to do is focus on the links we have in front of us," Cal said. He pointed at the tablet. "If Tephra was tasked by Halston to do ghost work, he either had to be killed"—he made air quotes—"or he had to go MIA."

"Exactly," Emit said. "He had no family and his only friends were fellow SEAL team members, but…"

Sitting forward again, he tapped the tablet screen and brought up a news release. "According to an official statement released by the *Washington Post* in an article buried in the back on the day Tephra was officially declared MIA by the federal government, Senator Halston is quoted as saying, '*Rory Tephra was more than a hero, more than a SEAL. He was like a son to me. The United States owes him a great debt and we will not stop searching for him. We will find him and bring him home. And when he does return, you can bet a hero's welcome will be waiting for him.*'"

Bianca tapped her foot under the table. "So Halston unofficially hired Tephra to perform ghost work after 9/11 to take out terrorists."

Emit nodded. "Those not in the spotlight like Bin Laden but still as dangerous. The war on al Qaeda shattered the Taliban and similar jihadists into a thousand tiny offshoots. It caused other anti-Western groups to rise up, many of which the smaller al Qaeda cells reached out to, in this country as well as others. A new decentralized network was spawned, and with it, more effective enemies."

"Like Otto Grimes," Bianca said.

Emit pointed at the blob of dots labeled Terrorists. "See this link?"

Bianca watched his finger trace a line from Otto Grimes' name to Senator Halston's. It made sense since the committee Halston headed went after terrorists.

"The last field mission Patrick Halston participated in before becoming a SEAL trainer involved Otto Grimes' father, Dago. Do you know who else was on that mission?"

Bianca and Cal shook their heads.

"Linc Norman's father. He was a field agent for the CIA

under deep cover in Grimes' network. Led Halston's team right to Dago. Dago and six of his men were killed."

"Setting up Otto's hate of Linc Norman," Cal said.

Bianca shook her head. "That's not right. I know everything about Otto Grimes. His dad died from cancer when he was a kid."

Emit and Cal both looked at her as if she were mentally challenged.

She of all people knew how much the government covered up. How many missions were kept secret. Taking a deep breath, she decided to let them run with their theories. "So you're saying the 'official' version of Dago's death was a lie, and that Otto Grimes has a vendetta against Norman and Halston. I see the connection, but I still don't understand why President Norman keeps challenging Grimes to a showdown—wouldn't it be the other way around? Grimes is the one with the vendetta, he's the one who should be going after Norman."

"He's been pretty aggressive with his responses to Norman's challenges. And for all we know, he did make the first move, only it wasn't a public threat made on YouTube. It may have been a private one made long before Linc became president."

"Do you think Halston sent Tephra after me?" She had to swallow before she could say the next words. "Or Jonathan? Neither of them know I overhead their conversation."

Cal's gaze was pinned on the table. He lifted his eyes and looked at her from underneath his brows. "Maybe it's not about that conversation at all. Maybe it's because you're married to me."

Emit tapped the edge of the table and nodded. "Someone wanted your mission to fail and leaked the information to Grimes. Cal, you weren't supposed to make it out alive, but you did. Whoever is behind this"—he motioned to both of them— "knows that between the two of you, you'll figure it out and blow the lid off their cover-up. That's why they sent assassins after you."

Theories weren't getting them anywhere. Bianca needed more. "But then, who tried to kill Halston and why?"

"It all comes back to this." Emit touched a small mass of red dots on the screen, enlarging them. "Everyone associated with Cal's mission is either dead or has a target on their back."

Bianca stood, her resolve returning at lightning speed. "We have to talk to Senator Halston."

"Security at the hospital is tight, and if I get you into his room—which is highly unlikely—he may not be able to talk."

She'd take the chance. "As I recall, you're much like Cal, Emit. You love a challenge."

He and Cal exchanged that look they'd always given each other when she irritated either of them. Emit shut down the tablet and stood. "I'll see what I can do."

"Thank you."

Soundgarden, the bodyguard from earlier, appeared in the doorway. "Sir? We have a problem."

Cal rose, his body seeming to go into fight mode instantly. Bianca moved closer to him.

"What is it?" Emit said.

"Feds." Soundgarden tapped the earbud in his ear as if listening to someone speak. "Roger that," he said, and then to Emit, "They're upstairs looking for Agent Marx."

Her stomach fell. "As in FBI?"

The bodyguard nodded.

"Is it Harris?" Cal asked. "The taskforce?"

Cooper was DEA. So was Thomas. Ronni was the only field agent who was FBI. Semantics, Bianca reminded herself. The real question was, how had they found her?

No time to worry about that now. "Cal and I have to get to the hospital and talk to Halston," she said to Emit. "Can you get rid of them?"

Emit started walking, pointing toward a back shelving unit of wine bottles. He motioned at Cal and the two of them pushed the heavy shelving aside. Behind it, Emit opened a hidden door.

"I'll do my best. You two head to the south end of the property. There are a couple of old trucks the monks use for harvest down there. Take one of them and get out of here. I'll catch up with you if I can at UC South."

Bianca couldn't help it. Against her natural instincts, she gave him a quick hug. "Thank you."

It wasn't much, but Emit responded with surprise and gave her a hard hug back. "Be safe."

Cal called Maggie over. "We will."

He and Emit did their man-hug thing and then Cal was tugging Bianca forward into a dark, cool tunnel.

CHAPTER TWENTY-FIVE

Like most teaching hospitals, UC South was a labyrinth of departments, hallways, and rooms. As a Level 1 trauma center, it also had a burn center, advanced stroke center, and cancer center. Outside, news vans and reporters hung around the ER entrance and main desk, waiting for updates on Senator Halston's health.

Cal and Bianca had parked in Lot A and left Maggie in the truck. Avoiding anyone with a camera wasn't easy, and asking for Senator Halston's room number at the information desk wouldn't work, so Bianca simply kept her head down and followed Cal.

He seemed to know where he was going. Bianca, being naturally curious, had to ask anyway. "Where are we going?"

He was busy keeping his face turned away from the cameras as he'd instructed her to do. They found a bank of elevators and he led the way into one and punched a button. "Internal medicine. From there, look for a throng of suits hanging around. That will be Halston's entourage."

Good plan. On the drive, they'd discussed how best to sneak into his room. Bianca would pose as one of his nurses. Cal would stay in the waiting room, pretending to be there for some other patient as he kept an eye on things and planned various exit strategies depending on how the situation went.

Bianca had already located the women's locker room and lifted a nurse's scrub jacket, complete with her ID tag pinned to the front lying on a bench. The nurse in question had been in the shower, singing away to Shakira, her shift apparently complete. Her jacket had Mickey Mouse ears printed all over it and Bianca hoped the gal didn't notice it and ID were missing before Bianca had a chance to break into the senator's room and get answers.

As the elevator stopped on the IM floor, Cal murmured, "Put that on and act like you don't know me."

The jacket was a little loose. She flipped the ID tag over in case anyone up here knew Charice Dolamar, RN. She was heavier than Bianca, but she was blond and wore glasses. Bianca hoped no one looked too closely if they did see the picture.

When the doors opened, she hung back, letting Cal get off ahead of her. They both avoided the nurse's station and as Bianca continued to follow Cal around a corner, she saw him duck into a nearby waiting room. As he did so, he covertly pointed down the opposite hallway, and sure enough, there were security guards posted on each side of the last door at the end, and a host of men and women in suits talking on cell phones and typing on laptops.

Bianca set her shoulders and continued down the hall. "Cell phones are not allowed inside the hospital," she said, as she breezed past the first woman talking on her phone. She pointed to all the people with phones growing out of their ears. "Please take your calls outside."

One of the security guys stopped her as she reached for the door handle. Brightly colored warning signs about isolation, gloves and mask required, and oxygen in use hung on the doorframe. The guard was big and black and imposing. "ID, please."

Bianca smiled and raised her badge. "Oh, sorry, guess it got turned around."

Thank goodness the picture of Charice wasn't the best. The guard eyed it, eyed her, looked a little suspicious.

Heart hammering, she smiled and pushed up her glasses.

"I've lost twenty pounds in the last month. The seaweed and kale diet. Ever try it? You have to use Korean seaweed. Anything else isn't as effective."

His brows tweaked ever so slightly but he waved her through.

She slipped inside and carefully shut the door, leaning against it for a second as she drew a deep breath. Senator Halston wasn't the only one needing oxygen at this point.

The room smelled of antiseptic. The oxygen tank droned loudly. On the far wall hung a white board with the date, the senator's condition, and the name of his nurse and CNA.

Near the window, the senator lay in a hospital bed with his eyes closed. Bars of sunlight fell across the white blanket tucked around him. Next to his head, monitors beeped and an IV dripped a steady flow into his veins.

Even though she wasn't a real nurse, donning plastic gloves and a face mask seemed prudent. The mask served to hide her features if another nurse, doctor, or member of Halston's troupe entered while she was talking to him. Plus, although Halston had ingested the poison, it didn't take much for a sick man to puke on you, and being exposed to cyanide wasn't on her bucket list.

Guilt over bothering him at a time like this rose up inside her. The poor man was pale and looked like he'd aged ten years since she'd last seen him. His normally stylish gray hair was sticking out in clumps, his jaw slack, his breathing, even with the oxygen, sounded congested and heavy.

But this might be the only chance she got. She had to know who he'd leaked the info to and why it was costing her and Cal their jobs...and possibly their lives.

Leaning over the bed, she shook his arm lightly and got close to his ear. She couldn't yell over the oxygen pump and let anyone outside the door hear her. "Senator? It's Bianca Marx. From Command and Control. Can you hear me?"

He didn't open his eyes, but his mouth moved. Only a gurgling sound came out.

She took out her phone and turned on the video. If he did say anything, she wanted it recorded. "Senator, I believe you were poisoned. I'm trying to figure out who did it, but I need you to answer a few questions for me. I know you feel awful, but can you open your eyes for me?"

His mouth moved again and his eyelids fluttered. Then they closed and he went back to breathing like he was asleep.

She shook him gently and said his name several times. *This is wrong. So wrong.* She should walk out and leave the man alone.

Ready to give up, she stared at the bars of sunshine falling on the senator's blanketed legs. How was she going to clear Cal's name now? Without Halston's admission or further proof that Cal wasn't to blame for the failure of Warfighter, she had nothing. She wasn't any closer to stopping Rory Tephra from killing her or figuring out the web of deceit and betrayal going on between all the players in those damn clusters of circles Emit had shown her.

"Agent...Mmm..."

Bianca's head snapped up. Halston's eyes were open and he was looking at her. His fingers rose and he tried to remove the plastic oxygen tubing from his nose.

"You need to leave that in place," she said, pulling his hand away. She drew the mask over her mouth down so he could see her face. "I'm sorry to bother you at a time like this, but someone is trying to kill both of us and I'm trying to stop them. I believe it has to do with Operation Warfighter. Do you remember what happened with that operation?"

He closed his eyes again and Bianca thought she'd lost him. The oxygen tank droned and the IV dripped, and she hated herself all over again.

He leaked info, Bianca. Information that got men killed. Wake him up and get him to talk. "Senator Halston, I don't have much time. If you know anything about Warfighter or why someone wants us both dead, please talk to me."

The senator's mouth moved, his lips puckering as he strained to say something. "J-j-j-he-wa-wants…"

J? "Jonathan? My boss?"

Before Halston responded, the door blew open and a heavyset gal in a floral uniform blew in. She already wore gloves and a mask. "How's our patient?"

Bianca quickly slipped her phone into her pocket and put up her face mask. "He's coming around a little."

"Great." The woman hustled over to the bed and started sorting out the drip line and monitor cords. Her badge had a blue CNA label below her name, Katy Smirtelny. "Radiology is ready for him."

"Radiology?"

"Ultrasound. Doc wants to check out his liver and kidneys."

"Oh, right." Halston was once again still. Bianca hesitated, not wanting to leave. "Do you need help moving him?"

The gal tapped a lever under the bed with her foot. "I never turn down help."

"What do you want me to do?"

The CNA gave her an odd look as she disconnected the oxygen line. "Release the break at the end of the bed?"

Brake. Right. Bianca found the lever in question and punched it with her foot. Grabbing the handles on her end, she guided the bed toward the door as the CNA pushed from her end and brought the IV pole along.

Bianca blocked the door open and wheeled the senator into the hallway. The security detail and the rest of the entourage came to attention. Before anyone asked, she announced, "Senator Halston is moving to the X-ray department for an ultrasound."

As the CNA wiggled the head of the bed through the door, one of the suits asked, "How long will that take?"

The woman locked eyes with Bianca for a second as if expecting her to answer. She had no idea. She'd had one ultrasound, with the second baby, but that was different, wasn't it? Hers had taken ten minutes. How long would one of the liver and kidneys take?

Like she'd told Cal, she knew how to bluff. This was a hospital after all. They ran on their own clock. "Half an hour, give or take, depending on what the doctor is looking for and what they find."

The CNA didn't contradict her and no one else did either.

Bianca drew a deep breath and smiled under her mask.

Two of the nurses were at the nurse's station desk, talking and laughing about something that had happened on *The Bachelor* last night. Bianca covertly glanced over her shoulder toward the waiting room, hoping to catch Cal's eye as she and Katy wheeled Halston by.

She caught it. He stood with a soda in one hand, leaning against the doorframe, pretending not to notice her even as he made brief eye contact and a muscle stood at attention in his jaw.

His posture was casual, yet as always, he radiated heat and danger, like a puma ready to pounce. She knew what was going through his mind. *Abort, abort, abort.*

No way. Halston had something to tell her and she was sticking with him until she found out what it was.

J... He hadn't gotten the whole thing out, but that's what it had sounded like. Her boss's name.

The elevator dinged and Bianca worked with the CNA to wheel the bed onto it. Jonathan had been high on her suspect list of who was having her followed, but would he send an assassin after her? The man who had trusted her with some of America's most dangerous secrets? The man who had trained her and believed in her analysis of any given situation more than he trusted the most sophisticated computers the NSA owned?

As the elevator doors began to close, Bianca saw Cal coming for her, his eyes now saying, *Where the hell are you going?*

She gave him a small *no-no-no* shake of her head. He needed to let her see this through.

Cal, being Cal, however, wasn't about to let her out of his sight for long. He'd almost reached the elevator when the big, black security guard from outside Halston's room stopped him and slipped his hand in between the closing doors. The doors slid open again. "Sorry, sir, this elevator is full." He slipped inside, working his way around the head of Halston's bed. "You'll have to wait for the next one."

Cal's eyes were hard as he met Bianca's. Clearly, he still wanted her to abort.

She reached up and tapped the end of her nose. A signal they'd used as kids when she wanted him to know she was all right.

As the doors once more closed, shutting her off from Cal, Bianca prayed she really was all right.

———————

The ultrasound would definitely take half an hour if not more, according to the tech Bianca and the CNA left Senator Halston with. The security guard went into the room with him and there was nothing Bianca could do but wait.

The CNA bustled off and Bianca loitered in the hall. Her phone had vibrated once with a text from Cal on the way down, but since entering the basement of the medical center, she had no service. She needed to go up a floor and text him back before he blew a nut, but the waiting room near the radiology unit was full and there were dozens of hospital staff, patients, and visitors walking the maze of halls. Trying to avoid the security cameras and get back to the elevators was a trial.

Plus, she had to pee. Like, now. All this undercover stuff was giving her hives and causing her nervous bladder to go into overdrive.

She was hustling down a hallway, looking for a restroom, when she thought she heard someone behind her say her name.

She stopped and did a quick check over her shoulder, and a man in scrubs nearly ran into her. Two women in street clothes went around them, a constant stream of chatter running between them.

"Sorry," Bianca said, starting to follow the women. They were probably heading to the restroom too.

The man grabbed her arm and held her in place. "No problem." His voice was light and cheerful. The women continued on. "In fact, I was just looking for you."

Goose bumps ran down her arms as she realized who it was. Jerking her arm back, she nearly lost her balance. "What are you doing here?"

Rory Tephra cocked his head. "Exactly what I was going to ask you, Agent Marx."

Before she could protest, he pulled her into a nearby supply closet and shut the door.

The assassin looked like an entirely different man in hospital scrubs rather than the get-up he'd worn at the beach house. His face was clean-shaven, his hair neat and trim. Posing as a doctor suited him...if not for the fact his creed involved taking lives rather than saving them. "I've been looking all over for you but never thought you'd turn up here."

"And why are *you* here? Come to finish what you started?"

He leaned his back against the door, blocking her only way out. "I told you, I'm not trying to kill you."

"I was talking about the senator. Why did you poison him?"

He glared. "I would never hurt Patrick. I'm closer to him than my own father."

Tephra was no doubt a skilled liar, but something about his demeanor and the tone of his voice made her believe him. "Did you go MIA for him?"

His eye twitched. It was subtle, but told Bianca she'd hit the mark. "Why do you think someone poisoned him?"

"Everyone tied to Operation Warfighter seems to have a target on their backs."

"I agree. Why?"

"You tell me."

He folded his arms across his chest. A gold bracelet around his wrist reflected the overhead lighting. "Did you figure out the numbers?"

"McConnell Place in Chicago. What's going down there?"

His tight smile told her she'd hit the mark again. "Besides the president's speech?"

"Is someone going to attempt to assassinate the president?"

Tephra snapped his fingers. "You are a smart one, aren't you? That's why, after I read your file, I knew you'd be the one to help me out of my jam here. Of course, with a bounty on your head, I had to make it look good. Had to make sure no one got the assignment but me."

"What situation?"

"Someone's going to shoot the president tomorrow night, but he's not the only one eating a bullet. I will too."

"You?"

"I'm coming out of hiding, you see. I wanted out, been trying to get out for years. Patrick agreed to help me, but we couldn't keep it quiet like I wanted. He had to get permission from the White House and it got turned into a big show. A hero's welcome home party. It's super top secret, all been arranged by the vice president. The party line is she and her team located me and sent in a Special Forces unit to free me from a Pakistani prison. That's where I've been all these years, you know, not doing wet work for my government."

He rubbed a hand over his face. He looked tired, defeated. "I'm supposed to show up in uniform tomorrow night and receive a medal. Shake the president's hand and tell the world the vice president is my hero. Get my picture taken with them while the Vice President Banner gets the credit for rescuing me. Norman will have to acknowledge her brilliance and astute military planning. Can you imagine? Haley Banner, an astute military planner? She's cunning, I'll give her that, but..." He waved off whatever he was going to say. "Someone pretending to be one of Otto Grimes' mercenaries will take a potshot at Norman and Vice President Banner. I'm to jump in front of the V.P. and take the bullet. I'm told Norman won't die and neither will I, but I don't believe it. The V.P. will stand there with our blood on her hands and vow revenge."

Bianca tried not to laugh. "You can't be serious."

"Trust me, it's all scripted like some goddamn reality show. I'm not supposed to know the details, and I was told not to worry, that the assassin won't aim for my vital parts, but they're full of shit. I'm a goddamned nightmare for them so they're going to kill me off. The V.P.'s approval rating will soar and it'll be a landslide vote next month when she's elected to president."

"You're delusional."

His eyes flattened. "You're delusional if you think this isn't true."

"Why would I believe you?"

"I haven't lied to you yet."

They stood there in a glare-off, neither backing down. Finally, Tephra pointed at her face, "How's the cheek, sweetheart?"

Bastard. "How's your shoulder?"

He grinned. "I bet you make Reese absolutely crazy."

"You hurt me again and he'll kill you."

He shrugged, held out his hands, palms up. "I'm already a dead man walking."

If she'd still had the Glock, he would just be a dead man. *He said he needs your help. Play along until you can get out of here.* "Why are you going along with the script?"

"If you knew someone was going to shoot the president, wouldn't you try to stop them? Besides, if I don't show up, Patrick will die. This little poisoning thing is a reminder to me to follow the script and not do anything stupid."

"Like ask me for help?"

"Banner wants another four years, but she wants it in the

president's seat. Patrick and I figured out this little stunt is to kill off Norman and pave the way for her to have an easy election win."

"Seems extreme for a reelection bid."

"For someone so intelligent, you're pretty naïve."

Gullible was more like it. As evidenced by the fact she was still standing there talking to an assassin. *Well, besides the fact that he was blocking the door...*

Tephra eyed her, waiting for a comeback.

She didn't give it to him. A tension, low but pervasive in her stomach told her she actually believed him. Rory Tephra, assassin and certified crazy person, was telling the truth. "How exactly do you think I can help?"

He blinked, and she may have imagined the look of relief that slid across his face, but she didn't imagine the sound of it in his voice. "I have to show up and play my part tomorrow night or Patrick will die. He's the only family I have and I owe him, big time, for many, many things you'd never understand. But you—you and Reese—the two of you can expose the V.P. and stop the assassination. Catch whoever is going to kill me and President Norman and make them give up Banner."

She really was gullible because she knew that was exactly what she needed to do. *If* any of this was true. "I need something from you in return."

"Besides me letting you live?"

"Who exactly wants me dead and why?"

"I can't believe you haven't figure it out."

"It's my boss, Jonathan, isn't it?"

"Jonathan? Hell, no, but you're not going to like the answer."

"Tell me anyway."

Just as Tephra opened his mouth to answer, all hell broke loose.

CHAPTER TWENTY-SIX

Cal was jogging down the corridor when a loud blaring started above his head and people began to scatter.

Fire alarm.

Threat.

Real or imagined? That was the question. If it was a drill, they couldn't have picked a worse time. From the way the hospital staff were acting, this was no drill.

But was there really a fire?

No. In his gut, he knew there was no fire. This was a ploy to get someone inside the hospital to come outside. Bianca? The senator?

You're paranoid. Well, he'd spent too many years in the field not to be. What better way to find a target than to set up on a nearby building and scan the crowds below? Easy as shooting fish in a barrel.

Evacuating the hospital wasn't the most brilliant idea, however, unless the assailant could cover all the exits. Hard to do with a place this size. Hard, but not impossible.

This part of the building was old, built before the laws requiring sprinkler systems. Cal skirted around fleeing people. Fire or no fire, he had to find Bianca. Keep her from running outside.

I can't lose her. Not again.

Bianca flinched and covered her ears as the alarm shrieked above her. "We have to get out of here!"

Tephra shook his head. "Could be a trap."

They locked eyes, the same thought suddenly dawning on both of them. "Senator Halston," Bianca said.

At the same time Tephra said, "Patrick!"

Tephra went for the door, Bianca followed him. "That way," she yelled, pointing to Radiology once they were in the hallway.

People were scrambling in all directions, the main stream heading across their path and to the left. An exit. Tephra grabbed Bianca's arm and pulled her behind him, forming a human shield as he plowed through the masses.

Someone knocked into her and she lost her balance. She didn't fall, thanks to the steadying hand Tephra had on her. *Protective. Just like Cal.*

Cal. She had to get to him, get a message to him. As she was jostled to and fro, she drew out her cell. Still no service. Of course not, she was in the basement.

They came to a T in the halls. "Which way?" Tephra asked.

Bianca looked down one and then down the other. Double wide swinging doors were at the ends of each. The shiny tile floors and overhead lights made everything look the same.

The alarm continued to shriek. Her brain was being bombarded with information. *Focus, Bianca.* She closed her eyes for a second, remembering the things she'd seen earlier, hoping she would remember some kind of landmark.

Her eyes snapped open, her attention turning upward. There. The colored stripes. The blue one ran to the double doors at the Radiology Department.

"Right," she told Tephra. "Beyond those doors."

They ran down the corridor, checking the gurneys and the nurses pushing them, looking for Halston. When they didn't spot him, they pushed on through the swinging doors and entered the x-ray department's waiting room.

Bianca pointed. "They took him behind that door."

Tephra again led the way as they ignored the warning signs and burst into the ultrasound area.

The room was empty.

Tephra double-checked behind several doors, but there was no one and nothing. He swore and motioned for her to follow him back out.

"What do we do now?" she asked as they left radiology.

He picked up a scrub hat someone had lost in the chaos and shoved it on her head, securing her ponytail under it. Then he brought the mask back up over her mouth. "The only thing we can do. We disappear."

CHAPTER TWENTY-SEVEN

From the moment he'd watched the elevator doors close with Bianca inside, Cal had felt a gnawing panic. He'd watched the light above the elevator as it illuminated each floor, stopping on 1. Problem was, once he'd gotten to the first floor, he couldn't find her. He couldn't find Senator Halston or Halston's bodyguard either. They'd all vanished.

And then, miracle of miracles, the CNA who'd been helping Bianca had hurried by. Cal had stopped her and turned on the charm.

Asking her where they'd taken Halston would have put the gal on alert and bring trouble on his head, so Cal took another route. He asked her about the cute nurse she'd ridden down in the elevator with. Where could he find her?

The CNA must have seen the honest truth in Cal's eyes— that he was smitten. "Lower level," she'd told him. "She's hanging around radiology waiting for the senator."

"Thank you."

He'd kissed her cheek with relief and she'd hollered after him as he sprinted back to the elevators. "Good luck!"

Luck. He'd needed luck, because when he'd gotten to radiology, Bianca wasn't there.

He'd lost her. *In more ways than one*, the voice in his head told him.

For some idiotic reason, memories of his lost friends flashed through his mind and stole his breath. Tank, the big lug, intercepting a football Cal had thrown and running it in for a touchdown during one of their breaks while waiting for orders in Afghanistan. Avery singing *Can't Touch This* and doing his MC Hammer routine after a successful mission saving a group of missionaries in a Colombian jungle. Butcher discussing quantum physics one night under the stars with an American professor they'd rescued from a Somalian prison.

All three men's bodies limp and lifeless.

Cal struggled to breathe, feeling like he'd been hit in the nuts with a baseball bat. *My fault.* Losing his friends, losing Bianca... *my fault.*

People swarmed out of various rooms, knocking into him. He plowed against the tide with one shoulder, his uninjured one, and kept looking for Bianca in her Mickey Mouse shirt. She might still be wearing a mask—smart girl—to help hide her identity, but there was no way he'd miss that white-blonde hair of hers and her purple glasses.

Radiology. Where the fuck was it?

Cal grabbed a passing nurse. "Where's X-ray?"

She jerked her arm out of his grip. "Sir, you need to leave. This is not a drill."

The fire alarm continued to blare and Cal had to yell over it. "My wife's in radiology. I'm not leaving without her."

"Radiology's been evacuated. The nurses will take care of her." Now she grabbed his arm. "You come with me."

He removed her fingers, not in a brusque way, but with force. "No, ma'am. Just point me toward the radiology department."

She must have seen the determination in his eyes. "See that blue line up there?" She pointed to the wall and a blue stripe of paint near the ceiling. A yellow stripe ran above it and a red one below. "Follow that. It'll lead you right to her. But I'm telling you, she's not there."

He nodded and took off, once more fighting against the stream of evacuating people, patients, and staff. The blue stripe turned a corner and so did Cal. This hallway was clearer and he raced down it, continuing to follow that damned stripe.

Another turn and he caught sight of the senator's bodyguard jogging around a patient in a wheelchair, headed for an exit sign.

"Hey!" Cal yelled, but the man didn't stop. Probably didn't hear him over the alarm and the noise. So he gave chase, even though that was the opposite direction from the blue stripe.

When he burst through the exit door, he found himself at a back dock, an ambulance backed up to the concrete and the senator being loaded into it by a nurse and two EMTs.

The bodyguard's hand went immediately to his weapon. The nurse glanced up.

But it wasn't Bianca's blue eyes looking back at him from behind her purple frames, or her blond ponytail swinging around the nurse's shoulders.

Cal pulled up short and raised his hands to let the guard know he meant no harm. "I'm looking for the nurse who rode down in the elevator with the senator. Have you seen her?"

The man shook his head and Cal turned on his heel and went back inside, yanking out his cell phone to see if he'd received any messages. *No service.* He nearly threw the thing against the nursing station as he passed by.

If Bianca had evacuated like everyone else, she'd be outside. Maybe she was at the truck, waiting for him with Maggie. He prayed she'd at least thought about the fact her assassin could be out there and had taken precautions.

But she wasn't a trained SEAL or even a field agent. His gut cramped so hard, he nearly doubled over. Fighting the emotion, Cal headed for the exit.

"Reese!"

Hearing his name called with such authority brought Cal up short. He spun around and nearly dropped his phone. Instead he snapped into a salute. "Senior Chief?"

Justin Lugmeyer strode toward him, seeming unfazed by the

fire alarm or the last few people running by. He gave a quick return salute. "What are doing here, SEAL?"

There was too much going on, too much to explain, and no goddamn time. "Trying to find my wife. What are you doing here?"

As the man drew closer, it dawned on Cal that Lugmeyer wasn't in uniform. "You missed your hearing this morning."

Not an answer. "How did you find me?"

Anger snapped in Lugmeyer's eyes. He wasn't used to being questioned. "I met up with Senator Halston to support him on his stops today. He became ill and I accompanied him here. I never expected to find you roaming the halls."

Cal's gut gave a funny twinge. "Huh, I didn't see you upstairs." At the narrowing of Lugmeyer's eyes, Cal added, "Sir."

The senior chief locked his pale eyes on Cal. "I stepped outside the hospital to make some calls earlier. The senator appears to have been poisoned. That may affect national security." He stepped closer, getting in Cal's face. "Imagine my surprise to find you here."

"I can explain everything, but right now I have to find Bianca."

Lugmeyer held his position, the sour look still on his face. "Where is she, your wife?"

"I don't know. She was with the senator, then disappeared before the alarm went off."

"Where's the senator?"

"They took him out back to an ambulance. I don't know where they are transporting him."

A muscle jumped in Lugmeyer's stony face. "Are you sure your wife is still in the building?"

"No, sir," he answered honestly. "But I have to find her."

"I'm sorry, son, but since you didn't show up for your hearing this morning, you've been declared AWOL. It's my duty to take you into custody and back to San Diego, regardless of what's going on with your wife."

Cal's pulse sped like a racecar. He wished someone would turn off that damned alarm so he could think. "With all due respect, sir, that's not going to happen."

He started to walk away, felt a strong hand grab his shoulder. "A good SEAL follows orders, Reese."

A good SEAL...

The words rang in his head. He'd heard those before. Heard them come out of Lugmeyer's mouth, but something clicked in his brain.

Warfighter.

Cal grabbed his head. A thousand images splintered in his brain, the jagged edges rising and falling but not coming together. Until they did.

———————

"Something doesn't feel right." The words had rolled off his tongue that night as Cal and his men watched the camp.

"It's too quiet," Tank had said.

"Where are the guards?" Avery had asked over his comm unit.

Cal had listened to the stillness. Too quiet was right, not even the barking of a dog from the village three clicks away or the scratching of a scorpion in the sand.

But he'd felt the presence of men. Many more men than in his team. Trap.

He had no proof, only his finely tuned instincts. That and the fact he knew Lugmeyer was keeping something from them. Something crucial to this mission. Cal had overheard him giving a promise to someone over the sat phone that this time the mission would be accomplished and the desired outcome achieved. "The warfighters will be eliminated," Lugmeyer had said. "No matter what."

At the time, Cal hadn't thought much of it. "Command, this is Eagle. Over."

Lugmeyer had responded. "This is Command, Eagle. Sit rep?"

220

Cal rattled off the bare facts, conveying his hesitation to enter the cave as best as he could.

"Eagle, this is a go," Lugmeyer said in his ear. "I repeat, Operation Warfighter is a go."

Warfighter. The reference was usually associated with soldiers. Cal had assumed in this case it referred to taking out Grimes and his soldiers, but suddenly Cal wasn't so sure.

He tried to shake off the nagging doubt. Lugmeyer, betray them? Never.

But after a minute… "Stand down," Cal told his men. He shook his head hoping for clarity. His guts churned. He always followed orders, but this time… "Abort."

Silence from his superior. Then, "A good SEAL follows orders, Eagle. Your orders are to engage the enemy. Now!"

"Lieutenant?" Tank's voice was solid in Cal's ear. "We follow you."

Damn. He couldn't do it. He just couldn't do—

Then from out of nowhere, the bullets started flying.

Shifting his shoulder, Cal tried to duck out from his superior's hold, but Lugmeyer put him in a choke hold and tried to sweep his feet out from under him.

Cal didn't hesitate. With anger rushing through his system, he threw the man over his shoulder and laid him out on the floor.

Lugmeyer looked stunned, his lungs struggling to draw air. Finally, he hissed. "You assaulted me."

"You assaulted me first. And you ordered me and my men into a no-win situation. You knew it was a trap, didn't you?"

Slowly, Lugmeyer sat up, then came to his knees, keeping a wary eye on Cal. "You're suffering from PTSD." He gained his feet, half bent over, and Cal took a step back in case he decided to rush him. "I'll forgive it this time, but if it ever happens again…"

The anger was still working through his veins. "This? This

221

isn't fucking PTSD. This is me putting you on alert. When I get back to San Diego, I'm going to see the committee for my hearing and I'm telling them what you did. But right now, I'm going to find my wife. Don't try to stop me again."

Lugmeyer lunged as Cal suspected, but he was ready for him. He cold-cocked his senior chief in the jaw, sending the man down. Lugmeyer did a belly-flop to the floor and didn't get up. Cal swallowed against the lump of acid in his throat, stepped over the man, and headed for the nearest exit.

The door led to a stairwell, the stairwell to the first floor and outside.

The hospital was a huge place with multiple exits so she could be anywhere, fighting her way through the crowds and looking for him. He couldn't see over so many people so he scrambled up on an ambulance and searched the crowd, calling Bianca's cell at the same time. The call went straight to voicemail.

The inside alarm ceased, leaving a ringing noise in his ears. In the distance, he heard sirens. The faces of his friends swam through this mind again and sweat trickled down the back of his neck.

How could you let this happen? How could you let her go?

They'd made it up a long tunnel and out into the sunshine. Outside, chaos ensued. Tephra's hand was fisted in Bianca's lab coat as he pulled her through the crowd. She thought he was simply helping her get clear of the throngs of people, but echoes of doubt kept looping through her head.

Everything he told me could be a lie.

He could still want to kill me...

...or Cal. I could be nothing more than bait.

The endless chatter inside her head assailed her to the point she couldn't think straight. She could be following Tephra right to her death.

A few feet from an alley, she pulled up short, knocking his hand loose from her jacket. "Enough," she said. "We're not going any farther until you tell me who hired you and why."

While she was panting from the run, he wasn't even breathing hard. His eyes darted around the area. His body was still primed for a fast getaway. "A third party. Someone the V.P. has at her beck and call." His eyes met hers. "Someone who knew all the *ground* details of Operation Warfighter."

Ground details. No one knew those except the men actually going in. In the Otto Grimes case, Command and Control gave the go-ahead and the parameters of the mission to a selected commander/officer-in-charge and his senior chief. They passed on the assignment to their elite squad and made the nitty-gritty details with the SEALs.

Bianca tried not to be shocked. "Lugmeyer?"

Tephra looked away. "He wants my job."

Her brain refused to process the information. "He sacrificed his own men because he wants *your* job? And I thought I was abnormal."

"Abnormal? You're weird and I'm stupid, but we're both loyal to our country. I went into black ops to serve. He wants my job because he's sick. He entered the military and became a sniper because he likes killing people. Twenty years of shooting the enemy, but then he made senior chief. No more sniping. Taking out his own team was to prove to the V.P. he was cut out for wet work."

"He killed his own men?"

He gave her that, *god, you're naïve* look again.

"But Lugmeyer was injured in the gun fight."

"He shot himself in the calf to make it look good. What better way to take suspicion off him if there was any?"

Sickness burned in her throat. "He let Cal live."

"He didn't intend to. Something went wrong with his plan."

Tephra tapped his temple. "And Cal probably saw or heard something that could prove his senior chief is guilty, but it's buried. He was betrayed by the one man he trusts above everyone. It's buried deep."

Bianca knew all about burying the pain of betrayal. Suddenly, her brain snapped to attention. "The PTSD. Cal is suffering from the trauma of losing his men, *and* he's dealing with Lugmeyer's betrayal."

"I'm not a psychiatrist, but I'd say that makes sense."

"Is Lugmeyer the one who's going to shoot the president tomorrow night?"

"That's my guess."

A ringing came from Bianca's pocket. "It's Cal."

"I have to go find the senator."

"Don't move." She hit the connect button, sensing Cal's relief through the phone when she answered. "Cal, it's me. I'm okay."

"Where the hell are you?"

Shadows darkened this side of the building. Tephra was trying to slip off and she grabbed the back of his scrub top. "East side. Can you make it to the parking lot? Rory and I will meet you at the truck."

"Rory?" Cal said at the same time Tephra said, "I'm not meeting anyone. I'm going to find Patrick."

"Senator Halston's gone," Cal said. He must have heard Tephra. "I don't know where. They took him off in an ambulance."

Tephra could easily have knocked her on her butt, but she held onto the scrub shirt and gave him the evil eye as she shifted the phone from her mouth. "You need to trust Cal. He can help you." Then she told Cal, "We're on the opposite side of the building from the parking lot, so it'll take us five minutes or so to get to the truck, but we'll be there. We have a lot to tell you."

"Don't hang up. Keep talking to me as you walk."

The connection was his lifeline. Hers as well. She released Tephra's shirt and made sure he was going to follow. He gave her a reluctant nod, then they started jogging, staying close to the brick building.

Bianca led the way. "We're heading for the southwest corner now. Near the cancer center."

Sounds coming from Cal's end suggested he was running as well. Fire truck sirens nearly drowned out his voice. "You're sure you're okay?"

"I'm fine." *But you won't be once we tell you the truth.* She tried not to think about how Lugmeyer's betrayal would crush the last of Cal's goodness. "Have you heard from Emit?"

"Negative. I'll call him once we're clear of the hospital."

The parking lot, truck, and Maggie were only a hundred yards away. Bianca had just started around the corner when a woman coming from the other direction crashed into her.

Bianca flew back when she bumped into the solid wall of Tephra. He grabbed her shoulders and stood her back upright.

"Oh, I'm so sorry," the woman said, also grabbing hold of Bianca's arm as if trying not to lose her own balance. She wore a floral top, her face covered by a mask. Bianca caught sight of her badge...Katy Smitrelny. The CNA.

Her fingers dug into Bianca's arm. She was still wearing her gloves. The latex felt sticky. Bianca knew she was only trying to make sure she hadn't done any harm, but Bianca couldn't stand the sensation of the gloves on her skin, the pressure of the woman's fingers. Why was she wearing a mask and gloves out here? Was she helping move patients?

Bianca jerked back. "No problem. Excuse us."

She skirted Katy and Tephra followed. When Bianca looked back, she saw Tephra slipping a handgun into the waist of his scrubs behind him.

"What was that?" Cal's voice came from her phone. "What happened?"

She stopped, covered the mouthpiece, and said to Tephra. "You pulled a gun on a CNA?"

He shrugged. "I pull a gun on everyone. It's second nature."

The thought actually made her feel safer. She uncovered the mouthpiece. "Ran into someone," she told Cal. "No big deal. Is Senator Halston safe?"

His voice sounded muffled, his breathing kicking up a notch. In the background, she heard fire trucks. "No idea. Where are you now?"

"Almost to Parking Lot B. There's a lot of people by their cars. Should we take the sidewalk to get to Lot A, or try to be more discreet?"

"You trust Tephra?"

She glanced over her shoulder. The man's intense gaze was analyzing everything in front of them as well as keeping tabs on the rear. If he was lying, he was the best she'd ever met. He'd been willing to shoot Katy to keep her safe. "Yes."

"Let him decide the safest route."

She fell back and gave Tephra a nod. "You lead. We're heading to Lot A across that divider."

The fire trucks surrounded the building, silencing their sirens. Bianca couldn't see any smoke or fire, so it was probably a false alarm. Tephra slowed, once again focusing on the path ahead of them. "Watch our six," he said to her.

"You got it." She lowered her voice as he walked away and whispered to Cal. "What's a six and how do I watch it?"

"Your backside. Keep an eye out for anyone coming up behind you."

Was it necessary to speak like they were in an old western movie? She checked behind her. The path they'd run was clear. No sign of Katy or anyone else. "Got it."

When she turned back around, Tephra was eyeing her. She saw police cars pulling up behind the fire engines. "We're both dressed as hospital staff, although your black slacks and heels are out of character for the nurses here. We should be able to pass normal people without question, but if there's an assassin in the area, you'll stand out." He pointed to the edge of the lot. "Hug that tree line and don't draw attention."

Bianca assented, then told Cal as she followed Tephra, "We're taking a circuitous route along the back of the lot."

He let out a heavy sigh. "Good."

Good? Cal never thought anything was good. "Are you okay?"

He was still running from the sounds of his hard exhales as he spoke. "Just never thought I'd be happy about you depending on him to keep you safe."

She stepped over a curb, following Tephra around a flowerbed. The shadowy tree line was only a few feet away. She checked the crowd on their right. Everyone in the lot was either in their cars or standing in groups, looking at the hospital and the fire trucks. Police officers had cordoned off the entrances and were starting to take statements. "You and me both."

Another curb hop and they made it. Bianca's heels sunk in the soft grass. Keeping her eyes pinned on Tephra's back, she stepped behind an oak tree, and kicked off her shoes. "We're almost there."

She ran to catch up with Tephra, which required her to hop over tangles of brambles and work her way through some tight bushes. They were passing by tall, skinny evergreens now, each tree nestled smack dab up against the other creating a wall. The branches prickled her skin but she had to keep grabbing them in order to keep her balance. The hospital needed a new landscaper. Of course, who saw any of this muck in the middle of the divider unless it was from the condo windows on the other side? "Twenty feet or so," she said to Cal, "and I should be able to pop out from behind the hedge and see the truck."

Tephra stopped suddenly, Bianca nearly plowing into his back. Her glasses slid to the end of her nose. "Hey." She pushed them back up. "The truck is in the next lot over."

"You won't be needing it," a man's voice said.

The voice was familiar. Bianca stood on her tiptoes and peered over Tephra's shoulder.

Justin Lugmeyer emerged from a second set of evergreens

across from them and stared back at her. He held a cold-looking black gun in his hands and pointed it at Tephra's chest. The barrel had an extension on it...a silencer.

"So you took up with the enemy, huh, Rory? What kind of soldier are you?" Lugmeyer was dressed in plain clothes. His eyes were hard and his jaw looked swollen on the left side. Or maybe that was only a shadow created by the trees. "Things will not go well for you or your mentor now. I suggest if you want him to live out the night, you move away."

Bianca dropped down, shielding herself behind Tephra's back. What the hell was Lugmeyer doing here?

Keeping tabs on Halston. Was he the one who poisoned him?

"Don't do anything stupid." Tephra raised his hands high in the air. As he did so, the scrub shirt rose and Bianca saw the gun handle peeking out of his waistband.

"Change of plans," she whispered into the phone. "You're going to have to come get me, Cal."

She dropped the phone and reached for the gun.

CHAPTER TWENTY-EIGHT

You're going to have to come get me, Cal.

Cal was closing in on the area behind Lot B when he heard the thud of Bianca's phone. Had she dropped it? A second later, he jumped a low-cut evergreen hedge and heard the unmistakable sound of a gun going off.

"Bianca!" he screamed into the phone, still running for the trees that formed a straight line behind the lot.

The only answer was a soft *pfft, pfft* sound. Almost too soft for the phone to pick up.

Cal knew that sound. *Silencer.*

His head felt like it would explode right along with his heart. Someone was shooting at Bianca. Again.

Defend. Sliding over the hood of a Beamer, he grabbed his gun from its hiding place while keeping the phone at his ear with his other hand. Someone in the parking lot—probably the owner of the car—yelled at him, but he kept going.

In his ear, he heard Bianca's voice, far away but still understandable. *"Tephra was bringing me here to meet up with you, Lugmeyer. He was going to kill me, but I wanted to talk to you first. I wanted to tell you you're an ass. You should have let me see my husband in Germany."*

The relief at hearing her voice was instantaneous. His knees, in fact, nearly buckled.

Another voice, this one more muted, answered. *"You're lying. Tephra didn't even know I was here."*

Lugmeyer. Firing on Tephra and Bianca? It didn't make sense.

His senior chief had been acting off since the Grimes mission, stress probably, but what was he doing going after Bianca?

"You don't have to kill Cal. He doesn't remember what you did in Afghanistan."

What was she talking about?

He hit the first tree and slowed, slipping behind a sizable oak and scanning the area. Two rows of evergreens formed a screen between the parking lot and the building next door. While they were well maintained from the parking lot side, here they were a tangled mess.

The phone was still pressed to his ear, a distinct silence raising the hair on the back of his neck.

Tephra and Bianca should have entered from the other end. How far down were they? He tried to align his internal compass with where he'd heard the echo of the gunshot. *Come on, Bianca. Tell me where you are.*

"But he might remember," Lugmeyer said. *"And I can't have that."*

"You killed Cal's men, didn't you?"

Like a flash grenade going off in his head, a new memory rose to the surface. The base of Tank's head, right where it connected to his spinal cord, exploding from a well-placed sniper shot.

But the shot hadn't come from the enemy they'd been approaching. The shot had come from behind their lookout point.

In rapid succession, Avery and Butcher had also gone down. Hit in the same spot.

Cal knocked the palm of his hand into his forehead. The PTSD had to be playing games with him. There was no way...

Lugmeyer's voice broke through the fog sending a chill

down Cal's already rigid spine. *"Warfighters sometimes have to die for the greater good."*

Cal's insides turned to stone. The truth bit deep. The man he had trusted above all others had turned on him. On Tank and Avery and Butcher.

I'll kill him. Rage seethed in Cal's bones. He locked his teeth.

A coldness buried deep in his gut spread through his system. Lugmeyer was shooting at his wife. Lugmeyer…

His fingers went numb. He dropped the phone, his hand with the gun trembling with the effort it took to hold onto it.

Fuck! He scrubbed his eyes, ground his teeth. This was not the time for an episode.

Control your focus. Slow down the adrenaline.

Every mission required the same discipline. He zeroed in on a tiny lizard pretending to be part of the tree. The animal's tiny eyeballs swung in circles, his body a mass of nerves in total flight node.

Not dissimilar to Cal's. Except he would never flee.

Oh, no. He was and always had been tuned for fight rather than flight. One of the reasons it had been better for him to go on mission after successive mission. The rage inside that he'd felt all these years had to be buried around Bianca. He would never let it get the best of him and hit her—never that—but he felt like he couldn't even raise his voice around her. Her mother's ghost always stood between them.

Closing his eyes, he fisted his open hand into a ball, drew a quiet breath, and thought of Bianca's smiling face.

His own lips drew up at the corners in response.

Protect.

I will not lose her.

His breathing slowed, circulation returned to his fingers. He opened his eyes and ever so slowly began stalking the assassin after his wife.

Cooper ran with Thomas and Emit across the crowded parking lot. "Where'd the fucker go?"

They'd found the truck Reese had stolen from the vineyard, had been on their way inside the hospital when the fire alarm had gone off. Emit Petit, smart man, had figured out quickly that all Cooper cared about was Bianca's safety.

He'd told Cooper and Thomas a hell of a story about Rory Tephra, Senator Halston, and Bianca's plans to prove Reese's op was compromised from an internal leak. Petit had even helped them locate the stolen truck. Thing was, Cooper didn't think even Petit knew the whole story behind whatever Bianca was trying to do.

"There!" Petit pointed to the other end of the lot where a double line of oak trees separated the hospital's parking lots from a high-rise condominium. "That's where the gunshot came from. That's where Cal was headed."

Cooper renewed his speed, diving around people and vehicles. He was a big man, so he tended to knock into people more than he avoided them. "Sorry," he said as he nearly took out a nurse. He whirled to his left and had to repeat the apology to bystander who swore at him. "Sorry."

What had happened inside the hospital? The firefighters and cops were clustered on the other side of building around the main entrance, but no hoses were lying on the ground, no water spraying anywhere. No smoke or flames came out of the building.

False alarm.

Which meant someone wanted to create chaos, either to escape or do something illegal inside. He needed to see the hospital's security tapes.

But not yet. He was *this close* to finding his agent. Her safety and well-being came first.

And then, once she was safe, she had a lot of 'splaining to do.

Somehow Thomas had gotten ahead of him. Cooper poured on more speed, hopping a curb at the edge of the natural divider and cutting the younger agent off as they entered the tree line.

They stopped, breathing hard, and stared into the shadowy hallway the trees created. Petit brought up the rear. "Oh, man, that's a frickin' mess."

Yes, it was. Twin oaks anchored the ends of the tree line but in between the two rows of evergreen shrubs planted only a few feet apart, the landscape was in disarray. "You sure he entered here?"

Petit nodded. Thomas drew out his phone, tapped the screen twice, and had an instant flashlight. He shone it around the area where they stood and Cooper saw the light hit metal on the ground. He bent down and retrieved a cheap cell phone. He held it up and wondered if Reese or Bianca had been using it. A noise came from the speaker and he realized it was an open line.

Cooper made a quiet motion with his free hand and held up the phone so all three of them could listen.

"According to the APA's Diagnostic and Statistical Manual of Mental Disorders—fourth edition, by the way—" Bianca's voice was slightly muffled, but Cooper recognized the tone and clip of her words. *"The 'lack of remorse, as indicated by being indifferent to or rationalizing having hurt, mistreated, or stolen from another' is a prime indicator of antisocial personality disorder. In present day culture, we often refer to that behavior as psychopathic, although that is not a medically recognized term."*

Thomas frowned and looked perplexed. *Who is she talking to?* he mouthed.

Cooper shrugged. Petit was grinning and nodding his head. "Sounds like our girl," he whispered.

Another voice, this one farther away from the phone, said, "What the fuck are you talking about?"

A male voice. Cooper glanced at Petit. *Reese?* he mouthed.

Petit shook his head and responded with a silent, *Tephra?*

Thomas waved his hand so Cooper would look at him. He exaggerated his lip movements. *Lughead!*

Cooper frowned. Lugmeyer must have followed Halston to the hospital, but what was he doing out here talking to Bianca? Had Lugmeyer fired that shot they'd heard?

And where was Reese?

"I happen to know a lot about personality disorders," Bianca continued. *"My mother suffered from several, and those were exacerbated by her drug and alcohol problems. You don't fit the classic psychopath criteria, but your case may be mild. Rory told me about your unhealthy need to kill people, how you went into the Navy in order to satisfy that need rather than turning to a less socially acceptable form of murder. I wonder why that is…perhaps you also suffer from narcissistic personality disorder? You should really be tested. You perceive your importance in the overall greater good, as you put it, as more than it actually is."*

"You're crazy," Lugmeyer said. *"I don't know how Reese puts up with you."*

Bianca seemed unfazed. *"I hate the word crazy, and for your information, Cal loves me."* She cleared her throat. *"It's possible you've suffered from a psychologically stressful event—I've had a few of those too—and you have PTSD like Cal. You probably refused to accept it so becoming a sniper was your form of stress inoculation training. In fact, your ultimate goal, your dream, has always been to assassinate the president, hasn't it? To show everyone how good you really are, what kind of warfighter you are. You took out your own SEAL team to prove something to the vice president, but it wasn't about taking over Rory's career with the CIA. You knew all along she'd come to you when she was ready to kill the president."*

Cooper frowned hard at the phone, lifted an eyebrow at Petit. The man shook his head and shrugged his shoulders. This was new information to him too.

Silence fell. A silence that made Cooper want to rush into the dense undergrowth and see what the hell he could find.

Seconds stretched into a minute and his skin itched. He

couldn't stand it any longer but as he was about to move, he heard Bianca's voice again. Not from the phone this time. From somewhere north of them. "Hello? Anyone out there?"

"He's gone," a muffled voice said. "You can come out now, B"

"That's Reese," Petit said.

Cooper held the phone to his mouth. "Agent Marx, can you hear me?"

A shuffling noise came through the phone, then Bianca's voice. "This is Agent Marx. Who is this?"

The air left his lungs in a whoosh. "Bianca, it's Cooper."

"Cooper? How did you get Cal's phone?"

Like that was the most important thing at the moment. "Where are you?"

"At the hospital. Behind Parking Lot B on the south side. Where are you?"

"The other end, behind Lot A. Stay where you are. I'm coming to get you."

In the background, he heard Reese say something, but he couldn't make out the words. Bianca covered the mouthpiece and said something back to him, then spoke to Cooper. "We need to get out of here, quickly. There are police officers approaching and it would be ill advised for them to take me into custody. Plus, there's an assassin after me. I can explain everything once we're someplace safe."

"Like I said, Agent Marx." Cooper started tramping through the brush, Thomas and Petit following. "Stay where you are. If you don't, *I'll* put a bullet in your ass. *Comprende?*"

A slight pause. Then, "Yes, sir."

CHAPTER TWENTY-NINE

Gifted or cursed? With her photographic memory and high IQ, Cal often wondered which Bianca was.

It was ten minutes after midnight. They'd returned to the winery and now sat in the room downstairs with the long table they'd eaten breakfast at the previous day. Everyone, except Bianca.

She was in a manic stage, pacing and writing on a rolling white board Emit had brought in for her. In one hand she brandished a black marker, writing furiously on the board as she talked to herself. In the other, she held several colored markers, using them for different people's names. Her system looked a lot like Emit's TrackMap, only messier.

"And then..." She stopped and wrote something Cal couldn't read. Maggie, lying next to his feet, lifted her head and whined softly as if Bianca's craziness worried her as much as it did him.

"But first...no that's not right." She used her other hand to erase what she'd just written. "Except he..."

Cal sat at one end of the table, Emit, Cooper Harris, and Thomas Mann lined up on his left. The three of them took notes on paper and computers. Coffee had been brought in while Bianca had recounted everything Tephra had told her at the hospital. Like Lugmeyer, Rory Tephra had disappeared.

And now Bianca was intent on connecting all the dots they had and filling in the ones still missing.

"If this hypothesis is true..." Bianca drew an arrow to a

bubble of words. "No, that timeline doesn't work." She slashed a line through the arrow.

Emit shot Cal a concerned look. Cal felt his already tense nerves tighten more. He'd seen this type of obsession in her before. When she was overly stressed or when she'd discovered something her logical brain couldn't figure out, she went into a mental meltdown.

Cursed or gifted?

Suddenly, she stopped, stepped back, and stared at the board, unmoving. Her hands fell to her sides. Her body became immobile, as if someone had flipped a switch, turning her manic side off.

Only, Cal knew it hadn't turned off. She'd gone inside her brain. Sometimes that was equally as scary.

"Agent Marx," Harris said. "You want to explain that chicken scratch to us?"

She didn't move, didn't respond.

"Agent Marx?"

"Yo," Mann said. "Earth to Bianca."

Bianca had once tried to explain to Cal how her brain worked—as if it were the sun, the nucleus of a solar system—and every memory, idea, and thought were the planets and stars circling around it. When she was in her manic phase, there was so much cranial activity, so many thoughts and ideas zooming around, she had difficulty latching onto only one. "It's like a meteor storm," she'd told him.

When she did grasp a single idea or thought, it consumed her focus. The other ideas and images floating by disappeared. Reality disappeared. She didn't hear people talking to her, didn't see what was right in front of her eyes.

Usually these breaks didn't last long, but he'd seen her become so fixated on a problem she would forget to eat and wouldn't sleep for days.

He sat forward and lowered his voice. "Give her time. This is her process."

It unnerved them. He could see it in their eyes. He sympathized. "She'll come out of it when she has a solution."

"How long will that take?" Harris asked.

He was a straight-forward guy. A little terse, but Cal liked that. You knew where you stood with Cooper Harris, and he seemed to have Bianca's best interests in mind, valuing her and her idiosyncrasies even though he didn't understand them.

He had listened patiently as Cal and Bianca had given him their accounts of what had happened in the past two days, and then he'd immediately been on the phone to the other SCVC taskforce members, assigning them jobs and telling them to get to Sacramento, pronto.

Harris's main concern now was what was going down at McConnell Place in Chicago and how they were going to prevent it. The clock was ticking. In less than nineteen hours, the President of the United States would take the stage.

"I don't know, but you can't rush her."

Emit poured himself a fresh cup of coffee and gave Maggie some water in a bowl. "Do you believe Tephra, Cal?"

Believing someone and trusting them were two different things. "Bianca believes him, and the only person who can confirm his allegations is in a coma."

Senator Halston had been moved to a private clinic. By the time he'd arrived, he was comatose. His prognosis had gone from bad to worse. Harris's boss, Victor Dupé, had increased the amount of security but they all suspected it might be too little, too late.

Mann's phone dinged. It had been going off constantly with messages from FBI Agent Ronni Punto. He read the message, said, "You're a wanted man, Reese. The Navy has issued a warrant for your arrest. You're officially AWOL and you're wanted on charges for assaulting a senior officer."

He should have done more than assault him. "What about Bianca?"

Mann scrolled through the text. "She's wanted too. The

usual criminal charges...aiding and abetting, harboring a fugitive, and, huh..." He glanced at Harris, then at Cal. "They're saying she pulled the fire alarm at the hospital. She's wanted for malicious intent, reckless endangerment, taking an action to falsely report a fire to cause panic...oh, and the fire department is seeking restitution for costs associated with personnel and equipment responding to the scene."

"What proof do they have it was Bianca?" Emit asked.

Mann typed something back, waited for a response. When it came, he frowned at his phone. "They have video footage of her setting off the alarm."

Everyone glanced at Bianca. As if she felt their stares on her back, she turned.

Her eyes were clear as she looked at Harris. "It wasn't me, but I know who did it."

"Who?" he said.

"Killer Kathy." She walked to the board and tapped the marker on a scribbled word. "AKA Katy Smirtelny."

This was how her brain worked. All the answers were there, like little electrical pulses, throbbing and begging to be put into order. Until she had that one final detail, she couldn't.

A detail like the alias of Killer Kathy. "Her real name is Kasia Wronski. She was born in Poland of Russian-Polish parents. She is one of a set of triplets, all girls. The three of them grew up to be nurses. Between them, we estimate they are responsible for at least ninety deaths throughout Poland, Russia, and the Ukraine while they worked at multiple nursing homes, a hospital, and two orphanages. One sister died five years ago of stomach cancer, the second sister was caught by officials in the act of giving a nursing home resident on overdose of muscle relaxants. Kasia, or Killer Kathy as she became known, escaped

Poland and offered her skills to any country who would pay her to kill people."

"What does that have to do with Reese's mission, Senator Halston, and an assassination attempt on the president?" asked Cooper.

By the look on his face he was tired. They all were. But he was also losing patience with her.

"Everything," Bianca answered. Her brain shifted into fourth gear again. "Remember how I told you earlier about when Thomas and Ronni were investigating her brother at the farm? I was checking satellite footage and listening for any phone conversations originating from there. I accidently picked up a conversation between a very high-powered official with top government clearances"—*my real boss*—"about an operation leak. He was talking about Cal's mission to take out Otto Grimes."

Thomas slouched in his chair, using the chair across from him to prop up his feet. "And you think Halston leaked that info to Killer Kathy. I get it, but why would he do that?"

"He didn't know who she was. I've seen her picture a dozen times, but I didn't recognize her in person today at the hospital. She's had facial work done and has gained twenty pounds at least. Even if the senator was familiar with her Most Wanted rap sheet and picture, he couldn't have known it was her.

"The point is, before I joined the taskforce, I'd been tracking her. I knew she was in Southern California and that she was after a specific target, but I didn't know what. I also knew Senator Halston had been seeing a woman. A woman whose identity he wanted to keep secret."

"And out of all the women in Southern Cali you decided it must be her?" Cooper asked.

Bianca bit the inside of her lip. This was the thing about people who didn't understand how her brain worked. And unfortunately, she couldn't always explain it. "It was a valid hypothesis based on her previous targets and the fact Halston is on the Senate Intelligence Committee."

"Wouldn't Halston have done a thorough background check on anyone he got close to?"

"That's why the senator and Kasia popped up on my radar before I was sent here. He asked his assistant to do a check on one Kathleen Wilmont, which she did, running her through the CIA, FBI, and Interpol. That search pinged my boss's, radar. He had me look into it. Her identity held up, but the one fault Killer Kathy has is her ego. She always uses some variation of her first name. Just like Katy Smirtelny. Kathleen, Kathy, Katy...all variations of her given name. Also, Smirtelny is a play on the polish word *smiertelny.*" Bianca wrote the word in block letters on the white board. "It's an adjective meaning death."

Emit grinned. "You know Polish? How many languages is that, now, Bianca? Eight? Nine?"

There was a difference between recognizing a foreign word and its meaning and being fluent in a language. "As an analyst, I've seen the word a few times in communications between terrorists."

She took a drink of water, purposely slowing herself down. She had to take this group of men from point A to point B to point C. Not vomit information on them the way it was blitzing her brain. "The identity Senator Halston was given was a backstop identity. One I was familiar with. I've seen that type of backstop in records of operations that our country has participated in since 9/11. Every analyst who builds a backstop identity leaves a signature. Something that ninety-nine percent of people would never notice. But I do."

Cal sat forwarded. "What are you saying, B?"

He'd been quiet—too quiet—the whole ride back and now during this discussion. He was keeping something to himself, she just didn't know what. She feared it had something to do with her and their relationship. Or that he was blaming himself for letting her out of his sight, and not capturing his senior chief who'd tried to kill her.

She looked at his stubbled jaw and the dark shadows under his eyes. As soon as she could get him alone, she'd find out what was bothering him. For now, there was nothing she could do but answer his question. "I know who created Kasia's Kathleen Wilmont identity."

"Who?" Cooper demanded.

"A former CIA analyst who's now in the White House."

All four men's faces blanched as understanding dawned. Cooper looked positively grim. "You're not saying…"

"I am."

Emit raised his brows. "Vice President Haley Banner?"

Bianca nodded. "It matches with what Rory told me. She's manipulated this whole thing. The senator may not have actually leaked anything about Cal's mission. Kasia knew the details from Vice President Banner, but Banner needed to throw suspicion elsewhere and she needed Kasia to get close to the senator so they could poison him at the right moment in order to force Tephra to go through with her plan."

Emit received a text, the chime of his phone interrupting her. He read it and looked up at Cooper. "Your people are here, Agent Harris."

"Good." Cooper stood as the door opened and Ronni, Bobby, and Nelson came into the room.

Ronni rushed to Bianca and grabbed her in a bear hug. Maggie jumped up, wagging and sniffing at the newcomers. "I'm so glad you're alive," Ronni said.

Bianca couldn't move. She fought her natural reflex to wiggle out of the embrace, forced herself to pat Ronni on the back. It was an awkward pat, but a pat nonetheless. "What are you doing here?"

"You're part of the taskforce. Where else would I be?" She broke the hug but kept her hands on Bianca's arms. Another form of affection that normally made Bianca uncomfortable with anyone but Cal. Somehow it didn't bother her with Ronni. "And from what Cooper's told us, sounds like you can use all the help you can get. Why didn't you tell us what was going on when this all started?"

Bianca glanced around. All these people. She hadn't wanted to draw anyone in, and yet here they all were, trying to help her and Cal. "I didn't know who was after me or why. I was afraid if I involved you, I would be putting your lives in danger as well."

Ronni's eyes were sad. "My God, Bianca, you're such a strong person."

Strong? She'd been called cold, calculating, and independent, but never strong. "I was simply being logical."

Cooper introduced everyone and brought Ronni, Bobby and Nelson up to date, using Bianca's white board to show the timeline and the connections between the players. "Any update on Tephra's or Lugmeyer's whereabouts?" he asked Bobby.

The man shook his head. "They've both disappeared."

"But we know where they're going," Cal said. Maggie had situated herself next to his feet again.

Ronni sat forward and nodded. "We need to alert the president."

Thomas brought her a cup of coffee and sat by her side. "We have to warn him about Vice President Banner and her plans."

Bianca wished it were that easy. "Banner will deny it, and who will President Norman believe? A disgraced NSA agent and her estranged husband, who are both fugitives? Or his running mate, the Vice President of the United States who's campaigned diligently for him and whom he needs to take the states of Texas and Ohio to carry his reelection?"

"But she's threatening his life," Nelson said. Like Cal, the stubble on his face suggested he was a day or two past his last shave. "If nothing else, we should alert the Secret Service."

Cooper had pulled his chair away from the table during this debate as if needing distance to think. Elbows on his knees, he stared at the floor, rotating a pen in his hands. "A call can be made to alert the Service to a potential threat, but Bianca's right. Banner and Lugmeyer have already laid the groundwork for discrediting her and Reese and we don't have an ounce of proof that any of this is true. Our witness, Tephra, and our possible assassin, Lugmeyer, are both in the wind."

Bianca felt numb. "And President Norman is closer to Haley Banner than he is the First Lady."

All eyes shifted to look at her.

"Are you saying…?" Thomas let the question hang.

"Yes." She paced to her white board once more, wondering why she felt terrible giving up a secret on a woman who wanted her and Cal dead.

Haley Banner was a hard person not to like. She was a friendly, tireless mother of two who brought democrats and republicans together on bills for equal pay and education reform as easily as she won over foreign dignitaries. Another reason it would be difficult to build any kind of case against her without solid testimony or proof of her actions. "She has all her bases covered."

The room fell silent and Bianca felt like a two-ton elephant were on her shoulders. *Analyze! This is what you do!*

There had to be a way to stop Banner and save President Norman.

Her mind went into hurricane mode again and she drew a circle around McConnell Place. "Lugmeyer will be in Chicago along with the president and V.P., but he'll stay off the radar. The only way to grab him is at the dinner before Tephra's presentation. He'll need a good vantage point to take his shot and then a clear exit path. Odds are Banner will bring out Tephra after the president's remarks and before dinner."

"What about Killer Kathy, Katy, Kasia…" Ronni said. "Whatever her name is. Will she be at McConnell Place?"

"No. She'll be here, trying to locate Halston, and staying close to him once she does. Even if Tephra follows the script, the vice president will probably have Kasia take out Halston once the president is dead. The senator knows too much and can figure out the rest."

Cooper, still staring at the floor, tapped the pen against his open palm. "Bobby, send all of this information about Kasia to Dupé and have him get it to the senator's security team."

Thomas glanced at Cooper. "So we're going to Chicago?"

Bobby, typing on his laptop, looked up. "I can call in some favors and score us tickets."

Cooper rose and stared at the white board, his gaze steering clear of Bianca's. "Not all of us, the taskforce will go in alone. Bianca and Reese will stay here with Petit and his team. Their mugs will be on all the no-fly lists, and if the V.P.'s as smart as we think she is, she'll have the FBI and Secret Service on the lookout for both of them. The FBI will be running everyone through facial recognition as they enter the dinner. No way will our fugitives get into McConnell Place without being arrested."

He was right, but irritation burned in Bianca's chest. "We can use Emit's private jet to fly to Chicago, and facial rec or not, Cal can get the two of us in."

All eyes landed on her. Cal's were the most surprised.

It didn't seem all that difficult to grasp. "He's a Navy SEAL. He could get us into the White House unnoticed if necessary."

"Bianca..." Cal started.

She cut him off, pointing a finger at herself. "My job is to protect the President of the United States." She pointed at him. "Yours is to protect its people. I'm not sitting here with the monks and protecting my own hide while the president's in danger. And if Banner gets in office, you and I are both dead."

Leaning on the back of a chair, she switched her attention to Cooper. "You and the team can't go in legitimately either. Lugmeyer will have alerted Banner that you may know what's going down, especially if Dupé alerts anyone with the Secret Service or his cohorts with the FBI. But Cal and I can sneak in. No one knows Justin Lugmeyer as well as Cal. He knows how the man thinks, knows his MO."

Cal made a disgusted noise in the back of his throat. Bianca ignored him. "I've studied Rory Tephra, and now that I've met him in person, I understand what motivates him and how dedicated he is to his country. Cal can shut down Lugmeyer and I'll find Tephra before they bring him out. We'll come up with a plan to expose the truth about Haley Banner."

Cooper finally met her eyes. "It's too dangerous, Bianca. I can't let you do that."

Frustration made her want to shut down. She'd never been a good team player.

But she wasn't about to let her emotions—those irrational, worthless things—cloud her judgment.

Taking a deep breath, she reached for logic, which never let her down, and took a different approach. "I strongly suggest the team go in under false identities in case Lugmeyer has in fact alerted Vice President Banner that you may know more than is good for you. Then you'll be present to back up me and Cal."

Cooper nodded at her. "Good idea, except for the part about you and Reese sneaking in." He cocked his chin at Bobby. "Can you make that happen? False IDs that will stand up to intense scrutiny from the FBI?"

Bobby looked offended. "Is my name Bobby Dyer?"

Thomas snorted and Ronni smiled.

Bianca tried on a smile too. *Time to be a team player.* "You'll need to analyze the layout of the building, any sites an assassin could hide, all the entrances and exits, and do a thorough check on all the people attending the dinner."

Bobby reared back slightly. "That will take hours, possibly days of prep work."

Bingo. Bianca turned her big, baby blues on Cooper. "Or you could let me help. With my memory and analytical skills, I could have it done in no time, improving your odds of a successful outcome by 96.2 percent. But that means, I'll have to come with you. And if I'm going, so is Cal."

A tense silence fell over the group. Everyone shifted their attention to Cooper.

He crossed his arms, leaned back slightly on his heels. His eyes were hard, challenging.

Cal cleared his throat, stood, and moved to Bianca's side. "She's right. You can't argue with her logic."

A sense of pride flushed her skin. She'd made up the calculation of the odds but as she'd pointed out to Cal on a day or two ago, bluffing was one of her strengths. If he considered it manipulation, so be it. For her, it was a way to make sure everyone was as safe as she could make them. She couldn't wield a gun accurately and she didn't know the first thing about being an undercover operative, but she knew how to analyze a dangerous situation in an instant, and that was one skill that could help all of them, including the president.

She met Cooper's challenging glare. "You keep saying I'm part of this team, so let me do my job."

"I'm not saying you can't help Bobby with the prep work." His eyes held hers. "But you're not going to Chicago."

Bianca straightened her spine. "Then we don't have a deal. You, Bobby, and the rest of the team are on your own, and Cal and I will be on our way. Know this, the team will fail. I guarantee it. You need me on this operation, and you need Cal. If you won't use us, then we might as well go on the run tonight. Vice President Banner won't stop until the two of us are dead, and you can't keep us here forever."

Ronni started to chime in, but Cooper raised a hand to stop her. "There's one thing I want to know," he said.

"What?"

"Did you find any dirt on Director Dupé?"

That threw her a curve. She hurried to regroup, her Command and Control training kicking in even after all she'd been through. "I don't know what you're talking about."

Cooper set his hands on his hips. "Stop lying, Bianca. Did you or did you not find anything incriminating about Dupé?"

Who did she have to be loyal to at this point? Her government or Cooper Harris? Easy call. "I did not. Director

Dupé is one of the few men in power who deserves it. He's dedicated to his job, he loves his wife, and he's never so much as got a speeding ticket. You're right to have placed your loyalty with him."

She shifted her weight and thought about going for the jugular...throwing Cooper's secrets in his face.

But she was tired of blackmailing people. Tired of being the drama queen Cal had so often accused her of. All she wanted to do was help and she'd told Cooper the truth about the odds, even if she had fudged the actual percentage of success. It was probably closer to fifty percent, but that was still better than if they went without her. "Look, this is what I've been doing with Command and Control—analyzing situations and the odds of operational success. I can tell you when and where to strike, when and where your *assassin* is most likely to strike. My life is worth nothing if this fails. You have to let Cal and I go to Chicago with you."

Thomas broke the tension with a stage whisper behind his hand. "Tell him you're his only hope."

Bianca frowned and looked at Thomas. "What?"

"You know," he said, "'Help me, Obi Wan Kenobi, you're my only hope.' From *Star Wars*? The way you've made it sound, Bianca, you're our only hope of success."

Ronni shook her head and rolled her eyes. "I'd like nothing more than to keep Bianca safe, too, Cooper, but she has a point."

Cooper screwed up his mouth. "What about you, Reese? You okay with taking your wife into the heart of danger?"

Cal placed a hand on her lower back. She was still wearing the nursing jacket with Mickey Mouse on it. Heat from his hand seeped right through the jacket and his T-shirt underneath. "Bianca knows how to handle danger."

Once again, pride rose like a swell inside her chest. She found his hand and grasped it with hers. A silent thank you.

Cooper rubbed the bottom of his chin, let out a deep sigh.

"All right then. It's on. Everybody catch a few hours of sleep. We'll meet back here at 0500 hours and figure out a plan." He caught Bianca's eye, gave her a nod. "The taskforce is going to Chicago. All of us."

CHAPTER THIRTY

No way was Cal letting Bianca anywhere near Chicago.

While everyone else said "goodnight" and "see you in a few hours" as they vacated the dining room, Bianca was attacking her whiteboard again like a madwoman. He could tell by her jerky movements and the way she muttered under breath that her mind was in overdrive once more.

Part of her process or not, it killed him to see her this way.

Stepping up behind her, he gently wrapped an arm around her waist and halted her writing by cupping his hand over hers. "You need to rest. Let's go upstairs. Take a break."

She tensed. "You know I can't."

He buried his nose in her hair, savoring the feel of her body against his. She still smelled clean from her earlier shower. "I can help you."

"You think I need help?"

"We all need help sometimes."

He felt her swallow hard. "Help as in...I'm turning into my mother and going loco?"

Her greatest fear. "Of course not. You're not suffering from a mental illness and compounding the problem with drugs."

"I wouldn't be sure about the mental illness part."

"Well, I am. I know what happens in your brain is sometimes unwanted, but think of all the good you've done in the world. All the people in this country you've protected."

Slowly, breath by breath, she relaxed into him. "I've wished for this."

He took the marker from her hand and set it in the cradle. Moving her hair aside, he laid a soft kiss on the side of her neck. "Wished for what?"

"You, me, working together, like I told you before. I've never been a team player, but you are. This was..." Her voice trailed off. "Tonight was a big step for me. I feel like a real member of the SCVC Taskforce, and I feel like you and I together, with their help, can actually stop the assassination of the President of the United States. I'm not just a desk jockey sitting in my cubicle, analyzing terrorists and giving the go sign for operations taking place half a world away."

"You've always been more than a desk jockey, and I'm sorry if I made you feel like less."

"You didn't know the details about my job, and I couldn't tell you." She sighed, tilting her head and giving him more access to her neck. "Secrets are not good for a marriage, especially the kinds of secrets I was keeping. I saw no way out. I felt like I had to divorce you in order to keep us both safe, and then you've always been so devoted to your career, it seemed like I was doing you a favor. You've taken care of me long enough. It was time I gave you your freedom."

He laid his forehead against the back of her head, his heart pinching in a way he hated.

Guilt. He'd always vowed not to screw her up more than her mother had done, and yet, somehow he had. "What's done is done. We can't undo the hurt we've caused each other, but we can start making up for lost time. Right here, tonight."

She turned in his arms, lifted her chin to look into his eyes. "And I want that, I do. But I only have a few hours to get the data I need and analyze it into some kind of plan. My brain is fully engaged and sleeping is out of the question."

He kissed her lightly on the lips and turned on the charm. If he didn't get her upstairs, his plan would be ruined. "I wasn't talking about sleeping."

She grinned, tugged at her bottom lip with her teeth for a second. "An hour. I'll go upstairs with you for an hour. Then I have to get back to work."

He took her hand and led her away from the whiteboard.

They took the stairs, but didn't get far before their hands and lips were on each other. The circular stairwell was cool and damp, the stones rough. Bianca pushed him against the wall and kissed him, hard and long. He gripped her ass cheeks and lifted her off the ground, her legs automatically wrapping around his waist. He would have taken her right there if he didn't need to get her into bed.

Fortunately, Maggie thought they were playing a game and began barking and jumping on them.

Keeping a tight grip on Bianca, Cal climbed the stairs with her legs still wrapped around his waist. Her tongue went down his throat and her hands locked around his neck. He couldn't see the steps but his feet found them without any problem. Maggie danced ahead of them a few steps at a time before running back and barking. At the next landing, Cal needed to catch his breath, not from the climb, but the intensity of Bianca's kisses. He took a moment to press her to the wall and cup her breasts.

She moaned against his lips and let her hand trail to the zipper of his jeans. Again, he had a fleeting thought to take her right there, but he needed her in the cozy comfort of the bed after their love-making in order to coax her to sleep. So he stayed her hand, lifted her once more off the wall, and carried her up the remaining flight of stairs.

Inside the main suite's bedroom, he tossed her on the bed, making her laugh. He put Maggie in the bathroom and came back, staring into Bianca's eyes as he shed his clothes. Bianca shed hers as fast as he did and set her glasses on the nightstand. She reached for him at the same time he reached for her, and together, they fell into the soft mattress, lips and tongues and hands finding the other's skin in a manic rush of longing.

He wanted to slow it down... *This could be our last time...*but the fire between them flared like a bonfire and he couldn't stop the animalistic drive to make her come hard and fast.

She spread her legs, her body arching and her hands guiding him in. Just the touch of her fingers on his cock made him crazy. The moment he got close to her soft, silky entrance, he couldn't help himself. He took her in one fierce thrust, her crying out his name as her body quivered around his in an instantaneous orgasm.

He gave her a moment to enjoy the sensation, then rode her hard, drawing out the waves of her pleasure. Lowering his mouth, he sucked on each of her nipples, pulling them gently through his teeth.

Without warning, he felt a second orgasm rip through her on the heels of the first, her body tensing, muscles clenching around him once more. This time he went over the edge with her.

He bucked, back arching and pushing himself farther inside her. She took him deep, pressing her hips up and clasping his ass cheeks to keep him pinned there. As his release pumped into her, everything else faded away except for those gorgeous blue eyes and that blond hair splayed across the pillow.

As the last of the orgasms drained from both their bodies, he memorized her face, now happy and relaxed. In the coming hours, he knew it would be the one thing that would get him through the choices he had to make.

In the aftermath, they spooned together, and as he'd predicted, Bianca was soon fast asleep. He waited until her breathing turned slow and deep, and then he slipped out of bed, cleaned himself up, and dressed. After he'd let her out of the bathroom, Maggie had taken her place at the foot of the bed.

Cal stood for a moment watching Bianca sleep. She'd never forgive him for what he was about to do, but in the end, the only thing he had left was her. He had to protect her at all costs.

Patting Maggie on the head, he whispered, "Keep her safe, girl," before he slipped out the door.

The night air was cool and heavy with an approaching storm. Emit waited for him in the garden behind the winery. His friend was dressed all in black. A heavy-duty duffel bag lay at his feet.

Weapons.

"You sure you want to do this?" Emit asked.

Leave Bianca? *Hell, no.* Hunt down Lugmeyer? *Hell, yes.* "It's best this way."

Emit picked up the bag, hefted the strap over his head, and let it fall across his chest. "She's going to kill you."

"At least she'll be alive to try."

Insects sounded off in the grass. An animal—probably a fox or raccoon—moved through the grapevines. In the distance, Cal could see headlights on the road heading north to Sacramento.

Emit kicked the bag at his feet. "Better check what I brought, see if there's anything else you want."

The duffel was standard-issue Navy. Inside was a plethora of handguns and ammo in their cases. Burn phones, two-way radios, and a few other electronic gizmos Cal had no idea about, rounded out the inventory. Emit always had to have his toys.

"Plane's waiting at the airport north of here," Emit said. "We'll be there in approximately four hours, maybe five, depending on the storm system moving in."

Taking Emit's private plane would strand the SCVC Taskforce, at least for a while, and it was at least a thirty-hour drive to Chicago. There was no way Bianca could get there in time for the presidential dinner.

Cal dared not look back over his shoulder to the top floor where he'd left the only two females he'd ever cared about. "Let's go."

A sprinkle of rain landed on his cheek, the grass under his boots was already weighted down from a heavy dew. They crossed the yard and headed for the pair of Emit's Range Rovers, hidden in the nearby grape arbor. As they approached the one closest to them, a dark shadow appeared on their right.

"Going somewhere, boys?" Cooper Harris's voice was low but still gruff.

Shit. They were made. Emit and Cal stopped. Cal tried not to sound annoyed. "Thought we'd do a pre-flight check, make sure the plane is ready to take off later."

"Bullshit."

"It's not what you think."

"You're going after Lugmeyer on your own. Trying to take him out before Bianca enters the picture."

Okay, so he did know. "I don't want her anywhere near Chicago."

Even in the shadows, Cal could tell Harris was pissed. "I gave her my word that I'd let her be part of this op. Hell, this *is* her op."

"She's not a trained operative." *And she's all I have.*

"She's better than a trained operative. She's got the smarts, the instincts, and above all, she's got guts. I've seen a lot in my years as a cop and a DEA agent, but I've never seen anything like her. You want to save your marriage? Stop treating her like a china doll. My team will be right there with her, backing her up all the way."

Marriage advice? Cal wanted to punch Harris's face. "I'll gladly sign the divorce papers and promise never to set foot around her again if it means she lives to see another day."

Harris let out a long breath. "Look, I get that, Reese. I was in a similar predicament with my girlfriend not that long ago. Bottom line, we can't eliminate every threat and keep them locked up. You have to trust her skills and you have to trust my team."

"My senior chief, a man I trained with, ate with, and spent more time with than I've spent with my wife over the past six years killed three of my men. Sniped them in the back of the head. Men he'd sworn to lead and protect and cover their asses at all costs. Forgive me if trust isn't one of my many virtues at the moment."

They stood, locked in silence for a long moment. Cal could sense Harris studying him, analyzing his stability, and calculating the odds of getting him to give up his plan.

"I'll let you go on one condition."

Emit, who'd been quiet, finally spoke up. "What?"

"You can have a head start, but I want another private plane on that runway ready to go for my team at 0800 hours."

"I don't have a second private jet," Emit said. "What about your helicopter?"

"It only seats two plus the pilot. If I have to take that, guess who the second person will be?"

Bianca. Damn. Cal again considered punching Harris in the face.

"And then," he added, crossing his arms over his massive chest, "she and I won't have my team to back us up."

"They could take a commercial flight," Emit offered.

"A commercial flight would take six to eight hours, depending on the layover, and the first one out of Sacramento isn't until twelve-thirty this afternoon."

Cal's head felt tight. "And if we don't agree to your deal?"

"I won't alert the authorities, if that's what you're worried about. But you can't do this alone, and if you try, it will blow up in your face. When it does, you'll be living with the death of your men *and* the death of the president on your hands. That's a lot of red to have in your ledger."

The back of Cal's neck heated even as cold rain began to fall. "You're a bastard, you know that?"

"And you're *not* a vigilante. You're a soldier and a decent guy who's been through hell. Your wife needs you, and this team could use your expertise to stop a killer. You go off on your own without considering the consequences and you'll regret it for the rest of your life. I guarantee it."

Emit shifted and Cal could feel his gaze on him. Cal thought of Bianca, sleeping peacefully with that look of bliss on her face. His leaving her would gut her. Reinforce exactly what she said was true...he was always leaving her.

"We'll take the head start," he told Harris. "And if we find Lugmeyer or gather any pertinent intel, we'll share it with you."

"And Mr. Petit, here, will find me another plane?"

"You sure about this, bra?" Emit said softly to Cal.

"Yeah, I'm sure."

"Okay, then." Emit adjusted the weight of the duffel bag. "I'll make arrangements, call a few people. A private jet will be fueled and ready for takeoff at 0800 hours."

"With a pilot," Harris added.

Emit's white teeth flashed in the dark. "With a pilot, sir."

Harris stepped forward, offered his hand to Cal. "I'll take care of Bianca until we meet again."

Cal forced himself to shake Harris's hand. "I'm counting on it."

CHAPTER THIRTY-ONE

Equal amounts cold fury and disappointment ate at Bianca's stomach. Maggie had woken her to an empty room and it didn't take her sleepy brain long to figure out what Cal was up to. She'd run out of the suite, down the stairs, and smack dab into Agent Harris. She'd told him her theory about Cal taking off without them, and he'd told her to stay put and let him handle it.

Rain now sheeted down on her, drenching her as she stood in front of the arched back door of the winery. In the nighttime quiet, a trillion reactions occurred in her cells every second as she overheard snippets of the conversation between Cooper and Cal. A trillion reactions keeping her heart pumping, her organs functioning, and her brain engaged. So why did she feel numb— dead inside—from her husband's words?

A single overhead bulb illuminated a golden circle on the ground at her feet as Cooper drew near. "You said you would stop him."

Water beaded in his short hair. "I tried." He walked past her, opening the winery's back door. "Come inside."

She kept her back to Cooper, hands clenched. Puddles formed at her feet. "Why did you let him go?"

A huff came from the taskforce boss. "I'm big and mean, Bianca, but do you really think I can stop a Navy SEAL without using deadly force?"

Cal was the deadly force, and now he was hunting Justin

Lugmeyer without a team to back him up. "He's always worked ops with a unit of trained men. He can't do this on his own."

"He has Petit."

"Who has a million resources, but no background in covert ops!"

Bianca's brain should have been trying to figure out ways to stop Cal, to intercept him, to get to Chicago first. Instead, it seemed frozen along with her heart. Arguing felt better than thinking. "If we don't leave until eight o'clock, they'll have a six-hour lead. What if something happens and they need help? We'll be too far out to do them any good."

"I've got eyes on the ground. As soon as they land, my people will keep tabs on them."

She looked over her shoulder, wiped rain from her face. "Who?"

"Dupé and Celina should be landing shortly. I sent them ahead in case we needed more boots on the ground."

"Celina, your girlfriend?"

"Before she became a CSI photographer, she was FBI."

"She brought down the Londano cartel and you kicked her off your taskforce."

Shadows flanked Cooper's jaw as he took his time answering her. "You did your homework on everyone, didn't you?"

"I'm an analyst. It's what I do."

"Then you know why Celina left the taskforce."

"Hard to perform undercover ops when your name and picture have been on *Time* magazine."

"So was your assignment to investigate all of us or just Dupé?"

"Only Dupé, but I was bored. I looked up all of you. Interesting skeletons in your closet, by the way. Does anyone know how you bribed a criminal with government money to keep your son, Owen, safe when you were still a cop?"

His face contorted and she knew she'd hit a sore spot, but God, she was so tired of secrets. Looking away, she stared out at the distant vineyards. "The real reason I was sent here wasn't to investigate Dupé, you, or the taskforce. That was my assignment, mind you, by my boss Jonathan, but I knew that wasn't the real reason. Haley Banner needed me out of D.C. to get me out of her hair and make it easier for Tephra to kill me. Lucky for me, he decided to ask for my help instead."

"Lucky for all of us."

She didn't want his words to affect her, but they did. A flicker of warmth nudged against her heart, pushing the numbness aside. "I've brought nothing but chaos to your team. Put their lives in danger. How you can say that?"

"I didn't realize the extent of your skills until these past couple of days. You're not only a valuable asset to this team, Agent Marx. You're a valuable asset to America. I'd throw my hat in with you any day."

Again, the force of his words slid under her defenses. Her heart seemed to beat again. "You don't think I'm crazy?"

"Only as much as the rest of us. And that's mostly because we have to put up with Thomas."

She almost smiled. "I kinda like him."

Silence fell with the rain. Cool night air seeped into her bones and made her shiver. "So Cal remembers what happened in Afghanistan?"

"Sounded like it."

"Do you think he'll get better now with his memory returning? Will he still need therapy?"

"I'm no shrink, but if it were me, the best therapy would be putting the killer behind bars."

Bianca rubbed her arms, trying to get feeling back into them. "Cal's justice will be more violent, I'm afraid."

"He won't kill Lugmeyer. He knows we need the man's testimony against Banner in order to take her down."

The small puddles at her feet merged into one. "There's nothing the US government can offer Lugmeyer as a bribe to turn on her. If he tells the truth, he'll be put in prison. In prison, he'll meet with an unfortunate accident. He knows that."

"Violence might be in order, then."

"Torture?"

"Persuasion."

Bianca had always been against such measures. Now, thinking about how Lugmeyer had nearly killed Cal and her both, she found her position wavering. "Why didn't Lugmeyer take Cal out at the hospital in Germany?"

"Perhaps you'll get a chance to ask him. My guess? It was too public, too many variables. He needed Killer Kathy to slip Cal a poison pill."

"But she was already cozying up to Senator Halston here in America."

"Exactly."

All the hours she'd spent in therapy talking about her childhood had never done her a bit of good. Talking things out with Cooper made her feel better. Not completely, but a little.

The realization surprised her. She eyed Cooper over her shoulder. Maybe it was the person she was talking to. "Are you sure you're not a shrink?"

He chuckled. "Are you ready to get to work, Agent Marx?"

Pushing her hair back, she stepped over the puddle and headed toward the door. "I have a few ideas that might help us."

On the plane, Bianca and Bobby immersed themselves in data.

Bianca had never been in a private plane before and might have enjoyed all the bells and whistles if she hadn't been cramming and analyzing. The onboard Wi-Fi allowed her and Bobby to collect plenty of information, and that was good enough for her.

They'd already gone over the blueprints of McConnell Place, all the entrances and exits, right down to the garbage shoots, loading docks, and interior duct work.

They'd gotten hold of the guest list and ran their own background check on every person attending. No one stood out.

Dupé had made a request to secretly join the FBI team running the event's facial recognition software and been granted access by the FBI's director.

There'd been no word from Cal and Emit—not that that surprised her or Cooper. Dupé and Celina had failed to locate them, nor had they seen anything of Lugmeyer. Another thing that didn't surprise Bianca.

By the time they landed in Chicago, Bianca had given each of the team members a job and Ronni had given her a makeover. Bobby and Ronni had built fake ID's for everyone and Ronni had used her FBI access to hack into the guest and staff lists and add their false identities. Together with Bobby and Ronni's help, Bianca had backstopped each member and added current photos.

As she stepped off the plane in Chicago, she was no longer Bianca Marx. She was, in fact, Beyoncé Arnold, a scientist with a privately-funded group interested in President Norman's stand on DNA profiling.

The sunshine was bright when they landed, the October air in Chicago biting. Her new credentials were tucked safely in her pocket. One of the buttons on the jacket Ronni had given her hid a camera. The brooch on the lapel, a hidden mic. Ronni and Thomas would be inside with her, their covers as wait staff. Cooper would cover the outside of the building with Bobby and Celina, watching the entry points.

Adrenaline rushed through her veins, sending jolts of nervous energy down her arms and legs, but her mind was clear, and when Ronni asked her if she was ready for her first official undercover assignment, Bianca gave her friend a thumbs-up.

"The hospital was my first op," she reminded Ronni. "Don't worry, I have your six."

She wasn't just ready to go undercover, she was ready to nail Haley Banner to the wall.

CHAPTER THIRTY-TWO

McConnell Place was abuzz with people. As Bianca stood on the upper balcony and watched the commotion below her in the auditorium, the movements of people circling tables, mingling with each other, and engaging in normal human interactions reminded her of an ant farm. A lot of industry from the worker ants as the soldier ants stood on alert. Everyone milling around, waiting for the queen to emerge.

Of course, the crowd *thought* they were waiting to see the president, but it would be the queen—his running mate and lover—who would steal the show tonight.

Unless I stop her.

Cooper had given her an assignment—get to Haley Banner—while Ronni and Thomas hunted for Lugmeyer.

She and Cooper both knew there was little chance she'd actually have a shot at talking to Banner and getting a confession, but Bianca loved her new boss just a little for giving her a chance to be part of the op, even if he was being like Cal and trying to keep her safe.

Won't Cooper be surprised when I pull this off?

There were too many variables at play for her liking. Lugmeyer could get past them and take out Tephra and the president. Tephra could be lying and setting them all up. Even if the taskforce found and arrested Lugmeyer, Vice President Banner could have a backup plan. Bianca had been over those scenarios and more multiple times. She had to get a confession one way or another from Banner. That was the only sure fire way to take the bitch down.

McConnell Place hosted a wide variety of entertainment and political events. There were hidden tunnels into and out of the bowels of the building that led to the stage and auditorium. Bianca had already told Thomas to get down to those tunnels during his search. Lugmeyer could be hiding in one.

The president had yet to arrive. The V.P. was already there, and if there was one thing Haley Banner loved, it was the spotlight.

As Bianca expected, Banner made her entrance several minutes before the shindig was to start—nothing too grand like later on when she'd be formally introduced, but acting like one of the "little people," entering from behind the stage curtain and catching people's attention as she walked down the stairs to the auditorium floor, waving and calling out to certain friends and acquaintances. Secret Service agents stayed close as people gathered and Haley started shaking hands with the president's supporters.

Bianca tapped her jacket button, heard Bobby in her ear comm unit. "You're a go. We're right here if you need us."

The balcony had been roped off, but from the blueprints of the building, Bianca had located a secret door that led to and from this spot for maintenance people to work on electricity and lighting behind the scenes. She'd thought it would make a perfect sniper's nest, but found it unoccupied. Now, drawing a fortifying breath, she slipped back through the door and worked her way downstairs.

She emerged on the auditorium floor a minute later and zeroed in on the V.P. Ronni sidled up to Bianca the minute she spotted her, wearing a black and white wait staff uniform and carrying a tray of champagne glasses. "May I offer you a drink, miss?"

Her hands needed something to do. She accepted a slender glass. "Thank you."

Ronni nodded, the said under her breath. "Tunnels are empty. No sign of target outside or in."

No Lugmeyer. No Tephra either. Maybe Tephra had found the man and killed him. Or they'd both fled the country. Who knew? If only the nerves in Bianca's stomach would stop fluttering like manic butterflies. If only she knew Cal was okay.

Bianca gripped her glass tightly and circled closer to Banner.

She was almost there, practicing in her head what she was going to say to bribe the V.P. to speak with her in private, when a hand caught her elbow. She pivoted and found herself staring at...

"Jonathan?"

The older man's thick eyebrows drew together, dipping low. "Bianca? What are you doing here? I thought you were in California."

Jonathan never left D.C., never left Command & Control. But here he was, dressed in a dark suit and tie, and looking strong and steady as ever. "I, uh...wow, don't you clean up nice!"

She was never tongue-tied, never speechless. And she sure as heck never gave ridiculous compliments to men old enough to be her father and smart enough to know a redirection when they heard one.

But this was bad. Really bad. Jonathan could blow her ID, could blow the whole mission.

The truth sprang to her lips. She tempered it by channeling Ronni and Cooper and even Cal, none of whom would give up anything relevant to tonight's operation. "I had a little trouble in California. I came here tonight to speak to Vice President Banner in the hopes of getting things straightened out."

"Trouble?" His gaze scanned the people milling around. His grip on her elbow tightened. "Perhaps we should take this conversation somewhere private."

Time was running out. She didn't have time to talk to Jonathan. In her ear, she heard Bobby say, *"Get away from him."*

"I have to speak to the vice president before dinner." She gave Jonathan a big smile and pulled her elbow out of his grip. "We can catch up afterward."

His hand latched onto her upper arm. "Now," he said, starting to drag her away.

"*Lose him*," Bobby said in her ear.

Bianca purposely tripped over her own feet and tossed her champagne in Jonathan's face. "Oh, dear, clumsy me. Let me get you a napkin."

He released her, and Bianca ducked out of sight.

A moment later, she took the secret entrance to the balcony once more. She had to catch her breath and regroup. *Fast.* Jonathan's appearance had completely thrown off her plans.

Down on the auditorium floor, she saw him looking for her. Staying back in the shadows, she placed a hand on her stomach and bent slightly at the waist trying to breathe. Her first undercover assignment and she'd blown it.

There had to be another way, she just had to figure it out.

"B?"

Cal's voice made her spin around. As if he'd materialized from the shadows, he stood behind her, three days of stubble on his jaw, his face tired but his eyes steady.

"You okay?"

What a question. Bianca threw herself at him, hugging him close. "You bastard. How dare you leave me."

He didn't hug her back, only patted her lightly with one hand at the base of her spine. "We didn't find Lugmeyer."

Which in his mind was a failure.

She dropped her arms. "He hasn't shown up here, either. He's probably not even in Chicago. Once he knew we were on to him, he disappeared."

Cal didn't respond. She could see it in his eyes; he didn't believe his former senior chief would give up so easily. Truth was, she didn't believe it herself.

Before they could say anything else, Vice President Haley Banner took the stairs to the stage and hustled up to the podium. There, she tested the mic and waited for the room to fall silent.

When it did, she gave the guests her biggest, toothpaste-commercial smile and said, "Folks, you're in for a treat tonight. Please take your seats, because the President of the United States has arrived!"

The crowd broke into cheers and applause. A moment later, President Norman took the stage.

"*Showtime*," Cooper said in her ear.

They were out of time, and even if no one had seen Lugmeyer, it didn't mean they were out of the woods.

Bianca scanned the balcony and the open beams above the arena. "Cal, if you were Justin and going to snipe someone, where you would set up?"

He rubbed a hand over his face. "Emit and I have been all over the place, even up here. So has the Secret Service and FBI. There's no assassin, Bianca, and even if Lugmeyer *is* here, there's nowhere he could set up to shoot the president on stage and then get away cleanly."

The president had emerged from the backstage curtains to thundering applause. He waved and helped the First Lady to her seat before sitting himself.

Bianca scanned the tables of guests. *Where is Jonathan?*

Vice President Haley Banner stood at the podium. "Before we get started tonight, I want to take a minute or two of your time." She looked over her shoulder and smiled at Norman. "I promise, it'll be worth it."

The president smiled back, nodded, and motioned for her continue.

Something isn't right, Bianca's brain insisted.

"Ten years ago, we lost a valuable soldier in Afghanistan. A Navy SEAL with over thirty missions under his belt and more commendations in his file than any of you could fathom. He's been hailed by his own men as one of the greatest SEALs to ever defend this country. For years, we didn't know what had happened to him. He was declared Missing In Action."

She paused, letting her words sink in. "But tonight…" A smile passed over her face and the lights reflected off tears welling in her eyes. "I'm pleased and honored to stand on this stage and tell you… I, along with a small team of dedicated individuals, have found Navy SEAL Rory Tephra."

A gasp from the crowd. The president sat forward.

"Senior Chief Justin Lugmeyer of SEAL Team Seven discovered Lieutenant Tephra's location in a remote Afghanistan prison on one of his last missions to the area, and…" She swept a hand toward the backstage curtain. "…with the help of former CIA Operations director, Jonathan Brockmann, we brought him home."

From the curtains, two men emerged. Tephra, dressed in uniform, and by his side, escorting him forward, was Jonathan. Jonathan, former CIA Operations director. Haley Banner, former CIA analyst.

Bianca's stomach twisted.

The crowd broke out into applause, people coming to their feet. The president and First Lady came to theirs as well. Vice President Banner smiled like a schoolgirl and rushed forward to shake Tephra's hand.

For a second, Bianca couldn't process how Jonathan had betrayed her. Betrayed his country. How had she missed that crucial connection between him and Haley? And here Bianca had ruined their plan.

And then she looked at Tephra's face.

Oh no. Nononono.

"It's still going down!" she said into her comm unit.

Then she tore off for the stage as fast as her legs would carry her.

"Bianca!" Cal reached for her, but came up with air as she jetted down the balcony stairs, yelling at the top of her lungs.

It's still going down. There was no way Lugmeyer had made it past all of them.

Unless...

In all the years he'd known Bianca, he'd never known her to be wrong about anything other than his intentions.

Protect.

Cal ran.

He jumped down the balcony stairs, avoiding the security guard who was chasing after Bianca anyway. The crowd was thick, on their feet still clapping, and Bianca was fast, losing the security guard and dodging in and around people, yelling over their cheers. "Get down! Get down!"

He was on her heels when she bumped into a woman and the woman teetered in front of Cal. He couldn't do anything but push the gal aside, and as she fell, jump over her.

The first shot rang out and Cal's heart squeezed. He looked up in time to see Rory Tephra, on stage, fall in front of the vice president.

Screams erupted, more gunfire. As people ducked and ran toward the exits, Bianca charged the stage.

Secret Service agents rushed to surround the president and V.P. Another shot. The back of Jonathan Brockmann's head shattered.

Cal froze. The man had been hit from the back.

The stage. The assassin was behind the curtain, shooting at them from the back.

Lugmeyer.

Bianca reached the bottom of the stairs to the stage. A female agent stationed there was ducked down, gun raised. At Bianca's frantic approach, the agent didn't hesitate. She charged Bianca and took her to the floor.

Anger exploded inside Cal's head. He had to move. Had to save Bianca.

Save the president.

"Don't touch me! I'm one of you!" Bianca shouted, wrestling with the agent. "I'm NSA!"

The agent tried to flip Bianca onto her stomach and secure her hands. Bianca ripped her hands away and cold-cocked the agent in the face with her elbow.

That's my girl.

Agents were scrambling, shouting orders. Guests continued to scream and fight their way to the exits. He pushed past fleeing people, aiming for Bianca, then heard another series of shots ring out.

Bianca gained her feet. She was about to take the stairs onto the stage, but he couldn't let her. Running for all he was worth, he caught up to her, shoved her aside hard, and ignored the raging pressure in his head. Reaching down, he grabbed the dropped agent's gun on the way by. "Stay the fuck down!" He took the stairs two at a time.

Startled, Bianca let go of a yip, but he didn't have time to see where she fell, his attention one-hundred percent on the horror that met him on stage.

Four Secret Service agents were down along with Tephra and Brockmann. The V.P. was crawling across the stage floor, past the president, who stood statue still over the body of his unconscious, and probably dead, wife. His terrified eyes were glued to the hidden assailant off stage.

Time folded backward on Cal, taking him back to that cold night in Afghanistan. The noise of the crowd fell away, the only sound a steady drone inside his head. He lived the scene with his SEAL unit over again in his mind. His men, the gunshots, the blood...

"Cal!" Bianca screamed, and instantly the present world came back to him—the here and now in a *whoosh.* If he went left, he could jump in front of the president and stop the bullet destined to kill him. If he went right, he could sneak behind the curtain and stop Lugmeyer before he fired.

Defend.

Over the noise in the auditorium, he heard the distinct click of a trigger, saw light bounce off metal behind the curtain.

But there was no shot, no falling president. Had the gun misfired or had Lugmeyer ran out of bullets?

Either way, Cal knew he didn't have time to get backstage. He leapt toward the president, shielding the leader of the free world.

And making himself a target.

As he slammed into the president, he heard Lugmeyer's gun explode, felt the bullet hit him in the left shoulder as he fell to the ground with Norman. They hit the floor, a pain, sharp and penetrating bursting inside Cal's chest as the bullet buried itself deep.

He rolled, releasing Norman and coming around to the other side. Catching the movement of a shadowy figure from the corner of his eye, he shifted, raised his pistol, and fired into the curtain.

For half a second, nothing happened, then he saw Lugmeyer's face, eyes wide, mouth frozen open, emerge from the shadows into the light. The forward motion of his body slowed, seemed suspended for a moment, and Cal caught the sight of the man's rifle pointed right at him.

Without hesitating, Cal fired again.

CHAPTER THIRTY-THREE

Twenty-four hours later

Bianca sat next to Cal's hospital bed, her brain in total shut-down.

Since the moment she'd seen him jump in front of the president and take a bullet for him, her mind had been blank. Totally locked up.

Cal had come through surgery with no complications. The bullet had missed his heart by a quarter of an inch. He'd need rest and physical therapy, the doctor had told her, but he was in great shape and should recover and be back to work in no time.

Back to work. She didn't want to go there. Of course he would go back to being a SEAL. The way he'd jumped in front of the president, saving him, and taking out Justin Lugmeyer, even with a slug in his chest, only proved that Cal belonged in the heart of the action. He was a hero, and his country needed him.

If only she didn't need him too.

Jonathan was dead. Command and Control was shut down. The First Lady was still in surgery but her prognosis was good. Tephra was not as lucky. He'd taken two bullets to his spine. He was alive, but would most likely be paralyzed.

Director Dupé and Cooper Harris were still behind closed doors with the heads of several agencies, including Homeland, the FBI, and the Secret Service. All had been dealt a crushing blow.

Bianca and the other taskforce members had been interviewed and cross-examined in the hours following the shooting. Their testimonies against the vice president had been met with shock and disbelief, but as the hours wore on and the circumstantial evidence grew, Bianca was allowed access to the NSA databases. While Cal had been in surgery, she'd been forced to focus on doing her job one last time. For Jonathan. For Rory Tephra.

For her husband.

She'd been able to systematically connect the dots she knew were there and show them to the team now assigned to sorting out this mess. And miracle of miracles, Nelson Cruz, back in Sacramento, had hunted down and arrested Killer Kathy. Kasia was now singing like a bird against Haley Banner in exchange for a lighter sentence.

Vice President Banner was under house arrest at the White House. The directors of the nation's security organizations were doing their best to keep a lid on things, but between the assassination attempt, the dead agents, and the fact Justin Lugmeyer, a SEAL team leader was the gunman, the media had plenty of wild theories to keep them busy for days.

Cal's chest rose on a deep inhale and his hand moved jerkily, then fell again to the white sheet.

Bianca's heart, the stupid thing, had the opposite problem of her mind. Emotions flooded her chest in a constant stream, as if she were the one hooked up to an IV. She couldn't stop crying. Couldn't stop the intense need to crawl into the hospital bed with Cal and hang onto the only steady, constant, and loving thing in her life.

Please don't die.

Illogical. He wasn't going to die, the doctor had said so.

Cal's hand jerked again. She grabbed it and gave it a squeeze. Seeing him pale, injured, and immobile in this bed was breaking her heart into a million pieces.

Worse, there was nothing she could do for him.

Failure. A rare situation for her to be in.

His eyelids fluttered, stayed half open and focused on her. "B?"

His voice was rough, his eyes cloudy from the drugs. Platitudes that came easily to others escaped her, so she said the only thing she could. "You saved the president. You're a hero."

His thumb rubbed lightly against her hand. "Are you okay?"

He'd been shot and had major surgery and the first thing on his mind was her? How sweet and...well, *that's just wrong.* He was in a hospital bed and she was sitting beside him with nothing but a few scrapes and bruises and he was worried about her. Her heart threatened to cave in on itself. "Are you in pain?"

"No." He closed his eyes again. "Woozy though."

"The doctor said you'll have another scar, but you'll live."

His thumb continued rubbing her hand. "I tried..."

"You did great. Don't worry, just rest."

He shook his head, licked his lips. "I tried to...protect you. I promised her..."

Cal's words cut a path through the fog in Bianca's brain. "Promised who?"

"...I'd protect you no matter what."

Her. The thread of what he was saying was right there. All she had to do was pick it up and run with it. She didn't want to.

But she had to. "Promised who?"

"...mother..."

A sick feeling bloomed in her stomach. "*My* mother?"

His eyes were still closed. He seemed to drift toward sleep, then snapped back. His eyelids cracked open again and he looked at her, but his eyes were still unfocused. "She made me promise."

Were the drugs making him delusional? "My mother made you promise her you'd protect me?"

He gave her a small nod, closed his eyes again. "Before she..."

The sick feeling spread, up, up, up, right into her overwrought heart. "Before she killed herself?"

"She...hated...her life. Wanted to be free. Wanted you...to be free of her."

Bianca swallowed the bile pushing its way up her throat. "She made you, a seventeen-year-old kid, promise to take care of me?" Horror and disgust hit her hard. "That selfish bitch."

"No." He shook his head. "She loved you. In her own...way."

Bianca pulled her hand away from his. "And she showed me that very clearly when she blew her brains out in front of me after she made you...oh, my God. Wait. Did you *know* she planned to kill herself that day?"

He shifted, grimaced. "I thought it was another play...for attention."

Her mother had attempted suicide multiple times before she actually got the job done. Pills, crack, meth...there had always been a drug involved. Never a gun, until that day. She'd finally been serious.

Bianca jumped up, knocking her chair over. "All these years, you've been honoring your promise to a sick, mentally unstable woman. Why didn't you tell me?"

But she knew the answer. He was a good guy. One who'd felt sorry for her and took her under his wing. One who'd given his word to her mother to take care of her and protect her so she wouldn't be alone in the world.

"Because I...love you," Cal said.

Love. Lust. Loyalty. Somehow they'd gotten all mixed up in his generous, incredible heart. He didn't love her. He felt the need to protect her.

Backing up, her foot caught on the metal chair leg, sending it banging into the wall. Cal opened his eyes and frowned when he saw the tears rolling down her face.

"B?"

She couldn't stay here. Couldn't look at him and not feel horrible guilt at the way her sad, pathetic life had chained his hands. How her mother had tied him to her, knowing that even as a kid, he was responsible and honorable and would do the right thing when she couldn't.

Coward.

Annabelle had played them both, right up to the end. The ultimate manipulator.

A sob broke from her lips. Her life was a lie. She'd been damaged goods then and she still was. Everything she touched, she ruined.

"I love you, too," she whispered. "But it's time you had a life without me. A real life, where you don't have to worry about me. You fulfilled your promise, Cal. Now go find a woman you can love with no strings attached."

"What?"

With her heart shattering into a million pieces once more, she bolted for the door. There she stopped and looked back at Cal. He looked too big for the bed, his gypsy eyes confused. "But I'm taking the dog. Go adopt a cat instead."

CHAPTER THIRTY-FOUR

San Diego
Six weeks later

The doorbell rang, Maggie barked, and Bianca looked up from her book. The sun was setting and the living room had grown dark without her noticing. She'd been so absorbed in JD Robb's *Reunion In Death*, she hadn't noticed her eyes were straining.

She rubbed her eyes. Her new contacts took some getting used to. She never read fiction, especially suspense or mysteries, since she could figure out the bad guy from the start. Most were filled with plot holes so big she wanted to throw them across the room.

In fact, *The Origin of Consciousness in the Breakdown of the Bicameral Mind* sat open on her coffee table where she'd left it. Next to that, was *What To Expect When You're Expecting.*

She was late with her period. Sick to her stomach as well. After two pregnancies, she knew the signs, but she couldn't bring herself to take the test sitting in her cabinet.

What were the odds? Even if she were pregnant—the universe sure had a sick sense of humor—her track record of carrying a pregnancy to term sucked. Although, after the last miscarriage, her gynecologist had discovered an abnormality with her cervix and corrected it with same-day surgery. Her odds were better now of carrying a child to term.

And her heart, oddly enough, wanted one.

Listening to her heart came easier these days. She'd found a way to shut off the logical side of her brain—she'd had to in order to stop thinking about Cal and what she should have, could have done to save their marriage—and Ronni had loaded her up with paperbacks that now consumed her when she wasn't working. After finishing the last *In Death* book, she'd tried diving into *Bicameral Mind*, but her brain had craved more fiction. *Reunion In Death* was number fourteen in the series and there were many more to go. A lot of chapters in the baby book to read too.

The doorbell rang again. No one but Ronni ever came to visit and she always texted first. Hope jumped in Bianca's chest. *Illogical.* No one knew where she lived except for Ronni and the taskforce. She'd changed her name, created a new identity for herself with the help of Bobby and the blessing of Victor Dupé. The secrets in her head made her a target for some very bad people and she wasn't about to leave herself an easy target.

Even so, it wouldn't be impossible for a good hacker to find her location. She'd anticipated as much. Slipping her hand under the sofa pillow, she drew out her handgun and flipped off the safety.

Making a mental note of her place in the book, she tossed it on top of the baby book and headed for the door. Maggie followed.

A check of the peephole revealed a familiar face on the other side. Not the one she'd hoped for, but odds were, she'd never see that face again.

And that was fine. That was what she wanted.

At least the logical side of her thought so.

Logic insisted the truth had set them both free. Bianca had no doubt Cal had felt a huge relief after he got used to her not being around and needing him. He'd probably run with his freedom to the nearest "normal" woman he could find. He was living a happy life with a healthy relationship.

And good for him. He deserved that.

On the other hand, the emotional side of her—which refused to go back into its hole—wanted Cal to realize he actually *did* love her, heart and soul, with no promises or personal codes of honor hanging over his head. She wanted him to break down the walls of heaven and the gates of hell to find her.

So far, logic was winning, just like always.

She unlocked the door and cracked it open, gun out of sight but still hanging by her side. Maggie rushed out between her legs and greeted the visitor, jumping and licking him, and making him laugh.

When the dog settled down to simply wagging and panting, their visitor looked up with a smile on his face and met Bianca's eyes. "Hey, Bianca. How's it going?"

"It's Bronwyn, now." Of course, he knew that if he'd found her residence. "Wyn for short. How'd you find me?"

Emit Petit wore his usual—black everything—and feigned shock at her question. "You doubt my skills?"

She doubted his intentions. This was no casual visit. He was Cal's friend, not hers. "What do you want?"

"Right to business. Some things never change." He patted Maggie's head. "Aren't you going to invite me in?"

"Nope."

He waited as if she might be kidding.

She wasn't.

He lifted one brow and smiled, hoping she would feel pressured and change her mind.

She didn't.

"Okay, okay." He stuck a hand in his coat and rustled around. "Two things actually. First"—he pulled out a pale blue envelope from the inside pocket—"we're having a birthday party for Austin next weekend. He's turning one. Lori and I would like you to come."

A social event. People, kids, food, and fun. Something she'd always hated. Something she might *still* hate, but she was working on that. Ronni and Thomas were helping her learn real world social skills. She'd already survived a party at Cooper and Celina's. It had only included the taskforce members but it had been nice. Not as overwhelming as she'd feared.

There were a dozen reasons why she shouldn't go to the birthday party, but only one that mattered. "Will Cal be there with his new girlfriend?"

Emit's brows drew together and he looked confused. "Nooo." His voice held a trace of a lie.

She took the invitation. "I'll think about it. What's the second thing?"

He reached into his coat pocket again. "This."

The envelope this time was legal sized and pale ivory. Her lawyer's name and address were in the top left corner.

The divorce papers.

Her heart cramped inside her chest. As usual, her instincts and her logic had been spot on. This was no casual visit. "Oh. I see. He finally signed them." *But he couldn't bother to bring them himself.*

Fingers shaking, she snatched the envelope from Emit's hand. "He could have just mailed them to the lawyer."

Emit scratched the back of his head, looked around. "Are you doing okay, Bianca? I mean, Bronwyn? Harris said you're consulting for the taskforce, but he said you won't come back to his team fulltime."

The envelope in her hand felt too heavy. She tossed it onto the foyer table and the stupid thing slid off. "I'm not an undercover agent, and there's a lot of stuff up here." She tapped her temple with a finger and focused on Maggie for a second to calm herself. The dog did wonders for her anxiety. "Criminals, terrorists, and foreign governments would like to get their hands on that kind of information. It's not safe for me to stay in one place too long or to form permanent relationships."

"Sounds lonely."

Ironically, she felt less alone now than she had before. It

would suck when she had to pack up and move, but Victor Dupé had already found several government consulting jobs along the west coast for her where she'd make new friends and have a decent income. "I know how to take care of myself. I'm fine."

And she was, except for the raging gap of misery in her heart.

"Well..." Emit hesitated. "I have a proposition for you."

"I'm not interested."

He held up a hand. "Hear me out. Business is good, but I need help. Help that I can trust. You'd be challenged and never bored, and you'd be safe. My team is made up of all crack bodyguards and they're smart. Not as smart as you, but I need the ultimate analytical mind to teach them how to fine-tune their skills so they can be better. I don't want them to just be meat bags that stop a bullet. I want them to stop the bullets *before* they fly."

Neurons in her brain fired. Her pulse sped up. What he was offering sounded too good to be true.

Which meant it was.

Maggie stood and looked down the sidewalk toward Emit's SUV parked at the curb. There was no one in the front seat, no one nearby.

"Offering me a job out of pity or because you owe Cal is low, even for you, Emit."

"No one in their right mind would ever pity you, Bianca, and I would never offer anyone a job if I didn't know they were the right person."

"Bronwyn, not Bianca." She didn't believe him. His eyes were sincere and his posture earnest, but there was a slight dip in his voice. "You're lying again."

He pinched his lips together, sighed. "Not about the job. I'm prepared to offer you a very substantial salary and all the perks that go along with management. You'd have your run of all my gadgets and I'd tell you all my secrets."

"I don't want to know any more secrets. Trust me."

He put his hands on his hips and gave her an exasperated look. "Tell you what, why don't you speak to my project manager. He can explain things better than I can."

He turned and motioned toward his vehicle. Maggie wagged her tail.

As the rear passenger side door opened, Bianca's heart stopped.

Cal exited the SUV slowly, shutting the door and standing on the sidewalk. He didn't move, just stared at her.

Maggie *woofed* once, then looked back at Bianca. She was too stunned to do anything but give the dog the command to go. Maggie rushed down the sidewalk and nearly jumped into Cal's arms.

Dog and master greeted each other, Maggie's enthusiasm pulling a smile from Cal's otherwise grim face.

Bianca tried to harden her heart. "What is he doing here?"

"What the hell do you think he's doing here?" Emit said. "He was afraid you wouldn't open the door if he showed up, so he sent me ahead to scope out enemy territory."

"Why. Is. He. Here?"

"Because he loves you, B. He's not going to sign those divorce papers so you may as well burn them."

The reunion with Maggie over, Cal started up the sidewalk, the dog slowing his progress by trying to get him to play.

It couldn't be true. He'd had Emit track her down. He hadn't signed the divorce papers. She'd given him his freedom and her blessing and he'd come back anyway.

Hastily setting the gun on the table, Bianca stepped out onto the porch. "Is it true?"

He was smiling. "Is what true?"

Emit backed away as Cal took the steps, sweeping her up in a bear hug.

She let out a squeak. Surprise, mixed with that fragile but tenacious spark of hope, made her giddy. But that hope was still tempered. "Do you love me for me and not out of a convoluted sense of honor and duty?"

He stared into her eyes, his own dark ones snapping with what looked like the same hope she was feeling. "I've always loved you for you. This past month, I worked on my rehab, and it was hell. I went before the investigative board and Congress and cleared my name. But the only reason I left you alone was to prove to both of us that we belong together. I can't imagine my life without you. We're a team, remember?"

She couldn't help it. She laughed. "Aren't you going back to the Navy?"

"You heard Emit. I'm his new project manager. And we need an analyst, badly. Emit can't keep up with the number of clients we have and something's going to slide through the cracks. A client or one of our men are going to get hurt or killed. I have the field knowledge, but you...you have the brains. The ability to analyze and predict outcomes. Together, you and I can make sure Emit's team stays safe and so do the clients."

"And," Emit added, "you won't need a fake name. You keep my men safe and they'll return the favor."

It was a big step. A huge one. The dynamics were mindboggling. Exactly the kind of thing she loved.

Emit peeked over Cal's shoulder at her. "What do you say?"

What could she say? She got her husband back and a new career.

She gave Cal a death glare. "How often will you be leaving me?"

"Did I not just say we're a team?" He grinned. "Where you go, I go, and vice versa. We'll travel to locations together to scope out security holes, and we'll brainstorm, plan, and execute operations together as well."

"Where will we live?"

"Anywhere you want," Emit said. "As long as it's here on the West Coast. We're doing more and more business in China and Russia. Keeping our base of operations here is more efficient."

"Do we have a deal, B?" Cal was still holding her. He lowered his voice, his gaze dropping to her lips and slowly working its way back up as if he were memorizing her features. "Will you be my wife again *and* my on-the-job partner?"

Her mind was spinning with possibilities. The complications.

A new adventure was waiting. A job that would challenge her mind and that came with one incredibly awesome benefit package.

Bianca didn't need logic to make this decision. All she needed was her heart. "On one condition," she said.

Both Cal and Emit lost their smiles. "What?" they said in unison.

"Maggie's part of the team too."

The two men released a collective sigh of relief. "Of course," Emit said.

"Not just as a pet," Bianca added. "Maggie likes to work and she's good at sussing out bad guys."

Emit shot Cal a quizzical look. "Sussing?"

"Never mind," Cal said.

"She has separation anxiety." Bianca ran her fingers through Cal's dark hair, touched the scar on his eyebrow. "Like a certain other female in your life, she doesn't like being left behind."

Cal grinned. "I think you've fallen for my dog."

"She's *my* dog, and surprisingly, I love your dog as much as I love you."

He kissed her, laughing against her lips. "By the way, we have one more addition to the team. Come meet her."

He set Bianca on her feet and led her to the SUV.

When he opened the door and stepped back, she peered inside. She saw no one. "Your new team member is a ghost?"

He pointed. "Over there. In my coat."

On the seat, a jacket was wadded up. Bianca leaned closer, and Maggie stuck her nose in, sniffing. Her tail beat a rapid-fire staccato against Bianca's leg.

A tiny ball of black fluff moved, stretched, and then blinked up at her. A small, pitiful mew came from its lips.

"A cat?" Bianca threw her head back and laughed. "You adopted a cat?"

"You told me to." Cal scratched Maggie behind the ears. "And I was lonesome. You stole my dog."

"I didn't steal her. She wanted to live with me."

Bianca drew out the kitten and cuddled her. Maggie tried to stand on her back legs to see it, but Bianca made her sit. Then she lowered the cat and let Maggie take a sniff. Maggie wagged her tail and the kitten mewed and licked Maggie's nose.

"Well, that's settled," Cal said, putting an arm around Bianca's shoulders.

She cuddled the kitten again, suddenly feeling very maternal. "Not exactly."

Leaving the security of Cal's embrace, Bianca hustled back to the apartment, carrying the cat with her and Maggie running by her side.

"What's going on?" Cal followed her inside.

Emit joined them, and Bianca handed the cat off to Cal. "What's her name?"

"She doesn't have one yet," Emit said. "We decided we both suck at naming things, so Cal was leaving it up to you."

"I see." She eyed the bathroom door at the end of the hall. "You guys grab a beer from the fridge and have a seat." Thomas had stocked her fridge with some kind of IPA while Ronni had stocked her pantry with chocolate PopTarts—her kind of friend. "I'll be back in about, oh, three minutes."

In the bathroom, she unwrapped the pregnancy test. Maybe the universe wasn't playing tricks on her. A new kind of hope took root in her chest.

The test didn't take three minutes. A plus signed showed up in less than one. Bianca hung onto the bathroom sink, staring at that little plus sign and trying not to hyperventilate. She laid a hand on her lower belly. "Hang in there, kid," she murmured.

"You have a very bright future if we can make it through the next few months."

She splashed water on her face and prepped herself to go back into the other room.

Cal was standing at the end of the hall waiting for her. When he saw her face, he frowned. "You okay?"

She marched into the living room, past him and over to Emit. The kitten was in his lap, purring and trying to go back to sleep. "What kind of maternity benefits do you offer?"

He'd made himself at home on her sofa, propping his feet on her coffee table and swigging her beer. Neither man seemed to have noticed the baby book hidden under *Reunion In Death.* "Why do we need maternity...?"

He stopped with the beer bottle halfway to his lips, his eyes bugging out.

Standing at the arm of the sofa, Cal looked like he was going to drop his bottle. "Are you...?"

She held up the stick with its pretty little plus sign. "I am, and I think this time we have a good shot at going full term. So you better make sure you know what you're doing, Callan Reese, because your team is about to expand."

With a loud whoop, he set down the beer bottle, picked her up, and spun her around. "Yes!"

They were both laughing when Cal finally set her back on her feet. "We're going to be one awesome team, Bianca Marx."

Maggie jumped and barked, delighting in the happy moment. The kitten opened one eye from the comfort of Emit's lap and looked disinterested.

"It's Bianca Reese, for your information," she told her husband, "and we're going to be an awesome *family.*"

NOTE FROM THE AUTHOR

Dear Reader,

PTSD affects between 11% and 20% of our military veterans. Service dogs can help traumatized veterans overcome emotional as well as physical challenges. Many veterans with PTSD report their dog companions soothe, draw them out of their emotional numbness, and allow them to sleep at night.

And that's just the tip of the iceberg. For some veterans, their service dog is not just man's (or woman's) best friend, but the one thing that keeps them functioning and connected with their families and friends. Bonding with a dog elevates a person's levels of the hormone oxytocin which can improve trust and overcome paranoia. The best part is that many organizations adopt shelter dogs and train them for this rewarding job. Being adopted by a service dog organization and trained to help a veteran is a dream come true for them as well as the person they help!

Please consider supporting one or more of the service dog organizations. You can learn more about a few of these organizations by visiting my website at http://readmistyevans.com/book/27/deadly-force.

A portion of proceeds from the sales of this story in the SCVC Taskforce series will be donated to service dog organizations providing support for our veterans.

Happy reading!

~ Misty

misty@readmistyevans.com

And now enjoy an excerpt from the first book in the
SCVC Taskforce Series

DEADLY PURSUIT
by Misty Evans

Cooper Harris wanted to hit something. Hard.

FBI Special Agent Celina Davenport—sexy siren of his daydreams as well as evil temptress of his night dreams—was sucking face with the biggest drug cartel leader in California and there wasn't a damn thing he could do about it.

Her soft voice coming through the mic as she taunted Londano to have sex with her on the beach gave him an instant headache of giant proportions. But it was the silence that followed, broken only by the sound of them kissing, that made him want to slam the wall of the surveillance van with his bare fist.

Sucker punched. That's what it felt like.

It's her job, idiot. She knows how to handle herself.

Didn't make him any happier. Which showed what a total sexist he really was. Sure, he felt protective about all the guys on his squad, but he never second-guessed them or their skills. He never went apeshit if they kissed a mark or led her on in order to get the information to take someone down.

Celina was female and a little one at that. Short, underweight, except for a few well-placed curves, and she had a soft, almost Southern Belle persona that totally belied her fiery Cuban roots. Push her buttons and you'd see that fire, but it took an ungodly amount of button-pushing for it to surface. He knew. Out of everyone on the SCVC taskforce, he'd managed to tweak every hot button she had at least once. Most of them he'd not only pushed, but punched into the stratosphere.

He loved it when the real Celina came out. Not the professional FBI agent she'd polished to perfection, but the holy shit amazing woman underneath. The one whose emotions rose up and took over, blasting him with her clever wit and overwhelming logic even as she flushed with anger and made gestures with her hands he'd never seen before.

Yeah. *That* was the Celina he'd fallen for.

But he couldn't ever let her know that. How she tied him up in knots. How absolutely gone he was every time he was around her. He was her boss. Head of the taskforce.

He was also fourteen years, six months and four days older.

She was a baby. A rookie. A Feebie, for Christ's sake. DEA agents did not play well with FBI agents.

And he was The Beast after all. His reputation would hardly hold up under the pressure if he robbed the cradle *and* got the female rookie Fed on his team hurt in the line of duty.

So he didn't cut loose and punch the wall of the surveillance van, didn't give into the surge of acid in his stomach. Instead, he scratched Thunder's tiny square head and batted away the image of Special Agent Celina Davenport kissing Emilio Londano.

FBI agent Dominic Quarters' gaze was heavy on Cooper's neck. Fucker had the hots for Celina, too. Cooper shot him an accusatory glance. Fucker could eat shit. "What the hell is your girl doing to our op, Quarters? This wasn't the takedown we had planned."

"Pull your shorts out, Harris." The shorter man eased back in his plastic chair and shrugged. The San Diego Mafia had been formed in the early 1970s by Jose Prisco. Thirty years later, his twin nephews, Emilio and Enrique Paloma-Londano took over the business. While most cartels gained international reputations for brutality and murder, the San Diego traffickers posed as legitimate businessmen. Their unique criminal enterprise involved itself in counterfeiting, kidnapping, and drug trade, but Emilio and Enrique passed off as law-abiding citizens, investing in their country's future and earning the respect of their neighbors and the general public. The Feds wanted them gone. The DEA wanted them gone. Even the CIA thought it was a good idea. Too bad it wasn't one of the spies he'd worked with before instead of Quarters sitting next to him. "She saw an opportunity and ran with it."

An opportunity? That's what this asshole called it? "She's going to get herself killed."

Quarters did the shrug thing again and Cooper's hand balled into a fist. Punching Quarters would be way more satisfying than punching the van's side panel.

The van slowed, following a discreet distance behind Londano's car and bodyguards' vehicle. "Perp is pulling off highway and parking approximately one-quarter klick from here," announced Thomas, a West Point grad who'd held a high profile position with the Department of Defense before defecting to the DEA. The T-man was Cooper's right hand man on this takedown.

Two keystrokes of Thomas's fingers and a night-vision view of the boardwalk appeared on the screen in front of Cooper.

The surveillance van wasn't the only vehicle in the area. A few diehard surf heads always parked near the beach overnight, only moving when the cops harassed them. There were plenty of cops in the area tonight, but none would be visible until after the sting took place, thanks to Cooper's friendly relationship with the police units from L.A. to San Diego. They all wanted Londano out of business and they knew Cooper's taskforce was about to do it.

"Perp is exiting car."

Like he couldn't see that. On screen, Londano and Celina headed to the beach. Thunder, in Cooper's lap, whined. Cooper was petting the dog too hard. "Sorry, hot rod," he murmured, never taking his eyes off the screen. He wanted to watch Celina. But years of intense training and experience told him to keep his attention on Londano. "Radio the other units in the area that this is going down here and now."

Thomas made a sound of acknowledgment and began notifying their backup.

Celina kicked off her high heels and strolled into the rolling Pacific Ocean. The moon and stars lit the beach with a surreal light that even the night-vision view couldn't compete with. Cooper could only shake his head at her stupid courage and undeniable sensuality. She glowed like a beacon.

A beacon that only reminded him he was trapped in a hell of his own making.

ABOUT THE AUTHOR

USA TODAY Bestselling Author Misty Evans has published over twenty novels and writes romantic suspense, urban fantasy, and paranormal romance. As a writing coach, she helps other authors bring their books—and their dreams of being published—to life.

Misty likes her coffee black, her conspiracy stories juicy, and her wicked characters dressed in couture. When her muse lets her on the internet to play, she's on Facebook and Twitter. Read more about her and her stories at www.readmistyevans.com.

Printed in Great Britain
by Amazon